READERS LOVE THE RYDER & LOVEDAY SERIES

'Insanely brilliant'

'I absolutely loved this book'

'Faith Martin, you've triumphed again. Brilliant!'

'If you haven't yet read Miss Martin you have a treat in store'

'I can safely say that I adore the series featuring Dr. Clement Ryder and Probationary WPC Trudy Loveday'

'This book is such a delight to read. The two main characters are a joy'

'Yet another wonderful book by Faith Martin!'

'As always a wonderful story, great characters, great plot. This keeps you gripped from the first page to the last. Faith Martin is such a fantastic author'

FAITH MARTIN has been writing for nearly thirty years, under four different pen names, and has had her 50th novel published recently. She began writing romantic thrillers as Maxine Barry, but quickly turned to crime! Her latest series of classic-style whodunits, featuring amateur sleuth Jenny Starling is now being reissued. But it was when she created her fictional DI Hillary Greene, and began writing under the name of Faith Martin, that she finally began to become more widely known. Her latest literary characters WPC Trudy Loveday, and city coroner Dr Clement Ryder take readers back to the 1960s, and the city of Oxford. Having lived within a few miles of the city, dreaming spires for all her life, (she worked for six years as a secretary at Somerville College) both the city and the countryside/wildlife often feature in her novels. Although she has never lived on a narrowboat (unlike DI Hillary Greene!) the Oxford canal, the river Cherwell, and the flora and fauna of a farming landscape have always played a big part in her life – and often sneak their way onto the pages of her books.

Also by Faith Martin

A Fatal Obsession
A Fatal Mistake

A Fatal Flaw

FAITH MARTIN

ONE PLACE. MANY STORIES

HQ
An imprint of HarperCollins*Publishers* Ltd
1 London Bridge Street
London SE1 9GF

This paperback edition 2019

1

First published in Great Britain by
HQ, an imprint of HarperCollins*Publishers* Ltd 2019

A catalogue record for this book is available from the British Library.

ISBN: 9780008330774

MIX
Paper from
responsible sources
FSC® C007454

This book is produced from independently certified FSC™ paper
to ensure responsible forest management.

For more information visit: www.harpercollins.co.uk/green

Typeset by Palimpsest Book Production Ltd, Falkirk, Stirlingshire
Printed and bound in Great Britain by
CPI Group (UK) Ltd, Melksham, SN12 6TR

For my sister, Marion.
Thanks for being my second pair of eyes!

Oxford, England, 1960

Prologue

The fine September morning had dawned that day with a very welcome and concealing mist. Even so, as a figure slipped cautiously into one of the many churchyards that were scattered about the city, it looked around quickly.

The clock in the bell tower was yet to chime six. Unsurprisingly, there was no one else out and about so early, save for the stray milkman or conscientious dog-walker. Yet the figure – who was dressed in a rather disconcertingly ghostly-looking pale-grey mackintosh – nevertheless made sure that the attached hood was up and pulled well forward, thus concealing their face.

A lone blackbird perched on a gravestone gave its familiar chinking alarm but the figure in grey ignored it, making quickly but carefully towards the oldest part of the graveyard. Here the stones were made illegible by lichen and time, and an ancient yew tree survived in defiant and baccate splendour.

The only living inhabitant of the graveyard looked anxiously around, making sure that their next action would remain unseen and forever secret, before reaching out and plucking several choice, wax-like red berries.

These precious berries were quickly picked and thrust into a small brown paper bag, which was then hidden out of sight in one of the mackintosh's large side pockets.

The anonymous figure in grey paused at the churchyard gate and peered carefully down the deserted small side street in either direction. As expected, nobody else stirred the early morning mist.

A clock in the city of dreaming spires chimed the hour, and the gatherer of berries paused to count them and smiled whimsically. Oxford. Here, in the hallowed halls of academe, the knowledge of the ages could be found. From the most obscure fact about a minor metaphysical poet, to the latest breakthrough in nuclear fusion. In this world-famous university city, with just a little time and effort, you could discover whatever you wanted to know, about any subject under the sun.

Like the properties of poison, for instance.

The figure slipped out of the churchyard gate and moved silently along the slick and damp pavement.

How many people knew that yew berries were poisonous? And of those that did, how many of them ever gave it a single passing thought that they could be so significant?

People were so complacent; so ignorant and oblivious to the ugliness in the world. So long as they were all right, and their own small personal universes were running smoothly, they cared little for anything or anybody else.

But as the person in the mackintosh headed quickly but cautiously for home now that the precious cargo had been safely harvested, they began to smile and nod. For soon the whole city would be made aware of just what the fruit of the humble yew could do. Oh yes. There would be a fuss made then, all right.

People always sat up and took notice when the young and the beautiful began to die.

Chapter 1

Grace Farley paused outside the garden gate of her old friend, Trudy Loveday, and took a deep breath. At just turned 22, she was a few years older than Trudy, whom she'd first met at their local primary school. But it had been a few years now since she'd last seen her, and she needed a moment or two to compose herself.

She was not at all sure that what she was about to do was the right thing. What if it all backfired on her? A worried frown creased her pretty, freckled face as she debated whether or not to just turn around and go back home.

Part of her was sorely tempted to do just that. After all, so much could go awry, yet things were getting increasingly desperate, and there was no doubt in her mind that she needed help. Everyone knew that Trudy had joined the police and was doing really well. Grace's Auntie May had heard from the hairdresser that Trudy had helped solved two murders. Mind you, everybody believed it was really one of the city's coroners who had been the true force behind the cases. But even so.

Grace, a pleasingly plump girl, with short, curly reddish-brown hair that lent itself nicely to the poodle cut she favoured, glanced around, knowing that she couldn't stand hovering outside the

Lovedays' garden gate all day long. People would begin to notice and wonder, and that was the very last thing she needed. Drawing attention to herself could be disastrous. Besides, it was getting on for six o'clock, and would soon start getting dark, so she needed to get back to her mum. She'd promised to help give her a bath, and...

Realising that she was still putting the moment off, she determinedly pushed open the gate, marched up to the front door and before she could stop herself, firmly rapped the knocker three times.

She realised then that her hands were trembling visibly, and quickly thrust them into her coat pocket. In her head on the way over here, she'd rehearsed time and time again what she would say, but most of it was swept away when the door opened, and there stood Mr Loveday, Trudy's father. She knew he drove the buses, though not the one she took into work each day.

She forced a bright smile onto her face, and said, somewhat breathlessly, 'Hello, Mr Loveday. Is Trudy in?'

Frank Loveday looked down at the worried face of the girl looking up at him, her big grey-green eyes open wide and unblinking, and gave her a friendly smile in return.

'Grace! Long time, no see. Of course our Trudy's in. Come on in, Barbara's just put the kettle on.'

'Oh, I don't want to put you to any bother,' Grace said quickly, stepping into the small hallway, and then following him down the little corridor to the back, where the kitchen was. Her own council house, when she'd lived in this area just a few streets away, had the exact same layout, as did their house once they'd moved to the other side of the city for her dad's job.

'Look who's come to pay a visit,' Frank Loveday said, ushering a suddenly shy and obviously nervous Grace into the kitchen. Cheerful yellow was the dominating colour, and the tiny space was filled with the appetising aroma of the shepherd's pie that the family had just consumed for their tea. Grace smiled uncertainly at Barbara Loveday, who was at the sink washing up. Quickly drying her hands on a towel, Trudy's mother bustled forward to give her a quick hug.

'Grace Farley! My, but you've grown into a pretty girl. Hasn't she, Frank?' Barbara demanded of her husband.

'She certainly has,' Frank agreed, taking his seat back at the kitchen table, where a copy of the local paper lay spread out at the sports section.

'How's your mother doing, Gracie?' Barbara asked, lowering her voice a few notches. 'Is she feeling any better?'

Her eyes sharpened in concern when the girl paled slightly, but Grace nodded bravely.

'Oh, well, you know, the doctors are doing all they can,' she said, with forced briskness. Then her eyes moved over the older woman's shoulder and met those of a tall, dark-haired girl with large pansy-dark eyes and a wide smile. 'Hello, Trudy.'

'Grace!' Trudy, who'd been drying the dishes as her mother passed them to her, put down her own towel, and correctly reading the appeal in her old friend's eyes said, 'I've had my bedroom redecorated since you moved away. Want to come and see it?'

'Oh, I'd love to,' Grace lied with a bright smile. 'I bet it's green. That's your favourite colour, right?'

'One of them.' Trudy laughed, and leaving her parents to listen to Tony Hancock on the wireless, she led her old school friend to the hall then up the narrow flight of stairs to her small bedroom at the back of the house.

Little more than a box room really, it had enough room for a single bed, a wardrobe and a small dressing table. As they had done when they were still both in pigtails, Grace and Trudy sat side by side on the bed without thinking, the years dropping away.

Although Trudy was glad to see her, her mind was nevertheless working overtime. The Farleys had left this area of town some four years ago now, and although she'd heard the odd bits and pieces of news about them from various sources, she had no idea what could have brought Grace back to her door.

She knew that her old school friend had a good job working as a secretary or book-keeper or something for some shop or business in the 'posh' end of town. She'd also heard, sadly, that Grace's mother was now rather seriously ill.

As if sensing her curiosity, Grace suddenly gave a wry smile, and began to nervously pleat and re-pleat the folds of the skirt she was wearing. It was a habit she'd had ever since she was little, and Trudy frowned, knowing that she only ever did it when she was upset or nervous.

'I suppose you're wondering why I'm here,' Grace said abruptly. 'I'm not sure, really, if I should have come at all. But I didn't know who else I could talk to. I mean, with you being in the police and everything.'

Trudy blinked in surprise. Whatever she'd expected Grace to say, it hadn't been that. For what on earth could someone like Grace want with the police? A more law-abiding, respectable family than the Farleys was hard to imagine.

'Blimey, Grace, that sounds ominous,' Trudy said, trying to force a touch of lightness into her voice. 'What's up?'

Uneasily, she wondered if it was possible that one of her family was in trouble with the law, and Grace was expecting her to help pull some strings? But if one of her relatives had been caught in some minor unlawful practice, there was really nothing Trudy could do about it. She was a mere humble probationary WPC – and as such, had no power or clout whatsoever. Even if she was inclined to do anything, which she wasn't, particularly. In her opinion, people who deliberately broke the law should take the consequences.

'It's about my friend, Abigail. Abigail Trent. The girl that died,' Grace said abruptly, the words shooting out of her mouth so fast and hard, that it was clear she'd been holding her breath without realising it.

For a second, Trudy was flummoxed. Died? It was nothing

8

petty then, Trudy thought with dismay. Nothing to do with an unpaid fine, or a car tax 'misunderstanding' or…

And then Trudy suddenly remembered. 'Oh! The girl who died from drinking poison,' she said, somewhat belatedly putting two and two together. She'd read all about the case over the past few days in the Oxford papers, of course. A girl aged around 20 or so had drunk orange juice laced with some kind of poison and had sadly died because of it. The inquest was due to open any day now. 'Wasn't it something to do with a poisonous plant. Berries or something?' she said.

'Yes.' Grace nodded miserably. 'Yew.'

'That's right. And she was a friend of yours?' Trudy mused quietly. 'Oh, Gracie, I'm so sorry. It must have been awful. Did you know her well?'

'Sort of. I mean, not that well, but…' Grace sighed and took a deep breath. 'The thing is, Trudy, everyone's saying that she committed suicide. At work, in the neighbourhood, people you overhear chatting in the café or on the bus… You know how people gossip.'

Trudy nodded. 'Yes. These things tend to get around. Everyone seems to know everyone else's business. They're saying she was depressed and moody, I expect?'

'Well, see, that's just it,' Grace said flatly. 'I don't think she *did* commit suicide. To begin with, I don't think Abby knew anything about poisons, let alone which berries were poisonous or how to turn them into something that could kill. I mean' – the older girl twisted a little around on the bed, the better to look at her friend – 'I don't know anything about that stuff either, I'm not a chemist or what-have-you. I didn't even do science at school, and what's more neither did Abby! But don't you have to distil stuff like that, or put it through some sort of process before it becomes really lethal? Surely it can't be something as simple as just… I don't know, pouring some hot water over some berries and then drinking it. Can it?'

9

Trudy looked at Grace's big grey-green eyes and saw how troubled she looked, and shrugged helplessly. 'I don't know either. But maybe it is? I'm sorry. But didn't she drink the stuff with orange juice to help mask the taste? That's what the papers said, anyway.'

Grace shrugged and sighed heavily. 'I think so. But I just know that Abby wouldn't have killed herself,' she insisted stubbornly.

'All right.' Trudy nodded amicably, not willing to argue. Clearly, her old friend believed she was right. But now that she was remembering more details, things didn't seem to quite bear out what Grace was saying.

Tentatively, she said, 'But didn't the people who were closest to her say that she was... well, rather moody? That she could be depressed sometimes? I think even her own mother was reported as saying that she could be a bit... intense?'

Grace again sighed heavily. 'Oh, that was just her way. She was only 19 after all, and yes, she could be a bit up and down. A row at work would get blown up out of all proportion, or a present from her boyfriend would have her walking on air. It was just her way. But that doesn't mean that she was suicidal!' Grace argued. 'Abby had great plans for her life. She talked about them often. And she enjoyed herself far too much to seriously want to die! For a start, she was looking forward to the beauty contest too much!'

Trudy blinked. She knew that a beauty pageant was being staged, of course, from the notices she'd seen around town, but it hadn't really registered with her much. 'Oh, she was in that, was she?'

Grace nodded, and with her hands restlessly folding and unfolding her skirt, began to speak rapidly.

'I work for Mr Dunbar, who owns Dunbar's Jams, Honey and Marmalade. You know, the factory up past Summertown?'

'Oh right,' Trudy said. 'You're his secretary or something?'

Grace gave a rueful smile. 'Hardly! I'm not that high up! I do the odd bit of book-keeping – petty cash mostly, and fetch the coffee, do the filing and some bits of typing that the other secretaries don't like doing... all tabs and... never mind that.' Grace suddenly waved a hand in the air. 'It's not important. What *is* important, is that last year Mr Dunbar came up with a plan to help promote his honey. He wanted to put Dunbar Honey up there with the famous Oxford Marmalade brand.' She paused to smile whimsically at this bit of obvious folly, and shrugged. 'So he came up with this idea of holding an annual Miss Oxford Honey beauty pageant.'

Trudy couldn't help but smile. Her friend, catching her look, laughed suddenly.

'I know – it's hardly Miss World!' Grace said, rolling her eyes a bit. 'But actually, it's quite a clever idea. All the papers will cover it, and Mr Dunbar knows someone who owns that old theatre just off Walton Street who's letting him hold rehearsals there for free. He's also agreed to host the beauty contest for the public one Saturday night next month. Tickets are already nearly sold out. That's one of the reasons why they decided not to cancel the event after Abby died. Everybody was so excited about it, it seemed a shame to call it all off. Not only that, he's got local shop owners putting up big prizes and acting as judges, so it's hardly costing him a penny.'

'He's obviously quite a businessman, your boss,' Trudy said, somewhat sceptically.

'Actually, he probably is,' Grace said flatly. 'But that's not really the point. I was asked to help out on the organising side of things, since I wasn't exactly indispensable in the office,' Grace laughed. 'And Mrs Dunbar...' For a moment the name seemed to catch in her throat, and then she smiled ruefully. 'Well, let's just say that Mrs Dunbar was adamant that her husband shouldn't spend time on the beauty contest or let it get in the way of the business of making honey!'

'Ah, I get it,' Trudy said with a wicked smile. 'She didn't want her husband spending too much time hanging around with pretty girls.'

Grace dragged in a large breath, but was obviously far too discreet to either confirm or deny her friend's interpretation of how she'd come to be the hands-on manager of the contest. 'So, anyway, a few weeks ago Mrs Dunbar drafted a piece for the newspapers, asking girls who lived in the city or within a twenty-mile radius, and who wanted to take part, to get in touch and sign up for the auditions. Obviously, they had to be over 18, but under 30 and well, er, they had to be, er...'

'Pretty and with good figures?' Trudy put in helpfully, when her friend seemed to struggle for a diplomatic way to phrase things.

Grace suddenly giggled. 'Well, you'd have thought that went without saying, wouldn't you? But some of the women and girls who turned up...' She rolled her eyes with yet another giggle. 'Well... let's just say that me and Mrs Dunbar and Mrs Merriweather – she's the old lady who's a Friend-of-the-Old-Swan-Theatre, and is helping us run the show – anyway, we had a bit of a job persuading some of them that they weren't... er... quite suitable for what we had in mind.'

Trudy shook her head. 'The tact and diplomacy must have been quite something!'

Again, Grace giggled. Then her face suddenly fell, as she remembered why she was there.

'Yes. Well... anyway, Abigail and her friend Vicky were one of the first ones to apply, and we signed them both up straight-away. Over the next week, we whittled the applicants down to about twenty or so. Actually, the process is still ongoing but, again, that's not what matters. The point is I got to know Abby, and... well, to put it in a nutshell, she was fairly confident that she had a good chance of winning. She was so looking forward to the competition night. She had stars in her eyes! What's more, she was so upbeat about her "talent" spot and she just loved trying on the evening gowns and… Trudy, there was just no way that girl killed herself,' Grace finished forcefully.

Her eyes were now open so wide, and were fixed on Trudy with such a glare, as if she thought she could make Trudy believe her by sheer force of will. 'And I don't know what to do about it. If they bring in a verdict of suicide, as everyone seems to think they will… it just won't be right!'

Her hands were shaking again, and Trudy reached out and held them firmly. 'Gracie, it's all right – just calm down a bit. But I don't quite know what you think I can do about it,' she told her gently. 'I'm just a probationary constable. And I didn't know this girl, or anything about the circumstances surrounding her death.'

'No, but you know this Dr Ryder man, don't you? He's a coroner, isn't he? Can't you ask him to help?' Grace asked quickly.

For a second or two, Trudy stared at her friend aghast. How could she possibly explain to her friend, who knew nothing about the police force and how its hierarchy actually worked, why her request was so impossible. For a start, if her boss, DI Jennings, ever found out that she'd gone behind his back about a case, he'd skin her alive! Especially since the Inspector was hardly a fan of the coroner.

But as if sensing what was coming, Grace got in first. 'Please, Trudy, can't you just speak to him? At least ask him to call me as a witness or something? I can testify to her state of mind, at least, can't I? Won't the inquest want to know that Abby wasn't feeling suicidal at all?'

'But, Grace, how can you be so sure?' Trudy asked helplessly. 'None of us know, not really, how someone else is feeling.'

Slowly, Grace's shoulders slumped. 'So you won't help?' she asked flatly, her gaze so accusatory that Trudy almost winced.

'It's not that I won't. It's that I can't,' Trudy tried to explain. 'I'm not even one of the officers assigned to the case,' she pointed out. 'And believe you me, my superiors… well, let's just say, they won't be in any hurry to listen to what I might have to say,' she added, a shade bitterly. The thought of the look that would cross her DI's face if she came to him with this tale was enough to make her shudder.

Seeing what she was up against, Grace decided that if she was in for a penny, she might as well be in for a pound, and took a deep, deep breath.

'It's not only this thing with Abby,' Grace said, sounding almost defiant all of a sudden. 'It's other things as well. At the theatre...' She paused, closed her eyes for a second, and then took the plunge. 'Things have been happening.'

'What do you mean?' Trudy asked sharply.

Grace shrugged, her eyes suddenly darting around the room so that they wouldn't have to meet Trudy's. 'Oh, just things,' she said, rather unhelpfully. 'Stupid things. Nasty little tricks... For instance, someone tied a string over the bottom step in the stairs that leads up to the stage, so that one of the girls took a tumble. Oh, she wasn't hurt – but she did have to rest her ankle for a few days, so she lost rehearsal time for her dance routine. And then something must have been added to one of the girls' jars of face cream which brought her skin out in a rash... It faded after a few days, but she pulled out of the competition anyway. Just silly little pranks like that.'

Trudy frowned. 'But isn't that likely to be a simple case of rivalry between the contestants? It sounds like the sort of mean tricks that some girl who wants to scare others into withdrawing from the contest might use.'

'Yes. That's what everyone seems to think,' Grace admitted reluctantly. 'But, Trudy, I'm not so sure. I have a bad feeling about it all. I think... Oh, I just wish you'd talk to your coroner friend about Abby! Perhaps you could come down to the theatre sometime, during rehearsals or something, and just take a look around? See if anything strikes you as... odd. But you mustn't tell anyone that you know me, or that I've been talking to you, because then I could lose my job,' Grace added hastily, suddenly clutching her arm and holding it in a tight grip. 'Mr Dunbar wouldn't like it if he thought that I'd been speaking out of turn. He's dead scared as it is that the papers will get to know about our little problems and give us bad publicity. So you mustn't come in uniform or anything... I know!' She suddenly beamed brightly. 'You could pretend to be thinking of applying to be a contestant or something. It would give you the perfect excuse for being there and having a look around. Oh, Trudy, please?'

Trudy, unable to resist the appeal in her friend's eyes, suddenly gave in. What could it really hurt, just to put her mind at rest? DI Jennings need never know about it. Besides, she was intrigued.

'OK. I'll go and see Dr Ryder and tell him what you've said. If nothing else, he can at least give us some advice. But I'm not promising anything mind!'

'Oh, Trudy! Thanks ever so much!' Grace leaned across and gave her a hug. 'Now, I've really got to get back to Mum,' she said. 'I don't like leaving her in the house for long with just Dad to look after her,' she admitted, and Trudy gave her a quick, fierce hug back.

'Of course!' she said, her voice suddenly thick with emotion. 'And I do hope your mother gets better soon,' she said. She simply couldn't imagine what she'd do, or how she'd feel or cope, if her own mother suddenly got so ill. The thought made Trudy feel quite sick.

She jumped up and ushered her friend downstairs. And with a quick 'goodbye' called out to the older Lovedays who were still in the kitchen, Grace was gone.

But as Grace Farley walked to the end of the street and caught the bus across town, she sat in her seat, swaying slightly and looking out at the darkening city with a growing sense of panic.

Had she done the right thing? What if it all backfired? What if Trudy didn't come through for her? Or worse yet, what if she did, but didn't get the results that she, Grace, so desperately needed her to get? And what if her old friend was really good at her job, and learned far more than was good for her?

Grace shifted on the seat, fighting back a growing sense of unease. What if she'd miscalculated, and it all went wrong?

For a long moment, Grace Farley felt chilled to the bone. She could actually end up in prison.

Or worse yet! What would her tormentor do to her if it came out that she, Grace, had brought the police sniffing around the theatre?

And yet... And yet, the risk *had* to be worth it.

She simply had to get something on her persecutor, before... well, before things got totally out of control.

Trudy Loveday was the only one she knew who might be able to find such ammunition. But she'd have to watch her old friend closely.

Chapter 2

Dr Clement Ryder watched his hand, which was lying flat on the tabletop, and scowled as it began to twitch slightly. Grimly, he used his other hand to massage the palm, and after a while, the twitching slowly abated. But he knew it would be back.

He'd self-diagnosed himself as suffering from Parkinson's disease whilst still a surgeon in London, which had led to him resigning from his medical career and embarking on his new life as a coroner in Oxford.

Although, so far, he'd managed to keep his condition a secret from everyone – his friends, family, and work colleagues alike – he was well aware that he faced an uphill struggle in the years ahead to keep the secret safe, as the disease inevitably progressed and worsened. And the symptoms became more and more obvious.

But at least, being a widower and living alone now that both of his grown children were off living lives of their own, his domestic situation put him in a good position to keep his private demons strictly private.

Which was why he scowled somewhat ferociously as he heard the doorbell ring. Visitors were seldom welcome. He glanced outside, saw that it was nearly fully dark, and wondered who could be calling at this time in the evening.

Although he was a man of influence and power, and often socialised with Oxford's movers and shakers, his real friends were few and far between, and all of them knew that he wasn't the kind of man that you simply 'dropped in on' to have a chat and a nightcap with.

He got up somewhat reluctantly from his chair, a tall man at just over six feet in height, with a shock of thick silvery-white hair. He was a few years off his sixtieth birthday, but looked comfortably closer to 50. As he walked out into the hall, he watched his feet carefully. The stumbling uneven gait of a man in his condition was a dead giveaway to well-informed eyes, and he was glad to notice that, so far, he was walking as well as he'd ever done.

Perhaps, in the future, he might have to feign some sort of leg injury to cover up any falls or mishaps? Or a touch of fictional arthritis might fit the bill? It would certainly give him an excuse to use a walking cane. He'd have to give it some thought.

He opened his front door with a peremptory sweep, and then blinked in surprise as he saw the young, tall, brunette woman standing anxiously on his step.

Trudy Loveday had never called at the coroner's home before. On the previous two occasions that they'd worked murder cases, she'd always gone to his office to make her reports or to meet up with him.

She'd found his name and address in the phone book and hadn't been at all surprised to have to find her way to the prestigious area near South Parks Road, where he lived in a terrace of large, Victorian houses, in a leafy street not far from Keble College.

'Hello, Dr Ryder,' she said now, launching nervously into speech. 'I hope you don't mind me calling on you like this... If you've got company, I can always come back...' She half-turned, almost wishing he'd say that he had, so that she could go away again.

18

For now that she was here, she was feeling distinctly uneasy. It was one thing to be assigned as this important man's police liaison by her boss, but that was a whole world away from coming to his private residence, out of uniform, and begging for a favour. It smacked of presumptuousness, and as such, was enough to send her face flooding with colour.

Which was why she'd come over barely ten minutes after Grace Farley had left, as she'd felt that the sooner she got it over with, the less fraught her nerves would become.

'No, no, I'm alone,' he reassured her pleasantly. 'Come on in, Constable Loveday,' Clement said, using her title rather than her name, since he'd instantly picked up on her anxiety.

Trudy forced a smile and stepped inside a small but – to her eyes at least – still rather grand hall, with black and white tiles on the floor, and a large oval ornately-framed mirror set over a narrow console table. She noted the private telephone that rested on it and was once again reminded of the differences in their status.

If the Lovedays ever needed to make a telephone call, they used the phone box at the end of their street, like everyone else.

'Come on through to the study,' he said, indicating the door that stood open to their left. 'I was just about to make some cocoa,' he lied. 'Would you like some?'

'Oh, no thank you,' Trudy said instantly. 'I won't stay long, and I don't want to take up your time,' she insisted. But even as she spoke, she wondered if it was true that the coroner had been about to drink so innocent a beverage.

Once or twice in the past, she'd wondered if he drank too much. Occasionally she'd noticed one or two signs that might indicate intoxication. But she watched him now as he led her into a pleasant, book-lined room with large sash windows overlooking the tree-lined street beyond, and he seemed to be alert and sober.

'Take a seat,' he offered, indicating one of the green leather button-back chairs that sat in front of a walnut desk. He took his own seat behind it as Trudy, still feeling very much the supplicant, lowered herself into the chair.

'The reason I've come,' she began, launching into her story before she could give herself time to chicken out, 'is that I've just had a visit from an old friend of mine. And what she had to say… I thought you should know about it.'

'Oh?' Clement asked, clearly puzzled but also intrigued. Which was, Trudy hoped, a good sign.

'Yes. It's about the girl who died recently from ingesting poison – the yew berry case, and she—'

Clement Ryder quickly held up his hand. 'Before you go any further, let me stop you just a moment. That's one of my cases – I'm holding the inquest the day after tomorrow.'

'Oh. I rather hoped it might be one of yours,' Trudy admitted. 'It makes things so much easier.'

Clement smiled wryly at her. He'd come to know Trudy Loveday quite well during the past year, and had come to respect her ambition and intelligence, but she could still be heart-breakingly young and naive sometimes.

'It might, or it might not,' he said firmly. 'But it's not really the done thing to discuss details of an inquest before it's even started. And if you're here to ask questions about the case, I'm afraid I simply can't discuss it with you. Even if you've been assigned the case in your official police capacity…?' He paused delicately, one eyebrow raised, and Trudy quickly shook her head.

'Oh no, I'm not,' she confirmed. And didn't need to say any more. Both of them knew that her boss wouldn't have assigned her to work on such an important case since DI Jennings preferred her to do office work, make the tea, and hold the hands of female victims of handbag-snatchings or lost cats.

Letting her work on a case that involved actual police work wasn't something that would have occurred to him!

'No,' Clement agreed, a shade heavily and with an ironic glint

20

in his eye. 'But even if you had been working the case—'

This time it was Trudy's turn to interrupt him, which she did, aware that she was blushing slightly.

'It's all right, Dr Ryder, I haven't come here to try and find things out. I'd never presume on our...' She found herself wanting to say the word 'friendship' and managed to alter her tongue just in time. 'Acquaintance. Actually, it's just the opposite. I've come here to tell you something that you might find relevant. Or not. I'm not really sure,' she said, suddenly feeling confused and not at all as confident as she had been that that this important man would be interested in Grace's opinion at all.

Suddenly, sitting here in this posh house and in this rather imposing room, Trudy began to wonder what she could have been thinking.

Had she been horribly stupid? When she'd set out, she'd been sure that, because he liked her and they'd got on well in the past, he would be glad to see her and interested in what she had to say. Now, she felt far less sanguine.

'Well, I won't know until I hear it, Trudy,' Clement said casually, amused by her sudden lack of coherence, and determined to put her at ease. She reminded him a little of a cat set down in an unfamiliar environment, and he was glad when she began to relax. 'So, tell me what it's all about then,' he advised her amiably.

Thus encouraged, it didn't take her long to recount the substance of Grace Farley's visit, and when she'd finished, she waited expectantly to see what he had to say.

Clement took only a few moments to process the information, and briefly consulted his memory – which, mercifully, was still functioning perfectly. 'The files on the case are all back at my office, of course, but I'm pretty sure Grace Farly isn't one of the witnesses on my list,' he finally admitted.

'Does that mean you can't call her as a character witness then?' Trudy asked, disappointed, and making Clement laugh softly.

'It's not a criminal trial you know,' he reminded her gently. 'I'll be calling the person who found her – which was her mother, I believe – along with medical experts and such like. And her best friend, I believe, who, presumably, will be saying much the same as your visitor?'

Trudy shrugged. 'I don't know if she will or if she won't. But Grace was really adamant that Abigail wasn't suicidal. I just thought you should know. And I promised Grace I would tell you, so…' She shrugged graphically.

Clement nodded. 'So now the ball's in my court, as they say. Both literally and figuratively speaking.'

She grinned, then looked wistful. 'I wish I could attend the inquest. I'm sort of interested now. But I don't think the Sergeant will let me have the time off! Not even if I make the case that it's all good experience for me.'

'Never mind. If you come round to my office when it's over, I'll fill you in,' he promised.

'Will you? Thanks so much,' Trudy said, already rising. He politely walked her to the door and was still smiling slightly as he shut it behind her.

Her youthful enthusiasm, as always, had lifted his spirits a little and helped lighten his mood. She might not have realised it, but the coroner was glad she'd come.

It wasn't until after she'd thanked him and was on her way back home, that Trudy wondered what he'd made of Grace's other concerns about the tricks being played at the theatre.

Had he been interested in that anyway? The rather catty goings-on of a bunch of would-be beauty queens couldn't have concerned him much.

In any case, it couldn't hurt to pop by the theatre herself one afternoon during rehearsals, just to satisfy her own curiosity. She knew from what Grace had said that the theatre's owner was happy for them to use the building during daylight, as long as they vacated the premises long before the evening performances began. Presumably the place didn't do matinees.

It sounded fun, in a way. She'd never seen a beauty contest being held before, and it had a certain appeal. All those pretty dresses and things. Mind you, she couldn't imagine stepping out in front of people just dressed in a swimming costume! The thought made her shudder.

But just to have a look around and put Grace's mind at rest – well, where was the harm in that? When Trudy had first started school, it had been a daunting time and the slighter older girl had been kind enough to take her under her wing. She'd even intervened once, when a playground bully had tried to push her into the sandpit. So far, she'd never been in a position to repay the debt, but now, finally, she could.

It never once occurred to her that by doing so, she might be putting her own life at risk.

Why would it?

Chapter 3

Mrs Christine Dunbar sighed over a large bunch of russet chrysanthemums that stubbornly failed to form into the shape she wanted, and began re-arranging them, somewhat impatiently, in a large cut-glass vase.

She was a rather handsome but large and fleshy woman, who was never seen out and about in public without wearing her corset. Her tightly waved, rather brassy blonde hair was always hardened into submission by a lavish application of hairspray, and her face was always made up with the latest and finest cosmetics. Only her rather boiled-gooseberry blue eyes caused her real concern, but, as her practically-minded mother had always told her, there was very little she could do about those.

Her grandfather had been a Tory politician for many years, and once, in his glory days before the Great War, had even been a member of the cabinet. And it was from him that, as an only child, she had inherited the large, whitewashed mansion just off the Woodstock road where she now lived. Sited firmly in the prestigious area in the north of the city, it boasted a large, well-tended garden, and a double garage.

Finally having beaten the blooms into submission, she carried the now perfectly arranged vase into the lounge and placed it on top of the grand piano. Neither she nor her husband could play the instrument, not being particularly musical, but it had stood in pride of place in the room, probably since Queen Victoria had reigned.

Her husband, sitting on the sofa and perusing the *London Times*, barely noticed her presence as she took a seat on the sofa opposite him, and reached for an embroidery hoop, containing her latest needlework.

She enjoyed making religious mottoes, usually surrounded by a flower border, which she then donated to the local church bazaar.

Now she looked over a rather fine pink peony that she had almost finished, and regarded her husband, Robert, without any obvious signs of enthusiasm.

In many ways, she believed, she had rather married beneath her. And yet she couldn't deny that in many other ways, her choice had been a wise and inspired one.

Robert was not, she admitted to herself without any undue sense of worry, a particularly handsome man. Of average height at five feet seven inches, he was now, at the age of 52, going slightly bald on top, but kept his hair nicely dyed black, which went with his nearly ebony-coloured eyes. The matching moustache was similarly obsidian, but his chin was undeniably weak. Her husband liked to dress well though, and at times, it sometimes occurred to Christine to wonder (rather uneasily and with a sense of rare self-awareness) if he might not have a better sense of fashion than she did. He was one of those men who radiated an immense sense of energy. The kind of man who was used to getting things done but also seemed full of humour and bonhomie; but that, as she very well knew, was merely a front for his rapacious nature.

Of which she approved enormously.

For although Robert had been born of distinctly lower-middle-class parents (his father had been a chemistry teacher at a second-rate boys' prep school) his ambitions had always been first-class. And she, on the market for a husband who could keep her in luxury, had been perspicacious enough to sense that he had the brains and the determination to succeed in life.

As, indeed he had. He had taken her not immodest dowry and turned it into a very profitable company producing jam, honey and marmalade to the discerning palate, nationwide.

Of course, it was 'trade', and as such, rather below what she was used to, but Christine had made it a point never to set foot in the actual 'works'. What's more, she had grimly ignored any behind-the-hand sniggering that might have gone on in her set during the early years of her marriage. It was now an immense source of satisfaction to her that, as income tax began to bite so hard and many of her friends had to tighten their belts or sell off the family heirlooms, she had been able to carry on spending as much as she had ever done.

It was just annoying that the 'works' had been allowed to intrude so rudely in her life in recent weeks.

Normally, whenever her husband discussed his plans for expanding the business or crowed over his latest scheme to bring Dunbar products more firmly into the public eye, Christine barely listened.

But this latest venture of his was causing her no end of anxiety.

When he'd first proposed establishing Miss Oxford Honey in a bid to make their own brands as famous as those of Oxford Marmalade, Christine had been almost speechless. Her conservative soul had shrivelled at the thought of something so utterly down-market as a beauty contest, and she could imagine the sniggering starting up all over again.

Surely, she'd protested to her husband, he had been in jest?

And just as surely, she'd come to learn that he was not. For whilst he had become used to acceding to her requests in the normal run of things, he was adamant that 'work' was his domain, and in this one area he would not be dictated to.

Eventually, therefore, she'd been forced to back down. But that did not mean that she was totally defeated. Instead, she'd magnanimously and cunningly offered to lend a hand herself, and 'help' him run the whole event.

In this way, she'd pointed out cannily, he wouldn't need to neglect the routine work, or the vital day-to-day running of the business, whilst still being able to make use of his brilliant marketing strategy.

In reality, of course, she'd only done it to ensure that her husband would have as little to do with it as possible, because... Well, as Christine had been forced to face, rather early on in her marriage, Robert had a bit of a roving eye.

It was annoying, of course. And when she'd been younger, overwhelmingly painful. But over the years, and by constantly telling herself that it was nothing really hideously embarrassing, she'd managed to ignore it. Well, mostly.

After all, many of the women in her set had to put up with men who strayed, especially wealthy men; men who were used to a certain amount of power and status. It was just their way. So long as it was handled discreetly, everyone could pretend it wasn't happening. And Robert, she had to admit, was always very careful indeed to be discreet. As he should be!

For a second, her rather unattractive face contorted with pain.

Although Christine had no qualms about letting her husband manage her money and capital, she'd been wise enough to keep it all under her own name. Which meant that Robert had lived for the nearly twenty-five years of their marriage well aware of which side his bread was buttered, and that keeping her sweet was definitely in his own best interests.

But she was, by nature, a deeply suspicious woman (and subconsciously at least, a very insecure one), so it hadn't taken her long to discover his succession of mistresses. These he kept in a discreet flat in High Wycombe, where Dunbar had a second factory, and which required Robert's 'input' once or twice a week.

This arrangement she'd been forced to accept with grace, as a woman of her intelligence and sophistication had been trained to do.

And she didn't – well, not *really* – believe that he would ever be so crass and stupid as to let himself get mixed up with some working-class dolly bird who had delusions of becoming a fashion model or some such thing, on the back of winning a local beauty contest.

Even so, it was a fact of life that Robert liked pretty women. And when men reached middle age… well, they could often get a little bit silly. The thought of letting him run free among so much temptation had definitely been enough to raise her hackles.

Luckily, she had a very good spy-in-the-camp in Grace Farley, whom she'd persuaded her husband to put in charge as the 'face of Dunbar's' during the running of the event. And she could always make sure Grace did as she was told. And, of course, she could rely on good old Patricia Merriweather to help her keep her errant husband on the straight and narrow.

A widow herself, the old lady knew how the world worked all right, and of course the Merriweathers were one of Oxford's 'old' families, whose ancestry went back even further than her own.

Yet, still, Christine felt vaguely uneasy about the whole thing.

Strange things had been happening. That incident with the face cream, for instance. And that poor girl taking a tumble from the stage steps. Not usually a woman given to picking up on 'atmosphere' or imagining things, even she was beginning to sense something… brooding, surrounding the whole competition.

And worse still, about a week ago, certain rumours had started to reach her ears about one of the girls boasting about 'hooking' a sugar daddy for herself!

So now Christine felt as if her whole world suddenly hung in the balance. Which was intolerable! As if she would let some silly little chit of a girl threaten her wellbeing and the pleasant, well-oiled orderliness of her life!

28

She glanced across at her husband thoughtfully.

She was fairly sure that he'd paid off the girl who'd come out in a rash to keep quiet about it. He must also be aware of the other instances of petty sabotage as well, since he'd made no secret of how worried he was that bad publicity might mar the first of what he hoped would be an annual event.

But at least things were progressing well in other ways. The Old Swan Theatre had seen better days, but it was still a respectable venue and ticket sales for the public show in three weeks' time were selling well. All the newspapers were lined up, and even the local radio station would cover it.

Several large local businesses, such as department stores and florists, were backing the enterprise, both by providing the prizes for the girls and by sitting in on the judging panel.

And wasn't she herself keeping a tight hold on the reins? She'd stepped in and taken control when she needed to and would remain in the driving seat until the whole debacle was over. There was certainly no way the contestants themselves – floozies and airheads all of them – could ever get the better of her!

Yet, lurking in the back of her mind, was the worry that her poor fool of a husband was in danger of forgetting himself and doing something monumentally stupid. So stupid that it would put their nice cosy world in real danger.

At this thought, Christine Dunbar stabbed her embroidery needle through the white fabric so forcefully that she pricked her finger. She stifled a very unladylike epithet and quickly sucked the blood from her throbbing digit before it could stain anything.

Her eyes when she looked across at her husband, still reading his paper in blissful ignorance, were narrowed and calculating.

Chapter 4

Dr Clement Ryder opened the inquest into the death of Abigail Trent right on time. As usual when he was presiding in the coroner's court, things tended to happen with clockwork efficiency, mostly because his staff both respected and feared him in equal measure.

He watched the jury assemble with a thoughtful eye, and then listened attentively as the witnesses were called. He was always diligent, of course, being ever mindful of the seriousness of his job, but he had to admit that the unprecedented appeal for help from Trudy Loveday had certainly sharpened his mind even more than usual.

He would not let what Grace Farley had to say influence him in any way, naturally, but he knew that he would be lying to himself if he didn't acknowledge that his curiosity about this case was definitely aroused.

As the morning went on, the story of the dead girl, via a series of interested and professional witnesses, slowly and clearly unfolded.

The medical facts, at least, were all clear enough, and the pathologist was very precise in his evidence. The girl had died as a result of ingesting a taxine alkaloid associated with yew berries

– namely the seeds contained within the berry. The actual cause of death came as a result of the cardiogenic shock that follows such ingestion. The victim would have suffered first arrhythmia and then heart failure.

On the day in question, her sister Miriam had come back to the family home in order to use her mother's newer washing tub. She disliked having to use the bowl-and-mangle that was all that was available to her in her own, rather new and as yet under-furnished, marital home. It was getting on for nine o'clock in the morning, so her mother had asked her to go upstairs to Abigail's bedroom and check that she had, indeed, already left for work. Her mother hadn't heard her youngest daughter come down, and although, since entering a local beauty contest, she didn't always eat breakfast in an effort to 'slim', she usually called in to the kitchen to have a cup of tea.

Miriam testified that she found her sister lying in bed, and had at first assumed that she was asleep. However, she'd been unable to wake her, and alarmed by her pallor and the coolness of her skin, had called for her mother. Mrs Vera Trent had taken one look at her youngest daughter and told Miriam to go to the telephone box and call for an ambulance.

But Abigail had been pronounced dead when a local doctor, also called by Miriam, had arrived first at the house.

This same doctor had noticed an empty glass on the dead girl's bedside table that had contained what smelt like orange juice, but still held some unknown residue which had clouded the bottom of the glass. Both Mrs Trent and Miriam had been aware that Abigail had been drinking orange juice a lot lately, as she had been told by someone that the vitamins in it were good for the complexion.

The doctor, not liking the signs he'd detected on the deceased, had insisted on calling in the police. The subsequent results of the autopsy had ensured that an inquest needed to be held.

These, then, were the facts.

31

Not quite so easy to ascertain were the more nebulous details surrounding the personality and circumstances of the deceased, in the weeks prior to her death.

Abigail Trent, according to all who knew her, was a pretty 19-year-old girl who had lived with her mother and father all her life. First that had been in Cowley, before the family moved to an area near Parklands on the outskirts of Summertown – a much more upmarket suburb of the city – when she was just 9 years old. She had three sisters and two brothers – all of whom were older than herself – and she had clearly been a young lady who had intended to 'get on' in life.

Unlike her sisters – who had married local lads before reaching their twenties – and her brothers – who both worked as labourers in a local construction firm – Abigail had always had (as her mother had proudly stated) ambition.

Being the youngest child, she had been the one to benefit most from the family's relocation to Summertown, especially since (after passing her eleven-plus exams) she had attended a very good local school, where the mix of children tended to belong to the more professional and mobile middle-classes. She had done fairly well at school, and her exam results – though nothing spectacular – had allowed her to go on and do secretarial training. She had subsequently gone on to find her first ever job as an office 'junior' in a small but well-respected solicitor's office.

But as her friends and contemporaries called to the stand to testify made clear, the dead girl did indeed have ambitions far beyond the environment of the office.

Dr Ryder had not added Grace Farley's name to this list of witnesses, as he hadn't wanted to complicate matters. As it was, her non-appearance hardly mattered, for Abigail's friends told pretty much the same story. All agreed that Abigail had been very popular at school, being good at sports and music, and aided, no doubt, by her obvious physical beauty. The coroner and jury were shown some photographs of the dead girl, who turned out to be a tall, leggy brunette with a very good figure and undeniably pretty face. She even had a mole, widely known as a 'beauty mark', just above and slightly to the right side of her mouth, giving her even more appeal.

So nobody had been unduly surprised when she'd answered the advertisement for an upcoming beauty pageant to find Miss Oxford Honey.

Her best friend, Vicky Munnings, testified that Abigail had talked her into applying as well, although she had been rather less keen than her friend, but when both of them passed the initial auditions, Abigail (or Abby as everyone who knew her called her) had been delighted.

'From that moment on, she was determined to win the competition,' Vicky stated. Her friend, according to Vicky, had seen winning the pageant as a step towards something bigger and better. Everyone knew that the winner of the pageant would be automatically entered for the Miss Oxford contest next year, and the winner of that would then go on to enter Miss England, who, of course, would then be a contestant in Miss World.

'Abby didn't have her head so far in the clouds as to think she'd go *that* far,' Vicky had defended her dead friend robustly. But she did feel that winning the competition would present her with more options. A life in London as an advertiser's model perhaps. Or a model for one of the bigger fashion houses. Maybe, Vicky had said through some tears, her friend had even seen herself as living in Paris.

But in order to achieve these ambitions, she needed to win.

'She became obsessed with beauty products and doing things to improve her figure,' Vicky testified. 'Like exercises to improve her bustline and slim down her waist.' She also took to periodic 'fasting' to lose weight, and had spent all her money on face creams and lotions, which, Abby constantly complained, were all so expensive.

'She was always reading in women's magazines about this

herbal stuff that you could make for yourself, to make your skin glow and all that kind of thing, that didn't cost the earth,' Vicky had added.

And it was here that Dr Ryder – and no doubt the jury and gentlemen of the press as well – really sat up and took notice. Because, finally, they were coming to the crux of the matter.

When Dr Ryder asked her if it was possible that her friend might have added something 'homemade and herbal' to her glass of orange juice in the mistaken belief that it would somehow help improve her looks or figure, Vicky hadn't been able to give a proper answer. She'd dithered a bit and had seemed frightened and nervous and unsure. Eventually, somewhat tearful and upset, she admitted that Abby had made some stuff for herself before her death – including some sort of oat-and-milk face pack, following a recipe she'd seen in a newspaper article. That had been followed by an experiment with a homemade shampoo that was supposed to make her hair shine more. And yes, Vicky admitted, her friend had got the ingredients from some sort of plant material that she'd picked herself, but Vicky hadn't bothered to ask what, because she hadn't liked the smell of it.

But whether or not she would make stuff to actually eat or drink – she just didn't know. When pressed, she was adamant that her friend 'wasn't stupid' and that, as children, their parents had always warned them not to 'eat berries from the hedges'.

But she also admitted that Abby, like herself, didn't really know anything about what was poisonous and what wasn't.

The parents' testimony, as usual, was heartbreaking. Yes, they'd heard the hurtful rumours going around that their daughter was sometimes moody and volatile, and that she'd drunk the poison on purpose. But such an idea was ludicrous. Their daughter had been young and beautiful and looking forward to being in the beauty pageant, and to being on stage at the Old Swan Theatre for the final public performance. Furthermore, she had been making plans for her future. Yes, sometimes she could be a bit moody and up and down, but a lot of girls her age were the same. She had certainly not been under the doctor for depression or anything else.

She had no real worries in her life; she had a good steady job, and a young man she'd been stepping out with, one William Hanson – although they didn't think it was serious – and no health issues. Why would she do something so dreadful?

The 'young man' in question, when called, admitted to 'stepping out' with her in the past, but that they'd seen less and less of each other since she'd started rehearsing for the beauty pageant, and that they'd more or less 'called the whole thing off'. He admitted to having a new girl now, but had backed up Abby's parents' claim that she had definitely not been the 'suicidal type'. He, too, couldn't believe she had deliberately poisoned herself. Why would she do it?

Clement wondered the same thing – and he could see that the jury did too.

By four o'clock that afternoon, all the available evidence had been examined, and Clement could see that the jury was looking uneasy and uncertain.

With his vast knowledge of both juries and human nature in general, it wasn't hard for him to read their collective state of mind. They clearly didn't believe it was a case of suicide. There had been no note left, and in any case, most juries were reluctant to bring in such a verdict, because of the effect it had on the victim's family.

There had been no evidence of 'foul play' either. Both her parents had testified that their daughter had gone to bed as normal and had obviously died in her sleep. There had been no evidence of an intruder or break-in at the house.

That left accidental death or death by misadventure.

Obviously the poison had been in the glass of orange juice (as chemical analysis had confirmed). But how had it got there?

Given what they'd been told, Clement thought it a good guess that they would bring in a verdict that the girl herself had made up a 'beauty' potion and had sadly and fatally poisoned herself in the process.

But Clement Ryder was not so sure.

So in his summing up, he very cleverly played on their confusion by stressing that an open verdict would give the authorities time to explore the matter further.

Thus feeling relieved at having the responsibility for giving a firm decision taken off their shoulders, they gratefully accepted this gift horse without so much as even a cursory look inside its mouth, and took less than ten minutes to return with the aforementioned open verdict – much to the chagrin of the police representative, who had hoped that he might be able to write this case off their books once and for all, with minimum time and effort.

The gentlemen of the press quickly fled to file their stories – for the 'mysterious death of a beauty queen' could run for days, if handled properly, thus saving them the time and effort of going out and hunting down real stories. Besides, death and pretty girls always sold well, making everyone happy.

Well, everyone except for Robert Dunbar of course, who would not be a happy man at all. He had been hoping that the demise of Abigail Trent would be settled quickly and discreetly, and would not be allowed to sully his first foray into the world of showbiz.

* * *

The next morning, another man who felt decidedly unhappy was DI Harry Jennings. But then, he never *was* particularly sanguine whenever Dr Clement Ryder chose to drop by his office. It nearly always meant trouble and inconvenience.

But for once, the Inspector was determined not to play ball. 'Sorry, you can't have WPC Truelove. She's been seconded on special duties,' he informed the older man smugly.

Since Trudy had already told him that said 'special duties'

required her to search the female suspects who were being brought in during a sporadic raid on the city's brothels, Clement didn't feel particularly impressed.

'That's a shame,' Clement said mildly. 'The press are going to be all over this case, whether we like it or not.'

'I don't see why there should be any trouble,' Jennings growled uneasily.

'Well, since there seems to be a joker at work in the theatre, the more ribald daily rags might make some play with it.'

The Inspector looked at him narrowly. 'What do you mean? What sort of joker?' he asked, feeling genuinely alarmed now. It seemed the wily old coroner was on to something that he didn't know about. And that was never a good sign.

'Oh, hadn't you found that out yet?' Clement asked casually. Luckily, Trudy had left nothing out when reciting Grace's woes.

'Apparently there's been trouble within the beauty pageant. Spiked face creams and trip wires across the stage steps and such forth.' He waved a hand casually in the air.

'That just sounds like petty rivalries to me,' Jennings said impatiently. 'It hardly sounds like anything serious.'

'Oh, I agree,' Clement said. 'But it does mean that you'll have to concentrate some of your efforts around this competition. Just in case the prankster went too far, and maybe didn't quite understand the poisonous possibilities of yew?'

'So?' Inspector Jennings tried to sound off-hand, but his unease was growing.

Clement shrugged. 'I think the owner of the theatre and the organiser of the contest, not to mention the girls themselves, might take it amiss having big-footed male constables tramping about all over the place. Catching them out "accidentally" in their undies during the changes, gawping at them in their swimsuits and generally making a nuisance of themselves.'

Inspector Jennings flushed. 'I hardly think that's likely! My men are professionals through and through.'

'Hmm. But men will be men. You don't think they're going to take advantage of so many pretty witnesses?'

'I do not!' Jennings huffed.

'Because if they do, and there are any complaints… Can you just imagine the headlines in the papers?' Clement gave a mock shudder.

'It won't happen,' Jennings said flatly. 'I'll make sure of that!'

'But why risk it? Don't you think, since you're lucky enough to have a woman police constable assigned to you, that it makes perfect sense to make use of her in a situation that's clearly calling out for her services?' he asked mildly.

The Inspector – who didn't feel at all lucky to have had a woman foisted onto his previously all-male police station – eyed the older man warily. He didn't like it when the old vulture talked in such a mild and reasonable tone. It made him feel very wary indeed.

Besides, he was damned if he was going to let the older man bamboozle him into doing what he wanted.

'WPC Loveday is too inexperienced to be given any real responsibility yet,' he said adamantly.

Clement, who was wearing his usual impeccable suit (today a dark-grey creation with a dark-red pinstripe so thin it was almost invisible), casually crossed one leg over the other at the knee, and regarded thoughtfully the short length of his burgundy-coloured sock which his actions had just revealed.

'But unless she's given the opportunity to gain experience, she'll never get to learn, will she?' he pointed out reasonably.

The Inspector sighed softly. 'This is an ongoing case thanks to y… to the verdict brought in by the jury,' he gritted. He was, of course, well aware that the coroner had directed the jury into the verdict, and was determined that the interfering old so-and-so wouldn't get his way this time. For once, he and his little pet would have to learn they couldn't win every time.

'And for that reason,' he swept on with a blithe smile, 'I've decided to appoint a more able police officer to continue the inquiries into Abigail Trent's death.'

Clement looked at him curiously. That the Inspector was being deliberately obstructive didn't really surprise him. But he wondered, idly, what was behind it. Misogyny perhaps? Or was it Clement himself that Jennings objected to?

Either way, it didn't really matter. He was in no mood to cross swords with such a feeble opponent. It was far easier – and quicker – to simply go over his head.

'Well, if that's the way you feel about it,' he said with a pleasant smile, putting both his feet to the floor and rising abruptly from his chair. As he crossed to the door, putting his hat on his head as he went, he was aware that the policeman was watching him with both surprised and wary eyes.

'Good day, Inspector,' Clement said pleasantly from the doorway, before walking through the outer office and nodding every now and then to the polite greetings from the few officers who were working at their desks.

Back in his own office, it took the wily old coroner only two minutes to decide which of his friends he needed to call. There were several men who owed him a favour – and now he thought of one in particular. Back in the old days, he'd saved one of his colleagues from making a potentially disastrous mistake when he'd misdiagnosed a patient with a rare condition. It had been a mistake almost any doctor would have made, but Clement had been lucky enough to have had a similar case early in his own career, and thus he'd recognised the very subtle signs.

His friend was now a VIP on a large scale, with thumbs in many pies, and had been itching to get out of Clement's debt for years. So it would make his day to hear that he could finally do Clement a good turn in exchange and feel that they were now even.

Ten minutes later, a fuming DI Jennings received a phone call from above ordering him to offer the coroner the police liaison services of WPC Trudy Loveday for the Abigail Trent investigation.

* * *

At that moment, Trudy was in the cells going through the handbags of several prostitutes while they watched, calling her names and offering her suggestions that would have made her mother's ears burn.

She gamely tried to pretend her own weren't burning at some of the more raucous jeering coming from the confined women, but in truth she was rather glad when she was relieved by another officer who told her that she was wanted in the DI's office.

Naturally, this set off a whole barrage of innuendo from her tormentors, and she could only hope that her cheeks weren't still burning when she knocked on the DI's door a few minutes later and was bade, crisply, to enter.

Right from the start, she could tell by her superior officer's sarcastic tone and short, sharp sentences, that he was in a right royal tizzy. But she hardly cared, when he told her the good news that she was going to be working with the coroner again.

And the fact that she was going to be working with the coroner again on Abigail Trent's case was the icing on the cake. Grace Farley would be so pleased!

At least now, Trudy thought with some satisfaction as she collected a bicycle and pedalled off towards Floyd's Row, where the coroner's office was situated, she might be able to give her friend some peace of mind.

Chapter 5

'So where do we start?' Trudy asked, beaming a thank-you smile at Dr Ryder's secretary as she delivered a tray containing a large pot of tea, three cups and a tin of Huntley and Palmer biscuits, and then left with her usual silent discretion.

By now, Trudy was beginning to think of Dr Ryder's office as a home-away-from home, and as she took a sip of tea, she looked across his big, but neatly ordered desk-top with an expectant look on her face.

'Well, I thought we might start with your friend Grace,' Clement said. 'I've taken the liberty of telephoning her at work, and she's agreed to come down here in her lunch hour' – he checked his watch – 'which should be in about ten minutes' time.'

Trudy nodded happily. 'So, what are your thoughts so far?' she demanded eagerly.

Clement smiled. 'I have none, in particular,' he said, amused, as ever, by her eagerness. He reached for a biscuit and put it on the side of his saucer and with no trace of tremor in his hand today, lifted the full cup of tea with confidence.

In due time, he knew his speech would become slurred, and he'd begin to shuffle. But with luck he could still eke out a few more years before anyone would guess he had serious health issues, and he might even get another year or more after that before anyone dared challenge him on it.

In the meanwhile, he was determined to make the most of these last precious, golden years of his life before enforced retirement and illness finally got the better of him. Besides, as he listened to the young girl in the chair opposite him, he was very much aware that acting as Trudy Loveday's mentor and champion was going to give him an investment in life for the foreseeable future.

'But surely you got a picture of what we're dealing with from the inquest? I only wish I'd been able to attend,' she added, a shade forlornly.

Clement contemplated lighting his pipe, then decided he couldn't be bothered to try and get it going, and leaned back in his chair with a sigh instead. 'The only things to be gained from inquests are basic information and a general "feel" for the case,' he pointed out patiently. 'It's not as if new evidence is ever revealed. It's a question of making official the facts that are already known to the police and the medical authorities.'

'All right,' Trudy said, trying to quash down a feeling of impatience. 'So what's your "feeling" for this one? Do you think she committed suicide?' she demanded. Now that her friend Dr Clement Ryder had become involved and the investigation was officially 'above board' with her superiors, she was eager to move the case forward.

'Your friend was adamant that Abigail wasn't suicidal, wasn't she?' he mused quietly.

'Yes. Why? Did the other friends you called as witnesses say otherwise?' Trudy asked sharply, and for some reason was rather surprised when the coroner shook his head.

'No. Her parents were adamant she wasn't depressed, of course, and her friends seemed to feel the same way. Nobody said that she seemed the "type" to take her own life. Not that there is such a thing, of course.'

'Oh. So all the gossip about her being moody and whatnot was just that? Idle gossip and speculation, and people being spiteful? Or…' Trudy's eyes widened slightly as a sudden thought hit her. 'Could it be that someone was deliberately spreading such rumours around to try and make people believe it was suicide, when it wasn't?'

'Maybe,' Clement said, a twinkle appearing in his rather watery blue eyes at her evident excitement. 'But it sounds a little far-fetched to me.'

Trudy sighed and reluctantly nodded.

'Then again,' the coroner swept on, 'she might have been moody and occasionally depressed without wanting to kill herself. Most of us are down from time to time, but we don't all go throwing ourselves off the top of tall buildings. No, the impression I got of her, reading between the lines, was of a pretty and ambitious girl, who was perhaps a shade on the selfish and self-obsessed side, and was determined to get on in life.'

'So not suicide then,' Trudy said with some satisfaction. 'When Grace gets here, she'll be pleased about that, at least. So – not suicide, and I take it we can strike out murder?' she offered, a bit more tentatively. She nibbled on a biscuit, her face thoughtful.

Clement verbally ran through the evidence – or rather lack thereof – for the case for murder. No break-in, no medical evidence of an attack or struggle, or that the poison had been forced into her system. Nor had the victim complained of being afraid of anyone, or of anyone menacing her prior to her death.

'Of course, none of that means that someone couldn't have sneaked the poison into her juice somehow,' he pointed out reasonably in summation.

'Which would put the people in the house with her in the spotlight,' Trudy mused, sitting a little forward on her chair now. 'Namely, her family.' Then she slumped back again. 'Can you really see her mum or dad or one of her siblings poisoning her?' she asked sceptically.

Clement had never met Trudy's parents, but he had been able to tell from the way she spoke about them, that she enjoyed a very close and loving relationship with them – as she did with her brother. So it wasn't surprising that she couldn't really believe in murder within a family.

However, he'd presided over too many cases (and read too many depressing news articles) to be unaware that one's supposedly nearest and dearest often *did* want to poison one another. And sometimes did just that!

'Her parents and the sister who found her seemed genuinely grief-stricken,' he temporised. 'Sometime soon I'm going to have to talk to them privately and in more detail. But I think *you* should concentrate on what your friend Grace has to say about this beauty pageant thing, and the strange goings-on there. Just in case there's a connection.'

Trudy nodded, then, picking up something in the coroner's tone, she shot the older man a look. 'You sounded rather disapproving of the beauty contest, Dr Ryder. Don't you follow the Miss World competition?' she asked, a shade tongue-in-cheek. Most men, she knew, liked looking at pretty girls.

'No, I don't,' Clement said, half-amused and half-appalled by the idea. 'I'd rather watch the cricket!'

Trudy shrugged. 'I suppose I can see why most of the girls doing them think it's fun. And the money prizes can be staggering – I did a little research on it after Grace came to me,' she admitted, seeing the doctor's thick eyebrows rise in surprise. 'But I think the Miss Oxford Honey only gives out prize money to the actual winner, and prizes for the runner up and winners of each round. Grace said the shop owners who are helping sponsor it are donating the prizes. You know, stockings from the clothes shops, and cosmetics from the chemists, and stuff like that. I think they're being rewarded for their generosity by getting to sit on the judging panel, along with Mr Dunbar and the owner of the theatre.'

'I'll bet they are,' Clement grunted, secretly thinking that most of them would be only too glad of the excuse to participate in a little glamorous showbiz under the auspices of a business banner.

'So, you think it's unlikely to be murder?' Trudy got the conversation back on track, trying not to sound disappointed. 'I suppose that leaves us with accidental death then? I mean, that the dead girl thought she was drinking something herbal and good for her that she'd made herself, and was in fact drinking poison instead. That's so sad. To think, she thought that what she was doing was going to help her reach her goals in life, when in fact, she was putting an end to her future once and for all.'

Clement blinked at this rather torturous statement and then shrugged. 'Or perhaps she didn't make the poisonous concoction herself, but was given it by someone else?'

'So you *do* think it's murder?' Trudy said, grinning with excitement.

'Or it's possible that the person who made the concoction made a genuine mistake, and is now too scared to own up to it?'

'Her best friend Vicky, perhaps?' Trudy proffered absently, reading the coroner's inquest notes in between chatting and sipping her tea.

'No, I don't think so. She didn't strike me as the adventurous kind. Not the sort of girl to try making up ointments and such,' Clement disagreed. 'She didn't seem that bright, for one thing. No, I got the distinct feeling she was more the follower, and Abby the leader.'

'Oh. One of her other friends then?'

'Or a rival in the competition, perhaps?' Clement mused. Although he considered it part of his remit to try and rein Trudy in on some of her more fanciful theories, he had to admit that it could be fun to let the imagination run riot now and then. 'Perhaps this prankster your friend told you about has struck again, but this time went too far? Possibly without meaning to?'

'Would that be murder then?' Trudy mused.

'Manslaughter, probably,' Clement said. 'But I'm not a QC, and besides, this is all idle speculation, remember.'

Just then, and before Trudy could reply, the secretary knocked on the door, announced the arrival of Miss Farley and ushered Grace inside.

Trudy took one look at her pale, tired face, and got to her feet. 'Grace. How's your mother?' she asked abruptly and urgently.

Clement took the opportunity to reach into his desk, unroll a pack of strong mints and pop one into his mouth. Another annoying side effect of Parkinson's was halitosis, and he had got into the habit of sucking on mints on a regular basis.

Grace, shrugging wearily and taking the seat the coroner rose from and offered her, slumped down rather heavily and gave a small smile.

'Oh, you know. She's been taking this new medication for a little while now, and at first she seemed to be improving. Now some of the doctors at the Radcliffe Infirmary seem to think that an experimental operation might be her only hope, but others are advising against it. So we're not sure what to do. Dad's at his wit's end. But you didn't invite me here to talk about all this,' she said, and with an obvious mental effort, stiffened her shoulder and looked across the desk.

'Thank you for calling me up Dr Ryder and for taking on Abby's case,' she said politely.

Clement, whose previous life as a surgeon made it easy for him to recognise all the signs of someone with a terminally ill loved one, poured her a cup of tea and insisted she take and eat two biscuits.

'I'm only too pleased to help,' Clement said and smiled at her gently. 'So, what can you tell us about Abby? How did you first meet her?'

Grace sighed, and then opened her handbag and reached inside for a packet of Camel's cigarettes and a small lighter.

She offered them around, but both Trudy and Clement refused.

'Well, I've only really known her since the beauty pageant started when Abby and Vicky showed up at the initial interviews. We're still having one or two girls coming in even now, though rehearsals are well under way.'

'I'm not sure I know just how a beauty contest works,' Trudy admitted, sensing that her friend was very nervous indeed. Whether it was because she knew that the morgue was so close by, or whether Dr Clement Ryder's somewhat imposing presence was getting to her, she couldn't tell.

'Well, neither do I really,' Grace admitted ruefully. 'But I know how Miss Oxford Honey is being run. Basically, we want girls from Oxford or within a twenty-mile radius to come for an interview so we can see if they're suitable. After that, they need to do a piece for the talent contest to make sure they have a certain flair – and that's really the main reason for the rehearsals, which is why we're so lucky to have the theatre. What's more, the resident make-up lady and wardrobe mistress are helping out with the evening wear section and swimsuit catwalk bit.'

'OK. And Abby was one of the favourites to win, was she?' Trudy gently led her back on course.

'Oh yes. Well, perhaps her and three or four of the others. Caroline Tomworthy is very exotic-looking, and a bit older, at 28. So she has a bit more glamour, I suppose, though 30 is the cut-off age,' Grace explained, puffing assiduously on her cigarette. 'Then there's Betty Darville and Sylvia Blane. And maybe Candace Usherwood. But she's only just 20 and acts much younger, so…'

'And how did Abby get on with these girls – the ones who were her main rivals?' Trudy asked curiously.

'Oh, I would have said they got on fine. I just can't imagine who's playing such nasty tricks on everyone. Just last night a girl's shampoo was doctored with glue! Poor thing, it took us all ages to wash it out. Even then, she had to have a hairdresser come in and cut her hair. Luckily, we all agree the shorter style suits her better than her long hair, but even so she was very upset...'

Grace sighed heavily. 'Poor Mr Dunbar is at his wit's end! So far the press haven't caught a whiff about the sabotage, but when they do...' She broke off helplessly, stubbed out her cigarette in the ashtray on the table and wearily folded her hands neatly in her lap. She didn't really want to talk about Mr Dunbar. She felt bad enough steaming open and reading his private mail, then reporting back the contents to his wife. It made her feel dirty and incredibly shabby. And that was not the only demoralising thing she'd had to do.

'So it couldn't have been Abby who was playing the tricks then,' Trudy said with a quick glance at the coroner. It wasn't a theory they'd discussed before – but it was obvious that if the prankster was still at work, then it couldn't possibly have been the dead girl who was causing the nuisances. 'Unless someone has taken over from her,' Trudy theorised. 'Maybe one of the girls might have known or suspected she was behind the pranks, and then decided to simply follow on where she left off? Especially if it was working, and some of the girls were being spooked into leaving the competition!'

Clement felt his lips twitch.

Grace looked at Trudy a little shocked. 'Do you think that's possible?'

'I think it very unlikely,' Clement interposed firmly. 'But Trudy has raised an interesting question. Have any of the girls dropped out?'

'Only two so far,' Grace said unwillingly. 'But most seem determined to try and win. Even the girl who had to get her hair cut shorter is carrying on. It's the prize you see – not the money so much, but the automatic entry into the Miss Oxford competition.'

'Did Abby suspect anyone of being the prankster?' Trudy asked abruptly.

48

'No, I don't think so. She never said anything about it to me if she did. But you should ask Vicky. She'd be the one who'd know. She and Abby were always thick as thieves. So if she'd told anyone, it would be her.'

'Did you ever hear her mention anyone who was trying to help her out by giving her beauty tips?' Trudy asked next.

'No. Oh, I know she and some of the other girls tried all sorts of homemade things to try and help. Some girl said putting cucumber slices on her eyes at night was marvellous for stopping her getting bags, and that sort of thing. But nothing about making concoctions and stuff to drink!'

'So you think it was an accident then, Miss Farley?' Clement put in smoothly. He was watching Grace closely and sensed a tension in the girl that seemed rather out of place.

Like Trudy, he'd sensed her nerves the moment she'd walked into the room. But again, like Trudy, he'd initially put that down to her being in an unfamiliar environment. The legal and medical professions made most people feel nervous, and here, at Floyd's Row, both of those combined. And, of course, a lot of people were uncomfortable around the trappings of death. As a coroner, he was used to people feeling unhappy in his presence.

But now he was beginning to think there was more to it than that. It seemed to him that Trudy's friend was holding something back. And he wanted to find out, at the very least, where to start probing for that information.

'An accident?' Grace echoed, her mouth suddenly going a little dry. She darted a quick look at her friend sitting beside her, then looked at the coroner, and quickly away again. It was one thing to try and manipulate Trudy Loveday, Grace suddenly realised, but rather a different thing altogether to try and hoodwink a man like the one now sitting across the desk from her.

'Well, what else could it be?' she heard herself say, and looked down into her lap. There, surely that sounded feeble and unsure enough? Or maybe it didn't? Maybe they'd just take the words

49

at face value. Clement could see that Trudy was frowning. Clearly she was perplexed by her friend's behaviour.

'Grace, if you know anything, you need to tell us,' Trudy said gently. She reached out and touched Grace's hand, still resting on the handbag in her lap. 'Even if you think it might not be important, or you don't quite know what to make of it. Just tell us and leave it to us to sort it all out.'

Grace quickly looked down, a feeling of relief flooding over her. It was all right. She'd done it. She'd planted the necessary suspicions in their minds. Surely her part was now done? She could just sit back and wait for things to unfold as they must. And then she'd be safe.

Wouldn't she?

She looked up at her old school friend, and took a deep breath. 'Trudy, you will come to the theatre, won't you? The Old Swan Theatre, you know the one, just off Walton Street? I'd feel so much happier if you'd just come and take a look around. It's run by Mr Quayle-Jones. He used to be an actor himself, but now he owns and manages the theatre.'

'Of course I'll come,' Trudy said, nobly ignoring Grace's nervous habit of waffling. 'But it'll have to be one evening, when I'm not in uniform.'

'Tonight?' Grace said urgently. 'There's a rehearsal on for the evening gown section of the show. Some of the dresses are on loan from the dress shops, and Mr Quayle-Jones has even said we can have our pick of some of the costumes. You have to see the gowns sometime, Trudy, they're sensational! Tonight won't be all that exciting since the girls will just be going through the motions in their normal clothes. But it'll give you a chance to meet everyone and...' Grace trailed off and shrugged helplessly.

Trudy smiled and patted her hand. 'I'll be happy to come!'

'Oh, I'm so glad,' Grace said, making a show of glancing at her watch and then getting up. 'I really have to go – I can't be late back from lunch. So I'll see you tonight then? About seven-thirty? Just go around the side entrance and knock. The doorkeeper will let you in. I'll let him know to expect you.'

She nodded across at Clement and left, her step much lighter than when she'd entered.

Clement watched her go and wondered what, exactly, the curly-haired young lady was up to. Because he was pretty sure that she had some sort of agenda that she wasn't sharing with Trudy Loveday.

'Poor Grace,' Trudy said, when her friend had left. 'She's got so much on her plate at the moment, with her mother being so unwell, and all this extra workload with the beauty contest. Still, if we can put her mind to rest about Abby, that'll be one less thing for her to worry about.'

Clement nodded. 'You two seem close?'

'Oh yes. Well, we were once, at school, where she sort of looked out for me,' Trudy felt compelled to add. 'But you know how important and intense childhood friendships can be. At the time, I felt I would have died if Grace hadn't been around.'

The coroner understood immediately that Trudy didn't suspect her friend of anything underhanded. And it certainly hadn't even crossed her mind that she might be playing some part in what was going on. He wondered, briefly, if he should say something to her about his suspicions, but almost instantly decided that it wouldn't be a good idea. For one thing, he might just be wrong (although he didn't think so!) But more importantly, he knew that if he told Trudy, she would begin to act differently around Grace, and as things stood at the moment, the more sanguine Grace Farley felt about things, the better he'd like it. She was far more likely to give herself away if she thought she was in the clear.

But he'd be watching her closely from now on, and one thing was for certain – when Trudy went to the theatre tonight, he'd be going with her.

'So,' Trudy said, 'where do we start?'

'What about the former boyfriend?' Clement said. 'He hardly spoke much at the inquest, and if anybody can tell us what sort of girl the victim was, it's bound to be him.'

'Great! Where does he work?' Trudy enthused.

'The council offices. He's a clerk in the roadworks department.'

Chapter 6

William Hanson looked surprised to see them but seemed willing enough to answer their questions. To avoid causing a disturbance in the office, however, he'd taken them outside to a nearby bench situated under an old horse chestnut tree, where they'd all sat down to watch some sparrows and starlings fighting over a discarded crust of bread.

'I thought I'd said all I needed to in court, sir,' he said diffidently, looking at Trudy in her uniform a shade uneasily and with real alarm in his eyes. 'I really don't know anything at all about how she came to be poisoned.'

'Oh, that's all right. All we need to know is more about Abby herself,' Trudy told him with a reassuring smile. It always made her feel rather unsettled to be feared by someone. Whilst she knew that it was her uniform that was instilling the fear in this rather pleasant young man, it still made her feel like squirming inside. So far, the shoplifters and handbag thieves that she'd mostly been dealing with had all treated her with either weary contempt or anger. It wasn't often that she experienced what it felt like to wield real power – the kind that your average man-in-the-street understood – and feared. And she was not sure she liked it.

'What was Abby like as a person?' she asked softly. 'We thought you could help us to understand her.' To her relief, William seemed to relax a little.

'Well, I only stepped out with her for a few months you understand,' he began cautiously. He was a good-looking young man, Trudy noted absently, with a haircut in the same style as the younger Everly Brother, and was wearing a well-worn but respectable suit. 'I knew her originally from school, but even when I got older I didn't dare ask her out. Well, not back then.'

'Oh, why not?' Trudy asked casually.

'Are you kidding?' William smiled ruefully. 'She was way too popular and scary. And I was nothing much. I mean, I wasn't captain of the rugby team or what-have-you. I had the feeling that she'd have withered me on the spot!' He laughed. 'Or maybe I was just too shy back then.'

'Oh, I get it,' Trudy laughed lightly. 'She was a bit of the "goddess" sort, was she? I'll bet she was good at everything. Lessons, sport, and had loads of friends? I wish I'd been that sort of girl.'

William glanced at her uncertainly. 'Oh I don't know. You're so pretty you must have been popular too.' He suddenly gave an audible gulping sound. 'I mean, not that I'm saying you're pretty... No, I mean you are, but I...' he began to stammer, clearly wondering if you could be arrested for sounding forward with a police officer.

Beside him Clement Ryder hid a grin behind a cough.

Before he could get himself more tongue-tied, Trudy laughed lightly and said casually, 'Thank you! But I understand Abby must have been really spectacular. I mean, to enter a beauty contest...?'

Clement, watching the by-play, admired her handling of the shy youth. Sitting back, prepared to watch and listen, he reached into his pocket and withdrew a roll of breath mints. He saw Trudy glance at him, at the mints, and then look away.

Trudy tried to concentrate on what William was saying, but in truth, she felt her mind wandering. For some time now, she had begun to wonder if the coroner might have a bit of a drinking problem. Once or twice she'd seen his hands tremble, and one of the older constables at the office had said that secret tipplers often used breath mints to try and hide the smell of alcohol lingering about them.

'Oh, she was very pretty,' William said, forcing her to concentrate on the matter in hand. 'Sometimes, I think she was too pretty for her own good,' he added a shade darkly.

'Oh? In what way?' Trudy asked curiously.

'Oh, I don't know,' William said. 'She could be… a bit bossy, I suppose. As if she thought the world owed her a living because she was so popular. You know what I mean?'

Trudy nodded. 'I think so. Somebody said she treated her friend Vicky more like a servant,' she lied smoothly. Nobody had actually said as much, but from reading between the lines, she felt fairly safe in tossing the supposition into the mix.

'Poor Vicky. Yeah, she hung on Abby's every word. It was a bit sad really – the way she was so anxious to please her all the time.'

'Everyone said they were best friends.'

'Yes,' he agreed, his voice a little uncertain. Catching her encouraging look, he swept on. 'The thing is, I often wondered if it was less about devotion and more about fear, with Vicky.'

'Oh?' Trudy frowned and wisely kept silent. She had already learned that sometimes keeping silent was the best thing when you wanted someone to talk.

'Yes. Abby was, well, the queen bee at school in many ways, and she made sure everyone knew it! And Vicky was, well, all right and pretty enough in her own way, and sort of smart. But she was nothing special, you know?'

'She wanted some of Abby's reflected glory, you mean?' Trudy asked.

But already William was shaking his head. 'No, not that so much. I think she buttered Abby up constantly so that Abby didn't relegate her. You know, a lot of girls wanted to be friends with Abby since she could be really cutting to the lesser mortals – especially the more plain girls. And the safest way not to be the target of Abby's scorn was to be in tight with her. You know?'

William paused, then looked at Trudy with a slightly puzzled look. 'That doesn't sound very nice, does it?'

'Oh, I remember school,' Trudy tried to reassure him. 'Everything was either black or white, wasn't it? You were either "in" or you were nobody. And if you were nobody... well, it was like being sent to Coventry. Nobody noticed you or talked to you. Sometimes it could make you miserable.'

William nodded. 'Yes, that's it. And I think Vicky was always terrified she'd do something to upset Abby and get sent out into the wilderness.'

'Is that why she joined the beauty competition, do you think? Because Abby wanted her to?'

'Oh yes, I'm sure of it. It's not the kind of thing she would have dared do if Abby hadn't bullied her into doing it. I know for a fact that Vicky's mum can't have approved.'

'But she's a grown woman now,' Trudy pointed out gently. 'They weren't at school anymore.'

William shrugged. 'Abby just had power over people. I can't really explain it. She could be wonderful, and then you felt lifted up, like you were flying among the stars. But woe betide anyone who earned her scorn. She could turn cold on you at the drop of a hat and without any warning, and make you feel utterly miserable.'

'Did she ever do that to you?' Trudy asked curiously.

William smiled. 'Yes. I know I shouldn't really say this, but when it became clear that she was getting bored of me, and finally threw me over, it was almost a relief. I'm much happier with Shirley now, anyway. You know where you are with Shirley.'

But Trudy wasn't interested in his new lady love.

'Did Abby ever talk about what was happening at the beauty contest?' she asked instead.

'What do you mean?' he responded, puzzled.

'Never mind.' Trudy changed the subject quickly. The less people knew about the trouble at the theatre, the better. 'Do you know anybody who might have wanted to hurt Abby? You said she could be a bit bossy and unkind. Can you think of someone she really upset?'

William's eyes shifted quickly. 'No, not really.'

Trudy shot Clement a quick look and he nodded back. Both thought that the young man was now lying.

'It's important, William,' Trudy insisted gently. 'If we're going to get to the bottom of what happened to Abby, it's important that we get a clear picture of what was happening in her life.'

'What does that mean? She drank that poisonous stuff by accident, didn't she?' he demanded, looking from Trudy to the coroner a little wildly.

'Perhaps she did, but perhaps she didn't,' Trudy said unhelpfully. 'So, did she ever seem frightened of anyone?' she tried again.

William shrugged, clearly unhappy with the turn things had taken. He'd obviously believed in the 'accident' theory and the prospect of something more sinister being at work was unsettling him.

Trudy could tell his mind was working overtime, and she shot Clement another look. He, too, was watching the younger man closely.

'Look, if I knew of anyone who could have hurt her, I'd tell you,' William finally said, sounding sincere enough. 'But I don't. And now I really have to get back to work. My manager won't like me taking too much time off.'

'All right,' Trudy said reluctantly, sensing that it would be pointless – at least at this time – to push him further. All three got up from the bench, sending the birds fluttering into the air.

They all shook hands solemnly, and Trudy and Clement watched the young man walk away.

'Well, that was interesting,' Trudy said quietly, when she was sure her witness was out of earshot.

'Yes. Wasn't it?' Clement agreed. He wondered if Trudy had picked up on the one really revealing thing that William Hanson had said during the interview and hoped that she had.

You have to pay very close attention to the things people say.

'I have to get back to the office as well,' Clement said now, glancing at his watch. 'I have another court case tomorrow and the paperwork is piling up. I'll pick you up at your house tonight, at about a quarter past seven?'

'Oh, you want to come to the theatre too?' Trudy said, sounding surprised. 'I didn't think beauty contests were your cup of tea,' she dared to tease him slightly.

Clement smiled. 'They're not. But I have a feeling that there are things going on at that theatre that need properly looking into.'

Chapter 7

Robert Dunbar watched a girl with long flowing blonde hair – but a rather ordinary face – sashay somewhat exaggeratedly down the middle of the stage. It was nearly eight o'clock at night, and the lighting wasn't as bright as he would have wanted it, as they were making do with the run-of-the-mill stage lights.

On the night though, when the paying public filled the seats, it would be time to pull out all the stops, and the businessman was confident that he could provide the city with a satisfactory spectacle – and get them buying Dunbar Honey in their droves.

'We need to make up our minds what music to play for this section,' his wife said fretfully by his side. They were seated in the fifth row of seats from the front, watching for flaws in timing and trying to imagine what it would be like when all the scenery was up, and the compere was there to keep things moving.

Tonight, however, that noted (but not quite so noted as he would have liked) thespian, Dennis Quayle-Jones was nowhere in evidence.

'I think we should have the quartet play something light but elegant. A waltz perhaps?' Christine said. 'It is evening wear, after all.'

Robert sighed. 'I was thinking perhaps something more

modern,' he said restlessly. 'Cocktail party music, that sort of thing. Where's Grace? Isn't she supposed to have…'

The Dunbars continued to bicker quietly.

* * *

Backstage, Trudy and Clement (having been let in by an octogenarian who had muttered constantly about the theatre's grand old days) were watching from behind the curtains as one girl after another walked down the length of the stage. A section of coconut matting laid out the route, but Trudy supposed that, on the night, it would be replaced with a genuine red carpet.

Beside them, Grace Farley was giving them the names of each girl as they passed, but had already indicated her employer and his wife watching from their seats.

'This is Sylvia Blane,' she hissed now, as a short, curvy girl with short blonde hair and big blue eyes did her stint on the matting. 'That old woman over there,' she added, pointing across the stage to the far set of curtains, 'is Mrs Merriweather. She set up "Friends of the Old Swan Theatre" years ago, when it needed some restoration work.'

Both Clement and Trudy obediently followed the line of her pointing finger to where an elderly woman stood, watching the action on the stage with a rather wry smile on her wrinkled face. She was very neatly and well dressed, but her shoulders stooped very slightly, marring what would otherwise have been a very elegant carriage.

Clement, as a medical man and a good judge of the human form, put her in her early seventies. She was of the lean and rather wiry variety of old lady, with iron grey hair that was short and curly. 'Her family are among Oxford's oldest and used to be very big landowners and in banks and shipping back when fortunes could be made in that sort of thing. Everyone around here makes sure to keep her sweet, obviously,' Grace added, with a rather cynical smile. 'Of course, Mrs Merriweather and the rest of the committee are quite happy to come and watch plays, but the beauty pageant isn't really her thing. Mind you, having said that, the old thing has been a bit of a sport about it all, and the girls are getting rather fond of her. She's a nice old stick, in a way. Sometimes she can be quite funny too – you know, witty. Oh, this is Caroline Tomworthy – I told you, she's the oldest of the competitors.' Grace broke off as another woman swept by them and began to walk gracefully down the stage.

Clement smiled at the young lady who looked to him to be about 22. Although he had to admit, after a second look, she had a certain elegance and élan about her that some of the girls in their late teens lacked. Perhaps it was because she was taller than most, and slim rather than curvaceous. She had long black hair and sloe-like dark eyes that hinted at some sort of Asian ancestry in her distant lineage. She had sharp cheekbones and a pointed chin, with striking-looking, rather than strictly beautiful, features. But she certainly had 'presence'. And he had no doubt she was one of those women who looked good in fashionable clothes. He could understand why Abigail Trent might have considered her a serious rival.

'Has anything happened to Miss Tomworthy whilst she's been here?' he asked curiously. 'Has she fallen prey to the prankster?'

'Not yet. Or if she has, she hasn't said anything,' Grace amended.

Trudy frowned. 'But why would anyone keep quiet about it? If something had happened, I mean?'

'Oh, Mr Dunbar has given us all a lecture. With the press on the alert after Abby died, he's warned us all that we mustn't speak about… you know, anything odd that might be happening. We've all agreed, naturally. We're only about two weeks away from the big night, and nobody wants anything to spoil it. That would be letting her win, wouldn't it?'

'Her?' Clement repeated sharply, and Grace bit her lip.

'The prankster, I mean. I sort of assumed it was a woman we're dealing with?'

Clement nodded thoughtfully. Looking around he could see that the vast majority of people around them were all women, with very few men in the mix. So perhaps Grace was right to conclude the joker in the pack was female. Even so, he had a feeling that Trudy's friend might have had someone specific in mind.

Or was he just over-reading things?

'Come on, let me introduce you to Mr and Mrs Dunbar,' Grace said nervously. 'I haven't told them who you are or that I've invited you over,' she added, feeling suddenly rather sick. 'I just hope I won't lose my job over this. Mr Dunbar might not be happy with the police being here.'

She shot her friend a nervous look. Even though Trudy, out of her uniform and wearing a long dark-green dress, didn't look in any way constabulary.

Before she could lose her nerve, she backed away from the stage and showed them where they could descend into the audience area via a narrow set of steps.

It was Christine who noticed their approach first and visibly nudged her husband in the ribs. Robert winced, and then frowned at Grace and the two strangers.

'Mr Dunbar, this is my friend Trudy, and, er, Dr Clement Ryder.' Grace introduced them in a rush. She didn't dare look at Christine. Only last night she'd ordered her to rifle through her husband's private chequebook at the first opportunity and report back any purchases of jewellery or flowers or other suspicious purchases.

Christine held out her hand to Clement, who took it with a polite smile. But her eyes immediately ran over Trudy, who had left her long, dark curly hair loose in a very attractive manner.

'Have you come to audition for the pageant, Miss... er?' she asked briskly.

'Loveday,' Trudy put in quickly. And then smiled ruefully. 'And no, definitely not. I don't think I'm beauty queen material, Mrs Dunbar.'

'Nonsense,' Robert said at once. 'You're just the kind of girl we're looking for. Can you sing or dance?'

Trudy blinked. 'Er, no,' she admitted, totally caught out by the question.

'Please, sir, I've brought Trudy here because I thought she might be able to help us,' Grace rushed in before either of the older couple could say anything really embarrassing.

'Help? With what?' Robert asked blankly, peering at Trudy more closely in the dim light. 'She doesn't look old enough to have had experience in the theatre.'

'No, sir. I'm a police officer,' Trudy said quietly.

Instantly, Robert Dunbar recoiled, and beside him his wife drew in her breath in a sharp hiss.

'You've brought in the police? You stupid girl,' Christine hissed at Grace witheringly, and Trudy felt her hackles rise on her friend's behalf as she felt Grace Farley quail beside her.

'Actually, Mrs Dunbar, she hasn't,' Trudy put in coldly. 'Not officially, anyway. But she has asked me to come down and… well, see what I could find out about your troubles here.'

Robert wasn't a man who had built up a small fortune without learning how to think quickly and adjust to life's challenges. His gaze sharpened on her thoughtfully. 'You're with the city police, you say?'

'Yes, sir,' Trudy said, and waited.

'Hmm. And what, exactly, has Grace taken it upon herself to tell you?' he asked tightly.

Grace paled slightly but stood her ground as Trudy ran over what she knew.

'And what do you think you can possibly do about it?' It was, perhaps inevitably, Christine who cut in with a voice as acid as a lemon drop.

'Well, I thought I could take a look around, chat to the girls. See if anything stands out as being odd.' But even as she spoke, Trudy realised how lame that sounded.

Beside her, Clement continued to watch man and wife thoughtfully. If he'd had to place money, he would have said the woman was the one who held the original purse strings, but he was not so sure if she was the one with the power. Her husband had the sort of force and energy that he'd encountered before in men (and a few women) that usually indicated single-mindedness.

And in Robert Dunbar's case, he was sure his single-minded purpose was the pursuit of money and prestige.

'I doubt you can learn anything in a few hours chatting back-stage,' Robert said now, his eyes narrowing thoughtfully. 'Mind you, it might be a good idea to have someone trained as an observer about the place, longer-term. To see if they can catch our mischief-maker in the act.'

'Robert!' Christine hissed warningly.

'But nothing official mind,' he added, staring at the nonplussed Trudy. 'We don't need you reporting back to your superior officers or such.'

Trudy blinked. What on earth was the man going on about? 'But, sir…' she began.

'I'll hire you privately. Pay you an hourly rate and a bonus if you can catch our troublemaker. What do you say?' Robert offered briskly.

Trudy, at that moment, was incapable of saying anything at all, and merely gaped at him.

'Of course, we've already got the perfect, whatchamacallit… "cover" that's it, yes, "cover" all set and ready to go. Rather obvious, don't you think? No one will suspect another compet-itor of being a nosy parker, will they?' Robert smiled, nodding happily. 'Good. You can start tonight. I'll introduce you as our newest entrant. Do you want to use your own name or make one up?' he steamrollered on.

Trudy decided enough was enough, and drew herself up to her full height. As she did so, she caught Dr Ryder's eye and he turned quickly away, his shoulders shaking suspiciously.

Trudy glowered at his profile. Laugh at her, would he, the old... old... vulture!

She turned a cold face upon Robert Dunbar. 'Sir, I have no intention...' she began imperiously, but was abruptly undone, as Grace quickly reached out and laid a hand on her forearm.

'Oh, Trudy, that would be perfect. You'd have the perfect excuse for talking to people and exploring backstage and all that. Who knows, the trickster might even try something on *you*, and then you'll have no trouble finding out who did it.'

Her faith in her was so touching that for a moment Trudy was tempted.

But it was ridiculous. Besides, there was no way she could 'moonlight' as some sort of private inquiry agent for Mr Dunbar.

DI Jennings would have a fit!

'I really can't—' she began but was again interrupted.

'I think that's an ideal solution,' Clement Ryder said, his face now deadpan, and his voice as smooth as the honey that Mr Dunbar was so eager to sell by the bucket-load to Oxford's discerning shoppers. 'I'll clear it with DI Jennings,' he added to Trudy with an arrogant sweep of his hand.

Trudy shot him a killing look.

Of course, both the Dunbars objected to Trudy's superior officer being informed at all, but were eventually persuaded by the coroner that it was a necessary evil.

'And since Dr Ryder will need a reason for being here too,' Trudy said sweetly, when he'd finished cajoling them, 'perhaps you can add him to the judging panel, Mr Dunbar?'

Clement Ryder blinked at being stabbed so neatly and unexpectedly in the back by his confederate, then reluctantly felt his lips twitch. Oh well – perhaps he'd deserved it.

'Oh, of course,' Robert Dunbar said, without much notable enthusiasm. 'Er… welcome to Miss Oxford Honey, both of you.'

Chapter 8

Clement left first and moved his Rover P4 to the front of the theatre to wait for Trudy to find her way from the side exit, which she did within a few minutes. He'd offered to drive her home so that they could have a serious talk before things went any further. In truth, he was feeling vaguely uneasy about the speed with which things had been happening.

He was just popping a breath mint into his mouth when she opened the passenger door and slid inside. As she did so, she shot him a puzzled look.

She had seen no signs that the coroner might have been drinking that night; in fact, nothing about his conversation or behaviour made her think that he had touched a drop. So perhaps he enjoyed the taste of mints simply for their own sake? She hoped so. She'd come to both like and enormously respect Dr Ryder, and the thought that he might have a problem with drink was a depressing one.

'Well, thanks for volunteering me to be a judge,' he said as he let a gaggle of student cyclists pass by before pulling out into the street. It was now fully dark, so he put his 'Aunty' Rover's lights onto dipped beam.

'You're welcome,' Trudy said with a smile. 'But we *did* both need a reason to be there, didn't we?' she pointed out reasonably. 'We couldn't just expect to wander around the theatre asking questions and not arouse suspicion.'

'Yes, I know that. But it worries me now that we arrived together,' Clement said.

'Why would that matt... Oh!' Trudy said, catching on quickly. 'Yes, of course. If there *is* something going on in the competition, and someone there tonight was responsible for what happened to Abby...'

'Exactly. They must be on the alert already. And then us two show up together... I don't like it,' the coroner said. 'In fact, I'm thinking it might be best to drop the whole thing. Oh, not the case,' he said as Trudy began to protest. 'Just your "undercover" assignment.'

For a moment, Trudy was silent, thinking things through. On the one hand, she hadn't really been all that enamoured with the idea of becoming a beauty pageant contestant! She didn't think she was a particularly shy or retiring sort of person, especially, but she *had* been raised by parents who had set ideas about what was and wasn't respectable. And some aspects of the contest made her want to squirm with embarrassment. So she was sorely tempted to grasp the excuse to pull out of it.

On the other hand, she was excited by the prospect of playing a bigger role in this case. The first two crimes she'd helped with had been very much Dr Ryder's province – or so it felt to her. This time around, being in the thick of it, as it were, she had been hoping to get more hands on. And she was reluctant to give that up.

In her hand she had a whole sheaf of papers, given to her by the Dunbars, that listed rehearsal times, competition rules, information on the behaviour that was expected by the competitors and all sorts of disclaimers and things to sign. It had all felt so thrilling and different from her usual run-of-the-mill existence.

Perhaps it was the atmosphere in the theatre, the sense of

excitement and 'something new' that pervaded the whole experience, but Trudy felt very reluctant to give it all up without a fight.

'But I don't think anybody actually saw us *arrive* together,' she said slowly. 'Except Grace of course, but she already knows about us.'

'And the doorkeeper,' Clement added flatly.

'Oh, but I don't think many people would talk to him or take much notice of him,' Trudy dissembled. 'I got the distinct feeling that he was very much a theatre-employee and the beauty contest people weren't really "theatre" people to him! I mean, actors and technicians and stuff. He just let us in and then went back to his cubbyhole. I didn't even see him again until he let us out. He struck me as the kind of old man who liked to complain a lot but kept himself to himself.'

Clement sighed. 'I still don't like it. For a start, it's bound to get around that I was the coroner on the Abigail Trent case. And if her killer is connected to the pageant, he or she is bound to smell a rat.'

Trudy had to admit that he had a point. Even though Robert Dunbar had promised to put it about that they needed another judge, and that Dr Ryder had always been on a shortlist as a city VIP, to an already alert and wary mind, that explanation might not sit well.

'Even so, they wouldn't have any reason to suspect *me*,' Trudy pointed out stubbornly. 'I'm just another girl in the parade, a hopeful, silly little girl, looking to wear a cheap-but-sparkly crown! Who's going to think I represent any danger? In fact, it might work out to our advantage,' she continued with renewed enthusiasm. 'You could be the stalking horse, attracting all the killer's attention, and whilst he or she is busy watching you, I can get on with things, unnoticed, in the background.'

'Thanks a lot,' Clement said dryly. 'I'll be sure not to drink or eat anything whilst I'm "judging". Is it down this way that you live?' he broke off to ask, not being particularly familiar with this area of town.

'Yes. Next turn on the left.' Trudy guided him to the front of her house – a semi-detached council house towards the end of a line of similar houses, and when he pulled the car to a halt, suddenly asked diffidently, 'Do you want to come in? I'm sure my mum and dad would like to meet you. I've told them all about you. Unless…' She suddenly looked unsure.

After all, why would an important man like the coroner be interested in meeting her family?

'I'd love to,' Clement said smoothly, turning off the ignition. 'One of these days, I'm going to have to get seatbelts fitted,' he said, changing the subject smoothly so as to give Trudy a chance to cover her obvious confusion. 'The amount of road traffic fatalities I have to deal with makes me shudder. There are just too many cars on the roads these days, and half the drivers don't seem to know what they're doing.'

Trudy, barely listening to him, walked quickly to the front door and opened it. Her father never locked the doors until it was time for bed. As she went into the tiny front hall, she called out quickly. 'Mum, Dad, visitor!' to give them ample warning.

She closed the door behind the coroner, took his hat and coat and hung them up on the wooden 'tree' that stood in the hall, then headed for the living room. As she did so, she heard the sound of the wireless being hastily switched off. Taking a deep breath, she pushed open the door and walked in.

Barbara Loveday rose from her favourite armchair by the fireplace, brushing down the skirt of her dress as she did so, whilst her husband rose from the sofa, looking surprised as he caught sight of Clement Ryder.

Clearly, the older man perceived at once and with some amusement, they had been expecting Trudy to have brought home a 'nice young man' for them to meet. It made him suddenly realise how little he knew about his young friend's private life.

Presumably she was courting?

'Mum, Dad, this is Dr Ryder. He's the coroner I sometimes work with, the one I told you about,' she added, for good measure.

'Oh, Dr Ryder, I'm so pleased to meet you,' Barbara said, holding out her hand and stepping forward. 'Our Trudy's been singing your praises for months now.'

'Mum!' Trudy blushed.

Clement smiled charmingly, and Trudy was suddenly aware of how alien her friend looked in this environment. With his smart suit and distinguished air, he looked so out of place in the ordinariness of her home. Her dad was wearing an old pair of trousers with his shirt unbuttoned at cuffs and neck, but as he shook hands with Clement, Trudy felt curiously proud of him.

He might only be a bus driver, shaking the hand of a social superior, but he was master of his own home and looked only friendly, hospitable and at ease. But then so too, she realised with something of a shock, did Clement Ryder.

'Mrs Loveday, Mr Loveday, I'm pleased to meet you at last.' He shook their hands in turn. 'You must be very proud of your daughter. She's certainly been of invaluable help to me this last year.'

'Please, have a seat,' her father said. 'We were just about to put the kettle on, weren't we Babs?'

'Oh yes,' her mother said at once. 'Would you like tea or coffee, Dr Ryder?'

'I'd love coffee if you have some. Milk, one sugar please.'

Barbara smiled and quickly left for the kitchen. She would return, Trudy knew, with a tray containing the best china, a plate of biscuits, and some slices of whatever cake she had made that day.

It was an unseasonably warm night, and the living-room window was slightly open. And just before either man could speak, there came the unmistakable sound of clucking.

Trudy recognised it at once of course – it had been a familiar and comforting sound throughout her childhood. Part of the Loveday garden had always been devoted to chickens – a mix of Rhode Island Reds and Buff Orpingtons. During the war nearly everyone in their street had kept chickens, of course, but unlike a number of their neighbours, her father had carried on keeping them.

'Is that a Buff Orpington?' Clement amazed her by asking, his voice warm with approval. 'I'll bet they give you good eggs,' he went on.

Her father, sensing a fellow chicken-fancier, immediately agreed. And Trudy, feeling rather disconcerted, sat and listened whilst the coroner and her father debated the merits of keeping a bantam cockerel, as opposed to a bigger bird.

Her mother came back with a laden tray, as prophesied, and Clement, with very clear and obviously genuine enjoyment, ate two slices of her Dundee cake and thus won her heart forever.

A half-hour later, and from the front door step, her parents helped Trudy wave Dr Ryder off, and she was left wondering what she'd ever been so worried about. The three most important people in her life got on like a house on fire!

'Now that's what I call a proper gentleman,' Barbara Loveday said, watching the coroner walk down the short garden path, her cheeks glowing. 'A really nice man. It makes me feel a whole lot better knowing that you're working with someone like that, our Trudy.'

Trudy bit her lip. She could have told her mother that she actually worked for DI Harry Jennings who was very much a different proposition. But she was far too wise to do so.

She knew her parents were still hoping that her choice of career was nothing but a passing fancy, and that she'd soon marry anyway, and cease working altogether. She understood why they worried about her, of course, so anything that made them feel happier about things was a definite bonus.

For that reason, as she bid them goodnight and went to her room, she didn't tell them about the beauty contest, or that she'd

72

entered it. Not that she had really 'entered' it, of course, in the true and proper sense of the word. She wouldn't be photographed by the official photographer, nor get her picture in the paper, nor yet be in the final public showing when it opened. This she had insisted upon when negotiating the terms of her undercover work with the Dunbars. And she certainly wouldn't be appearing in any of the publicity opportunities arranged to advertise the competition. Her mother wouldn't have known where to put her face! And her dad would have put his foot down and ordered her to not set foot in the theatre at all.

No, she would be very careful not to do anything that might embarrass either her parents or DI Jennings.

Thinking of her superior officer, she couldn't help but wonder, with some trepidation, just how he'd take the news that one of his most junior officers was now working undercover at the theatre. Although she had perfect confidence that Clement Ryder could, as he'd promised, 'handle' the DI, she also knew that she would be in for some teasing back at the station.

Oh well. It wouldn't be the first time she'd been the butt of the station jokes. Besides, it might be worth it just to try on some of the sumptuous gowns that Grace had told her about. Gowns that the likes of Bridget Bardot, Doris Day and Audrey Hepburn might wear. Or even Elizabeth Taylor!

Of course, she knew the dress shops of Oxford and the wardrobe mistress of the Old Swan Theatre couldn't actually run to the real thing – the genuine St Laurent, Chanel, Dior, or Balmain creations that such luminaries would take for granted. Nor would their hair be done up like…

Suddenly Trudy's thoughts ground to a halt, and she clapped a hand over her mouth, as her eyes widened with horror.

For thinking of actresses and performers made her suddenly realise that, in order to blend in and act like a real beauty pageant contestant, she'd have to do a 'talent' spot at the rehearsals, along with everyone else.

And as she'd told Mr Robert Dunbar, she could neither sing nor dance!

What on earth was she going to do?

* * *

Clement Ryder poured himself a weak whisky and soda and slumped gratefully into his chair. It had been good to meet Trudy's parents at last. They played such a large part in her life still. And since they'd done such an excellent job of raising her, he'd been sure that he'd like them, and he had. Very much. Indeed, Barbara Loveday reminded him of his favourite aunt, a warm-hearted woman he used to visit as a child and who insisted on baking him scrumptious cakes. And Trudy's father was very much a man who was happy in his own skin and his lot in life. Which was a trait that seemed to be getting rarer and rarer these days.

He wondered briefly what they'd made of him. Had they liked him so well, or had they merely made him feel at home out of an innate sense of hospitality?

He'd never really much cared what anybody had thought of him – with a few notable exceptions – and he didn't intend to start worrying about such things now! He snorted as he took a sip from his drink. And yet with the Lovedays... it mattered somehow.

Perhaps it was because he could see how close-knit a unit they all were, it highlighted how his own family seemed to have drifted apart. He rarely saw his children nowadays. But then, they had flown the nest and had their own lives to consider. Which was how it should be.

With another snort, Clement Ryder took another sip of his nightcap. Good grief, he was in danger of getting maudlin! Soon he'd be sounding like a lonely old man...

Two days of frantically practising on her old school recorder in her spare time (much to her parent's bemusement) had left Trudy hoping like mad that on her next scheduled visit to the theatre, they wouldn't be rehearsing the talent spot!

And as luck would have it, they weren't. It was something almost worse!

The first intimation she had of it was when she walked into the dressing-room area backstage and saw two girls in swimsuits. Tonight, clearly, they were doing a full dress rehearsal of the swimwear part of the contest. Of all the segments of the pageant, this one had caused her the most anxiety.

Like most girls in her street, Trudy had rarely been to the seaside. Aside from a few day trips, the Lovedays had never been able to afford proper holidays by the sea. And at school, her main sports had been hockey and cross-country running, not swimming. So wearing a swimsuit had never been something she'd had to do often.

She wasn't even sure she had a swimsuit that fit her. The one she had lurking in the back of a drawer somewhere at home was probably fit only for a 12-year-old – not a grown woman.

Alas, the fact that she hadn't brought a swimming costume with her didn't allow her to wriggle out of anything though. Before she'd even had a chance to find 'her' spot in the changing area, Grace was bearing down on her with a white one-piece draped over one arm.

'Ah, Miss Dobbs,' Grace said loudly. 'There you are.'

For the briefest of moments, Trudy forgot that her name, for pageant purposes, was now Trudy Dobbs. She, Grace and the Dunbars had come up with the name the other night.

Catching Grace's grim smile, she suddenly forced herself into action, and said enthusiastically, 'Oh hello, Miss Farley. Am I late?'

'Not really,' Grace said, 'it's just that most of the girls get here early.' She glanced around, and said, 'Here, this is yours, you can change behind the screen in dressing room three. I think Miss

Tomworthy and Betty Darville will be sharing it with you tonight.'

She handed over the swimsuit to the unhappy Trudy, and nodded in through the open door.

Trudy's role as a beauty contestant was about to begin in earnest.

She could only hope that she didn't look as nervous as she felt as she walked into the room and met the interested eyes of its two inhabitants.

'Hello – you must be the latest masochist to join up for the parade!' the girl with lots of red-brown hair said. She was sitting in front of a stage mirror, wearing a long white towelling robe. She looked, even sitting down, to be a tall and lean-looking girl, with very pretty and distinctive sherry-coloured eyes, almost the exact shade as her hair.

'I'm Betty Darville,' she said with a grin, holding out her hand.

'Trudy Dobbs,' Trudy said, shaking hands vigorously, then cocking her head to one side. 'You look familiar,' she lied smoothly. 'I'm sure I've seen you before?'

'Are you a bit of a bookworm?' Betty asked.

'Oh, I love reading murder mysteries,' Trudy said, truthfully enough. She had always loved reading the classic whodunits of the Twenties and Thirties. But she was also thinking that, if she were to go around asking questions, she might as well play up the fact that she was a bit of a mystery fan. That way she could always say that having a 'real life' mystery to solve was proving too much for her! 'I adore trying to work out who the murderer is,' she gushed.

'Ah, then you've probably seen me in that big bookshop near Carfax? I work there, for my sins,' Betty said. 'It's one of the things that sometimes becomes of girls who have been blue stockings at school, I'm afraid! I may be only 22, but I sometimes feel ancient!'

'Oh, that'll be it then, I love that shop,' Trudy again lied. She always got her books from the local library, never having been able to afford the extravagance of buying her own.

'And this is Caroline,' Betty said, turning and nodding at the other inhabitant of the room.

Caroline was also dressed in a robe, but hers was a silk kimono, heavily embroidered, with a curling Chinese dragon surrounded by peony flowers. Jade green in colour, its exotic design amplified the older girl's dark eyes and black hair.

'Hello,' she said, casting a quick, assessing eye over Trudy.

Trudy immediately sensed that, although Betty Darville might not take the competition all that seriously – hence her amusing opening remark, this woman most definitely did.

Which made Trudy wonder what this rather elegant creature must be making of the new competition – probably not much! She hadn't bothered to put on any make-up after leaving work at the police station, thinking that she'd only have to put more on at the theatre, and she'd simply pulled her hair back in a basic ponytail to keep it out of her eyes. She was wearing a simple skirt and blouse outfit in plain black and white. And she felt, suddenly, very stupid to think she could pass herself off as a beauty contestant.

Betty must have sensed her discomfort at being the object of the other girl's open scrutiny, because she suddenly patted the seat next to her own. 'Here, sit next to me before you change into your costume, and I can give you the run-down on this madhouse.'

Grace, taking that as her cue to stop hovering in the doorway, muttered a general goodbye and an admonition not to be late for the rehearsal, and moved off.

'So how did you hear about us?' Betty asked. As she did so, she leaned forward in her seat, and turned her head this way and that as she studied her image in the mirror. 'Do you think I should leave my hair loose or put it up?'

'Oh, leave it loose,' Trudy said at once. 'It's too pretty not to!'

Betty beamed, genuinely pleased by the compliment. 'Thanks!'

She paused as Caroline Tomworthy rose and left the dressing room without another word.

In the mirror, and meeting Trudy's surprised gaze, Betty grimaced. 'Oh don't mind her. She's an unfriendly cat! She slinks about on silent paws, and watches you with that aloof, amused look that all cats have. You know, like they know something you don't? Most of us here are a good lot, you know, we'll help you out if you put a run in your stockings or run out of face powder or whatever. But don't expect anything like that from Caroline. She's strictly in this thing to win it. And boy, does she expect to!'

'All right, thanks for the warning,' Trudy said, then eyed the white costume Grace had given her with disfavour. 'I suppose there's no use putting it off. I'd better change into this thing.'

Betty laughed. 'Feeling shy? Don't worry, we all felt a bit odd about it at first. I mean, we're all amateurs here, right? Not a professional model among us, so we felt rather self-conscious at first, parading around. But you get used to it after a while. You can change behind that screen.' She nodded towards a folding wooden screen. 'I can lend you a spare dressing gown if you like. Or Maudie can probably find you one from the theatre.'

'Maudie?' Trudy repeated, retreating behind the screen and beginning to undress quickly, before she could really stop and contemplate what she was doing.

'Maud Greenslade – she's the wardrobe mistress here at the theatre. A bit of a grumpy old stick, but underneath it she's all right really. She just doesn't see us as "proper" actresses. Which we aren't, of course!' Betty laughed.

Trudy, relieved to find that the white one-piece fit her perfectly, stepped a little nervously from behind the screen and scooted back to her seat. There she released her own hair from the pony-tail and began to brush it vigorously. She was used to wearing it up in a tight bun underneath her uniform's cap, of course, so it wasn't often it was left loose.

Her long dark hair had always been naturally wavy, and she was rather glad of that now. She'd also washed and dried it before leaving home and now she was pleased to see it shine. At least that was one thing about her that looked 'glamorous'.

'You should leave your hair down too,' Betty said at once, and Trudy grinned back at her.

'We can be a pair of long-haired moppets together,' she agreed.

Just then, another girl popped her head around the corner. She looked around the same age as Trudy herself, (although for some reason she had an almost child-like air) and had similar dark curly hair and large brown eyes with a gentle expression, reminding Trudy of a doe or a young calf. She was also very pretty, in a sort of cutie-pie, Shirley Temple way.

'Betty, you don't have a spare pair of shoes, do you? Only the heel's just broken off mine,' she wailed tragically.

'Aren't we doing it barefoot?' Trudy asked, surprised.

'Oh no,' Betty said, with a knowing grin. 'Mrs Dunbar thinks that would be too common. Of course, swimmers don't normally wear shoes on a beach, but she prefers us in high heels. And sorry, Candace, I don't. This is Trudy Dobbs, by the way, the latest recruit. Trudy, Candace Usherwood.'

'Hello.' Candace, now looking distinctly woebegone, came a bit further into the room to shake hands. 'I don't suppose you have a spare pair of shoes, do you?' she asked hopefully.

'Sorry, I don't even have a pair to wear myself. I came in my usual pair of lace-ups!' Trudy lamented, getting into the swing of things.

'She's still new to all this.' Betty came to her rescue as the other girl sighed heavily.

Trudy reached into her bag for her make-up kit. It was interesting, getting to know the ins and outs of life backstage, and she was at least beginning to get a feel for some of the girls involved. Betty was obviously a good sort, even if Caroline was a bit of a cold fish. Candace looked like she was about to sulk.

She was wearing a yellow and blue bikini, and her figure was rather plumper than that of either Trudy or Betty. 'Puppy fat' her mother would have called it. But for all that, she certainly looked appealing, and Trudy could understand why she'd had the nerve to enter the contest.

'I'm a bit worried about my skit,' she said now to Betty, who snorted rather inelegantly.

'You've nothing to worry about and you know it,' Betty said, then looked across at Trudy. 'Candace does a little comedy monologue for her talent spot and she's brilliant! Has us all in stitches – even though we've heard it three or four times now. She's almost as good as Joyce Grenfell!'

Trudy gulped, hoping nobody was going to ask her what her non-existent 'talent' was.

Candace suddenly giggled. 'That reminds me! I've just thought up another little idea. What do you think of this?' She struck a pose, standing up with her hands on her hips and adopting a confiding attitude. '"I call my house Lautrec." Now you say, "Oh why do you call your house Lautrec?" And I say, "because it has two loos.". Get it? Toulouse...'

The girl certainly had a sort of impudent charm, and Trudy could see it going down well with a live studio audience.

Slowly, Trudy had begun to relax – and feel less exposed in her swimming costume – as the two girls began to compose more jokes, whilst Trudy industriously applied her make-up.

Grace came back ten minutes later. 'All right, five minutes and then it's rehearsal time,' she chivvied them. 'Betty, this is for you – someone left it at the ticket office counter.' She handed over an envelope and withdrew. 'And, Miss Dobbs, next time you need to bring in high-heeled shoes and a robe of some kind.' She tossed one over her shoulder.

'Yes, Miss Farley,' Trudy said, mock-meekly at Grace's departing back, making Candace grin.

If the other contestants were all like this pair, Trudy mused,

80

she would pretty soon be able to rule them all out as being a potential killer. She simply couldn't see the slightly dotty Candace or the straightforward Betty wanting to kill anyone. In fact, Trudy warned herself sternly, nothing might come of all this 'undercover' work at all. Abigail Trent's death might have no connection with the prankster at the theatre anyway.

And come to that, she mustn't let herself be disappointed if nothing more happened on that front either, she told herself firmly. It was always possible that, having scared off all the girls who were likely to frighten easily, the person responsible for the trouble had simply stopped. Or it might be days and days before anything more happened…

It was at this point that Betty Darville suddenly gave a little shriek and began to cry.

'What on earth's the matter, Betty?' It was Candace who reacted first, standing up and going to her friend, her arms going around Betty's shaking shoulders.

Trudy got up and moved up to her other side.

'It's horrible!' Betty gasped shakily, putting a hand up to her face and wiping away her tears angrily. 'Who would write such a thing!'

Trudy quickly glanced down and realised that the other girl had opened her letter and read it. It was written in thick, black, large letters, all in capitals, with what looked like some sort of marker pen.

She could read it easily.

FLAWED SO-CALLED 'BEAUTY QUEENS' HAVE NO BUSINESS PUTTING THEMSELVES FORWARD AS EXAMPLES OF FEMININE PERFECTION. BEWARE ALL VAIN WOMEN. REMEMBER YOUR DEAD COLLEAGUE – ANOTHER FLAWED SPECIMEN – AND WHAT HAPPENED TO HER!

'But what does it mean?' Candace Usherwood said, looking rather sick, her hand held up to cover her mouth.

Trudy saw Betty's tear-streaked face rise up to meet her reflection in the mirror. Her sherry-coloured eyes looked darker with tears and shock.

'Is this a death threat?' she said. But whether she was asking Trudy or Candace – or herself – Trudy couldn't be sure.

Chapter 9

'I don't understand,' Trudy said, looking and feeling a little bewildered by the poison pen's somewhat obscure message. 'I mean, what can this "flaw" be that it mentions? Do you know?' she asked Betty, trying to give her something else to think about to help her get over the nasty aftertaste that must have been left by the anonymous letter.

'What?' Betty said vaguely, and then, with a visible effort, pulled herself together. She frowned slightly and then shook her head. 'I'm not sure. There was nothing wrong with Abby. She was a really beautiful girl – and one of the favourites to win. She certainly didn't need to kow-tow to the cat.'

For a moment Trudy didn't understand what on earth the other girl was talking about, then suddenly she did. So Abigail and Caroline Tomworthy hadn't seen eye to eye. Perhaps that was not surprising, with both of them being hot favourites to win the competition.

'Unless it refers to her mole?' Candace put in uncertainly.

'What? Oh, her beauty spot,' Betty said. And then frowned. 'But it can't mean that, can it? I mean, if it does, then we're all in trouble! I mean, none of us are absolutely perfect. No human being is. Even Caroline has just a slight twist to that patrician

83

nose of hers. You must have noticed how, when she's rehearsing, she always manages to make sure her face is partly in profile whenever she's in front of the judge's panel, instead of looking at them straight-on?'

Candace, Trudy noticed with interest, suddenly began to look very scared indeed. 'Oh, I feel sick,' the younger girl moaned, and with a sudden dash for the door was gone.

Trudy looked at Betty, who was staring down at the letter with distaste.

'Do you know who might have written it?' Trudy asked her gently.

'Not a clue,' the other girl responded flatly.

'I mean… you don't think… maybe Caroline…?' Trudy offered tentatively, just to see what the other girl would say.

But after barely a second's pause, Betty shook her head firmly. 'I can't say I have any great affection for the cat, but I just can't see her stooping to this sort of… of…' She nudged the edge of the letter with a finger, her lips twisted in a grimace of distaste. 'Anyway, even if it *was* her, why would she send it to *me*?' she wailed. 'Sylvia Blane is far more competition than I am. So is Vicky Munnings if it comes to that. If it was the cat doing it, she'd be targeting her nearest rivals, wouldn't she?'

Trudy didn't know.

She so badly wanted to scoop the letter and envelope up in order to preserve the evidence that she could feel her fingers literally itching, but she wasn't quite sure how she could set about doing that without attracting attention.

Then she had a bit of a brainwave. 'Do you want me to get rid of it for you?' she offered solicitously. 'I dare say you don't want to even touch it again. I can burn it for you, if you like?' she fibbed shamelessly. 'Unless you want to show it to someone in authority – Mr Dunbar, perhaps?' she asked cunningly. For she didn't think that the other girl would want to do any such thing.

'Oh no, not him,' Betty said at once, endorsing her confidence. 'I don't want him to think I'm a troublemaker or anything. It might affect my chances of winning!'

And at this, Trudy just had to hide a smile. For all Betty's so-called certainty that either Caroline or Sylvia or Vicky were the real favourites, she still clearly wanted to win the crown herself – and thought she was in with a chance.

'So what do you want to do?' Trudy pressed, itching to get possession of the note. Out of all the 'pranks' played at the theatre, this was the first one that offered up any real evidence in tangible form.

'Oh, do what you like with it,' Betty said at last, and with a final shudder, rose to her feet, leaving the note and envelope lying on the tabletop. 'I'm going to the stage. You'd better come too – you don't want to be late for your first rehearsal.'

'OK, I'll be right behind you,' Trudy promised. Then, the moment the other girl disappeared, she quickly picked up a tissue paper and manipulated the letter back into the envelope, then wrapped the whole thing up in her handkerchief and slipped it into her handbag.

She was fairly sure that the culprit wouldn't have left any fingerprints on it, but she was taking no chances.

When she made her way to the stage, with her borrowed dressing gown wrapped tightly around her, she found that Candace had already spread the news of the letter, and several groups of girls were standing around, gossiping nervously and looking over their shoulders. It quickly became clear that nobody had seen who had left the letter at the ticket office counter, but Trudy wasn't surprised. Their joker was far too canny to be caught in so simple an act.

There was definitely an air of tension and unease in the theatre, and Trudy didn't feel immune to it either. After all, she was one of the 'flawed beauties' herself now, and as such, was presumably just as much a target as anyone else. It was odd quite how vulnerable and exposed she felt, wearing just a bathing suit and in bare feet.

Suddenly, Trudy began to appreciate her robust uniform and sensible shoes.

'All right, ladies.' Grace Farley's voice suddenly rose above the hysterical-tinged babble. 'Let's make a start. Line up – everyone is wearing their numbers, yes? Now just imagine there's some appropriate music playing, Frank Sinatra or something… The compere will be here…' Grace moved to a spot on the stage and Trudy watched her friend, fascinated. It was odd to see Grace in such a position of authority.

'What did she mean by "wearing their numbers"? What number?' Trudy hissed at Candace, who looked startled, and then held up her hand automatically.

A round white cardboard disc with the number '12' on it was secured around her wrist with an elastic band. 'We all have a number so the judges can easily make a note of us and mark down points. It's easier for them than having to try to remember all our names, Mrs Dunbar says. Haven't you got one?'

'Not yet,' Trudy whispered back. Presumably Grace would give her one before too long. Although something inside her instinctively rebelled at being regarded as a mere number.

'Don't worry, you won't get number thirteen,' Candace promised solemnly. 'Nobody would have it, except Caroline. She just smiled like a cat with the cream and graciously offered to take it. I think that woman's probably a witch!'

Trudy grinned. Well, either that, or she just wasn't superstitious.

'All right. We'll go in order – number one, off you go please.'

Trudy watched as 'number one', a rather short redhead with a round but attractive lightly freckled face, swayed obediently towards the end of the stage, did the hands-on-hips classic turn at the end, and sauntered back.

Trudy watched her in dismay. Good grief, was she supposed to actually walk like *that*?

Apparently she was, as the next girl did the same. Presumably, being a very late arrival, she'd missed out on the training sessions on how to parade for the judges. How could she possibly manage it in her bare feet? At least high heels made that exaggerated swaying a little more accessible.

Number ten was a girl with lots of naturally honey-blonde hair and a very good figure indeed. 'Who's that? Her legs are marvellous!' Trudy whispered to Candace.

'That's Vicky Munnings. She was best friends with the poor girl who died,' Candace said, then opened her eyes wide and clapped a hand to her mouth. The gesture was, Trudy suspected, something of a habit with Candace who probably spent much of her life saying the wrong thing. 'Oh, sorry, we're not supposed to talk about her,' she said. 'You won't tell Mrs Dunbar I did, will you? We're not supposed to say anything that might reflect badly on the show!'

'It's OK, I'll keep mum!' Trudy promised.

'Thanks – oh it's my turn next,' Candace said, and shot forward as number eleven left the stage.

Trudy was still chewing over all this 'numbering' business. Why couldn't the compere just announce their names as they came on? Were the judges so lazy, or so illiterate, they couldn't just write down a name on their notepads as easily as a number?

Since she didn't know her order in the group, she hung back until last, and after removing her dressing gown (and perforce in bare feet) did her best to mimic the 'catwalk' sashay to the end. She felt incredibly stupid doing so, even in an empty theatre. Luckily, it was soon over.

'Thank you, girls,' Grace called. 'We'll take a little break then do it again. Miss Dobbs, I'll get a number card for you – and see if I can find you some shoes to practise in.'

Trudy's lips twitched helplessly. 'Thank you, Miss Farley' she sing-songed. Just wait until she got Grace alone. She'd give her 'practise' indeed!

There was a stand set up backstage where soft drinks and snacks could be had, and as Trudy accepted a glass of orange squash from someone she took to belong to the theatre staff, she wandered about wondering who to talk to first.

Over in a corner, the Dunbars conversed briefly, then split up. Patricia Merriweather, the old woman who was on the committee championing the theatre, was talking to a rather distinguished-looking man who looked both familiar, and most definitely theatrical.

This, Trudy knew, must be the actor-cum-theatre owner, Dennis Quayle-Jones. Although her mother had never attended a theatre performance in her life, she'd always subscribed to a cinema and theatre magazine. After going through some of the back-issues, Trudy had come across a piece on the great man himself when he'd been playing some minor role or other in London's West End.

An early glittering career – and most of the wealth that came with it – seemed to have dwindled over the years, however. Nowadays, he wasn't quite so matinee-star good-looking, nor quite so slim, but he still undeniably had a certain 'presence'.

Trudy gave him a wide berth. She couldn't imagine any scenario where a man like that would be interested in sabotaging a beauty pageant or murdering pretty young women. Especially since it would bring his theatre into disrepute!

Instead she drifted and aimlessly chatted, always contriving to bring the subject around to Abigail. Some girls openly talked about her, others, minding the Dunbar's taboo on the subject, shied away.

But the news about the nasty letter cast a definite pall over the whole affair, and naturally, speculation was running rife. Trudy could only hope that she wouldn't be asked to give up the letter to somebody in authority before she managed to get away from the theatre.

Then she spotted Vicky and casually strolled over. 'Hello – I'm Trudy, the new girl. I don't think we've met?' She smiled and held out her hand, and the other girl, after a moment's hesitation, reached out and shook it.

'It still feels very strange to me, all this' – Trudy cast a quick hand around to encompass the theatre – 'but I understand from the others that you and your friend were among the first to join up,' she carried on, trying to sound a little gushing. In her experience, a little bit of hero-worship put people quickly at ease. 'I have to say I envy you your confidence!'

'Oh, well,' Vicky Munnings said vaguely. She looked about to walk off with barely a few words so Trudy had no option but to force the issue a little.

'I just wanted to say I was so sorry to hear about your friend. Abby, was it?' She took a deep breath. 'Somebody told me what happened. You must miss her awfully.'

Vicky went a trifle pale, then slowly nodded, but for a moment she looked a shade uncertain. Perhaps, Trudy thought, with a quickening heartbeat, the two girls weren't as close as people thought?

'Abby was one of a kind,' Vicky said carefully, with a brief flash of a smile that was more a twist of her lips than anything else.

'Oh, one of *those*,' Trudy decided to gamble. 'I used to have a friend like that. Very popular and everybody loved her and all that, but' – she leaned a little closer to Vicky, who froze on the spot – 'underneath… well, I could tell you a thing or two! She wasn't as angelic as people thought.'

She paused, hoping that Vicky might now trade confidences. Instead the girl looked decidedly alarmed.

Damn, Trudy thought. She'd come in too strong.

'Well, I have to go,' Vicky said next, confirming her fears. 'It was nice to meet you.'

'Sorry, I hope I didn't offend you,' Trudy said quickly. 'I didn't mean anything by what I said. I'm sure *your* friend was very nice,' she added, desperately trying to salvage the situation.

Vicky Munnings shot her a quick, rather wry look, and said dryly, 'Are you?'

And before Trudy could reply to that enigmatic response, the other girl smiled determinedly and moved away.

Trudy watched her go in frustration. Clearly, it would be no good pressing the other girl now – she'd only get suspicious, or worse, uncooperative. But at some point soon, she'd have to try to talk to her again and find out what the dead girl's best friend meant by her last remark.

There was something more to be learned in that quarter.

* * *

The picker of yew berries was having a wonderful time. The atmosphere was so tense it could be cut with a knife. And watching everyone flutter around like a flock of alarmed starlings was really most entertaining, not to mention gratifying.

Everyone was casting everyone else sly looks, no doubt wondering who the culprit could be. Pretty soon all the camaraderie and trust they'd built up would erode away altogether. Already they must be wondering. Was the death of their fellow contestant really connected to the run of 'bad luck' at the theatre, or wasn't it? Of course, none of them wanted to think that it was.

But now they must be seriously wondering.

Well, that was all well and good. Let the poison pen work its magic. Before long, they'd be left in no doubt at all that Abigail Trent was only the first of them who was going to die.

Chapter 10

Trudy had no idea that the judges were due to arrive for the second run-through of the swimwear competition until she noticed a rising level of noise front-of-stage, and looking through the gap in the curtain, saw a middle-aged man take a seat in the front row.

Nervously, she sought out Betty Darville, who sighed heavily and confirmed that tonight was indeed a 'judging' night.

Trudy went hot, then cold.

'They don't come every time, of course,' Betty explained patiently. 'Only when we have a full dress rehearsal mainly, like tonight.'

'Oh.' Trudy gulped. Out there, presumably, Dr Ryder was already taking his place along with a whole group of perfect strangers – all of them intent on judging her appearance and performance. And here she was – barefoot, green as a cabbage, and still not sure how to 'sashay' properly!

'Oh hell,' Trudy muttered under her breath.

* * *

91

By refusing to look anyone in the eye, especially Dr Ryder, and simply concentrating on putting one foot in front of the other, Trudy managed to get through the second run-through. Afterwards, somewhat to her surprise, the judges joined them behind the curtains backstage, and helped themselves to the refreshments.

Trudy had changed out of her swimwear right away, and was thus the only girl to be fully dressed as she mingled with the judges. Although Mrs Dunbar had insisted that all the other girls put on a robe, it was clear that this didn't stop the majority of the contestants from allowing the judges, up close and personal, to judge just how well the bathing costumes fitted!

She watched with almost shocked eyes as Sylvia Blane flirted outrageously with a rather nervous-looking but attractive man of around 40 or so.

'Mr tall, dark and handsome is Rupert Cowper,' Betty said with a smile, sidling up to her and offering her a glass of sparkling wine. 'When the judges come, Mrs Dunbar lets Grace spend a bit more of the "entertaining" budget!' she explained, shaking her half-filled glass in explanation.

Trudy accepted the glass and eyed it casually, hoping that her curiosity and excitement didn't show, because she had never actually tasted wine before. Although her parents sometimes drank it at Christmas time, she'd always been told that she could have some only when she reached the age of 21.

Obviously, she couldn't refuse the offering or she'd look silly, so Trudy thanked her, took a cautious (and somewhat guilty) sip and found that she didn't really like it! It tasted a bit like sour lemonade to her, and made her wonder what all the fuss about drinking alcohol was all about.

'They do make a striking couple,' she said, masking her disappointment in the Liebfraumilch and nodding instead at the short, blonde-haired Sylvia and her captive audience.

'They sure do, and doesn't our Sylvia know it!' Betty giggled, making Trudy wonder how much wine she'd already consumed before coming over. 'Rupert Cowper owns Cowper's Florist, in the covered market – do you know the one I mean? But he also has several shops all over the place – Banbury, Bicester, Witney. He's providing the flowers for the stage on show night, which is why he's on the judging panel. Even more interestingly, he's a widow with nearly grown children. Mind you, with his looks, he'd be quite a catch even without all that money.' Betty sighed. 'It's no wonder Abigail and Sylvia were scrapping over him.'

At this, Trudy's ears pricked. 'Oh? That must have made for bad blood between them?'

'Oh, it did,' Betty agreed blithely, draining her glass and then looking longingly at the table, clearly wondering if she dared get another refill.

Trudy hoped it was just the shock of finding that nasty letter that was behind her need for alcohol. 'Do you want mine?' she offered kindly, holding out her glass. 'I've barely taken a sip.'

'Oh thanks, don't mind if I do,' Betty said eagerly, exchanging her empty glass for the full one. 'It doesn't do to... Oh hello, Mrs Merriweather.' She broke off as the old woman appeared beside them.

'Don't think I didn't see you snaffle that second glass, young lady,' the old woman said, then at Betty's dismayed face, suddenly smiled widely. 'Don't worry, your secret's safe with me. When I was a deb I used to snaffle whole bottles of champagne and sneak them out to the garden to drink with my friends! So drink up.'

'Thanks, Mrs M, you're a brick,' Betty said. 'Oh, this is Trudy Dobbs, a new recruit. Trudy, Mrs Merriweather. She's one of the judges and works on a committee to help keep the theatre going.'

'Nice to meet you,' the old woman said, shaking hands politely. 'I must say, I think you did a good job on that walk-through without any shoes.'

Trudy blushed. 'I must have looked awful!'

'I doubt anybody thought that,' Patricia Merriweather said,

with yet another smile. 'Don't worry, you'll soon pick it all up. It's been a bit of an eye-opener for me as well, I can tell you, watching all you young girls go through their paces. In my younger day, the older generation would have had a fit.'

Betty giggled. 'It's 1960 now, Mrs M,' she said with slightly drunken smugness.

'Indeed, it is. And I suppose all of you who are now just out of your teens think you're so grown-up and sophisticated! But I still wouldn't have let my granddaughter take part in something like this,' she said firmly. But her eyes, Trudy thought, looked a shade wistful. It was only then that Trudy noticed that Betty suddenly looked a bit disconcerted, and with a vague murmur, quickly excused herself.

'Poor Rupert *is* looking rather cornered, don't you think?' the old woman continued the conversation with a bit of a grin. 'You'd have thought a man who looks like that would be better able to take care of himself, wouldn't you? Between you and me, I think poor Rupert is a bit of a sheep in wolf's clothing!'

Looking at the couple again, Trudy had to agree that the judge did indeed look a little alarmed at the way Sylvia was holding on to his arm and leaning forward, to give him a better view of her undoubted charms and assets. 'I'd better go and rescue him, I suppose,' Patricia said with a sigh. 'Good-looking middle-aged men are apt to get themselves into all sorts of difficulties, if you let them. And Sylvia, who has to be 24 if she's a day, has had time enough to learn some very interesting little ways.'

Trudy hid a smile as the unlikely Sir Galahad sailed forth to do battle on behalf of the florist.

Then she had a sudden thought. Florists were used to dealing with all kinds of flora and leaves and that sort of thing, weren't they? So wouldn't Sylvia's potential beau know all about yew? She was pretty sure it wouldn't be used in big flora displays, since the leaves were too spiky and dark to be pretty, but florists also made up Christmas wreaths, didn't they? If they used ivy and holly, perhaps they used yew too. Yews had bright red berries too. Which meant...

She nearly jumped out of her skin as Clement Ryder crept up behind her. Putting aside her idle musings about florists and yew trees, she launched instead into an account of what she'd been dying to tell him ever since she'd learned that he was in the theatre. Keeping her voice low, she related the rest of the evening's events.

'I've got the letter in my bag,' she concluded. 'But I'll have to hand it over to DI Jennings straightaway. As you know, there's now an official police investigation into the case running parallel with ours, and the officer in charge will want to see it.'

'Hmm. Too bad,' Clement mourned. 'Whilst there was nothing definitive to link the beauty contest and Abigail Trent's death, the Inspector was prepared to indulge us. Now it looks as if there might be a connection after all, we might find ourselves sidelined.'

Trudy sighed. 'But the message is a bit... well... up in the air, isn't it? Do you think the killer actually wrote it? Or was it just someone here taking advantage of Abby's death to make everyone scared of their own shadows?'

Clement shrugged. 'No idea yet. I'm going to chat to the theatre owner, see if he has any ideas on what's been happening in his theatre, right under his nose.'

Dennis Quayle-Jones knew a man of importance when he saw one, and although he had no idea who Dr Clement Ryder was on sight, the moment the man walked up to him and introduced himself, the actor-cum-theatre-manager was on his best behaviour.

'So you're the new judge,' Dennis said, wracking his brains for all he'd heard about this man. As a leading light of Oxford society himself, he liked to keep himself informed. So he knew the coroner had friends in very high places, didn't suffer fools gladly, and was both respected and feared in equal measure.

'Yes. It was my unpleasant duty to oversee the inquest into

the death of one of your girls here. Abigail Trent?' Clement decided to take the bull by the horns. 'Did you know her?'

'Oh, poor Abby. Yes. No. Well…' Dennis took a breath, pulled himself together, and managed a light smile. 'I didn't know her as a person, not really, but I had talked to her, naturally, on and off during the rehearsals and whatnot. Some of the girls are total novices, as you'd expect, and I was happy to give them some pointers on stagecraft. You know – how to stand, walk, and especially talk during the interview segment. I keep telling them – you need to project your voice. It's no good talking to the compere, even with a microphone, as if you were just chatting to the boy-next-door. Even with something as banal as this, they needed to emote.'

Clement found the actor-manager's verbosity annoying, but he nodded wisely.

'And did Abby take direction well?' he asked urbanely.

'Oh yes. Most of them do. Mind you, I think most of them are a bit stage-struck, and see this competition as a way into show business. Poor lambs.'

'And Abby was no different?'

'Like I said, I didn't really know her,' Dennis prevaricated, straightening his cravat. He was dressed theatrically in a velvet lounge jacket of dark green, and everything about him screamed 'famous' actor. There was almost something desperate about the man's desire to 'be' someone, and Clement found himself feeling sorry for him. What, he found himself wondering, did the man do when he was alone at night without a play to direct, or people to impress or bedazzle?

'Her unexpected death must have been felt keenly here, I imagine,' Clement mused gently, glancing around at the milling girls, the Dunbars, judges and theatre workers.

'Oh, it was. She was so young, you see – barely into her twenties and quite lovely.'

'Did you think she was in with a chance of winning?' Clement asked, not really interested in that, but wanting to keep the conversation on track.

He was rather surprised at the quick flash of alarm that crossed the other man's face. In a second it was gone, and the smooth mask was back in place.

But it left the coroner feeling wrong-footed. What on earth had pierced the man's armour like that?

'Oh, who can say? A lot of the contestants are capable of winning, aren't they?' he said off-handedly.

'But you're one of the judges,' Clement pressed. 'Don't you have some idea by now who you're going to vote for?'

'Good grief, no!' Dennis said, in his best (and often portrayed) horrified manner. 'I'll just wait until show night and make up my mind then. I expect that's what most of us will do. Mind you, some of my fellow judges may have been thoroughly corrupted by then,' he said with forced gaiety, nodding towards a good-looking man who was being charmed by a pretty blonde.

'One of the perks, is it?' Clement asked, wondering if his companion's sudden unease had its basis in a guilty conscience. Had he been making promises he couldn't keep to one girl in particular, in return for a little appreciation? Somehow, he didn't think so. Unless his intuition was way off – and it seldom was – the fairer sex was not the one that held any interest for Dennis Quayle-Jones.

'Naughty! And no, it most definitely isn't', Dennis said archly. 'You'll have Mrs Dunbar breathing fire and brimstone down on you if you try any fraternising with the beauty queens. That woman terrifies me! I can see her heading this way right now, so if you don't mind...' He adroitly slipped away, and with a thoughtful glance, Clement let him.

As the actor turned away, however, the coroner noticed that one of the contestants – a very striking-looking woman with raven hair and wearing a Chinese silk kimono that he recognised as Caroline Tomworthy – was watching the actor-manager's progress across the room with a small smile that played intriguingly at the corners of her mouth.

So what did *she* know, that he didn't? Clement mused, with a slight frown. Clearly, there were undercurrents within undercurrents at the Old Swan Theatre. And again, he felt uneasy that Trudy Loveday was right in the thick of things.

Perhaps he should ask DI Jennings to intervene and put an end to her undercover assignment here? Although he knew Trudy might never forgive him if he interfered, he also knew that he could never live with himself if something happened to her.

Or was he just over-reacting? So far, they'd found no evidence whatsoever that Abigail Trent had even been murdered in the first place. And the latest poison-pen incident might be a totally empty threat.

Clement sighed. He would wait and watch, and if he thought that Trudy was in the slightest danger, then whether she liked it or not, he would do what needed to be done.

* * *

Trudy had been trying to corner Vicky Munnings all night for a second chance to talk to her, but somehow seemed to keep missing her. She was just pretending to drink from a second glass of wine when Sylvia Blane went to move past her, almost jogged her arm, and then had to stop and apologise.

'Sorry, I didn't see you there,' she muttered gracelessly. 'Truth be told, I'm only seeing red at this moment,' she fumed.

Trudy grinned. 'Bad as all that? What's up?'

'Interfering old busybodies, that's what up,' the blonde girl muttered mutinously. 'First it's that old bat Mrs Merriweather poking her nose in where it's not wanted. Then Mrs Dunbar. Honestly – it's getting so that a girl can't even talk to a man without somebody coming down on you like a ton of bricks.'

Trudy smiled sympathetically. 'Mr Cowper *is* very good-looking isn't he,' she said mildly. Then, when the other girl's eyes narrowed on her, hastily held up her hands. 'Pax! I'm not interested in him! He's too old for me,' she added, wondering what the other girl would have to say about that.

Sylvia merely tossed her blonde curls and gave a slightly condescending smile. 'I prefer mature men. They're so much more interesting than mere boys!'

Trudy blinked a few times at this, but wisely said nothing. Then she sighed as she saw Vicky Munnings slip behind the curtain and head back towards the dressing rooms. Apparently, she was going to call it a night.

Oh well, Trudy thought. There'd always be another time.

Then she turned her attention to Sylvia, realising that she couldn't afford to miss the opportunity of picking up more of the gossip. 'I see Vicky Munnings is leaving early. I suppose it must be hard for her to carry on with all this, now that her friend's dead? Didn't someone tell me that it was Abby who was the one who persuaded her to enter the competition in the first place?'

Sylvia gave a sudden snort of laughter. 'Yes, she did. And if you ask me, she was beginning to regret it.'

'Oh? Why?' Trudy asked sharply.

Sylvia shrugged. 'Well, you had to know them, really. You got the feeling that Abby was the queen bee, and little Vicky was just another drone, you know? A worker bee, only there to support her majesty.' Sylvia gave a little giggle. 'From what the rest of us could tell, Abby had been lording it over her all the way through school.'

'You sound as if you didn't like her much,' Trudy slipped in.

'I didn't. She was much too sure of herself for one thing.' Sylvia huffed. 'Mind you, after a few sessions in this place, she was beginning to get taken down a peg or two,' she added with some satisfaction. 'Oh, she might have got that poor mouse, Candace, under her thumb in short order, and one or two of the others. But she definitely couldn't bully Caroline! It was rather funny, really, watching the cat run rings around her. Then Abby would get so mad and frustrated that she'd take it out on Vicky. Poor kid – the things she had to put up with. Abby treated her like a servant!'

Trudy sighed. 'I'm surprised Vicky didn't just withdraw from the competition if it got that bad!'

'So was I, at first. But then it became clear that she'd got the bug.'

'The bug?' Trudy echoed blankly.

'Yes. The contest! Vicky… I don't know, in these last few weeks, she's begun to really blossom. She was always quite pretty, but she'd always been in the queen bee's shadow. But this place' – Sylvia waved a hand around the theatre – 'was beginning to set her free. She started to wear better clothes, use her make-up with more skill, come out of herself a bit. She had her hair cut properly and began to, you know…'

'Gain confidence?' Trudy proffered helpfully.

'Exactly.'

'I don't suppose Abigail liked *that* much,' Trudy remarked carefully. 'Losing her best worker bee and all that.'

'Oh, she didn't,' Sylvia said with relish. 'Especially when Vicky began to get talked about as a real possibility for winning the crown. By the time Abby died, they were almost at daggers drawn!'

'Oh,' said Trudy, her eyes shining. 'I had no idea that was the case.'

And wasn't it interesting?

Chapter 11

Clement accepted a cup of tea from Vera Trent and smiled his thanks at the grieving mother as she sat down opposite him.

He'd called on Abigail Trent's family home at ten-thirty in the morning, expecting her father to have gone to work, since it was primarily the dead girl's mother he wanted to talk to. Mothers, in his experience, knew far more about their daughters than did their fathers.

The house was a new-build council house in a small cul-de-sac on the ever-spreading outskirts of Parklands, a desirable suburb in Summertown. Here, the new houses rubbed shoulders rather uneasily with Victorian and Georgian buildings, and rows of what the tourists would no doubt call 'quaint' workers' cottages.

'Thank you for calling in, Dr Ryder,' Vera Trent said, her voice rather slow and weary. The doctor in him wondered what sedatives her family GP had prescribed for her.

'I just wondered if you had any questions about the inquest, or wanted to ask me anything,' Clement began gently. 'When you go through such a traumatic event, as you have, sometimes you don't think to ask questions right away.'

'No. Well, I suppose I'm not sure what happens now?' Vera was a woman who was not quite tall, not quite thin, and not quite pretty – but looked as if she missed all three by just a whisker. Her daughter, in contrast, had clearly had no difficulty in achieving beauty, as the many framed photographs of her distributed about the living room showed.

'Well, when the circumstances surrounding a death are unclear, the police continue to investigate, of course,' Clement said, but didn't mention his and Trudy's secondary involvement. The less people knew about it, the less likely it was that Trudy's undercover role at the beauty pageant would be discovered. 'What do *you* think happened to Abigail, Mrs Trent?' he asked, taking a sip of tea. It was hot and strong and unsweetened, just as he'd asked for.

'She didn't kill herself, that's for certain,' the dead girl's mother said, with the first signs of animation Clement had seen in her. But no sooner had she got the words out, than her shoulders slumped and she became weary and apathetic again. 'My Abby was full of energy and confidence and had all of the rest of her life to look forward to.'

With these words, Clement felt a wave of sadness wash over him. In his former life as a surgeon, of course he had lost his fair share of patients. But it always struck hardest when it came to losing the young.

'Yes, she did,' the coroner agreed softly. 'So you think it was an accident then? That she'd made up a potion thinking it was safe, and it wasn't?'

'I suppose so,' Vera said, but didn't look convinced. 'But it wasn't as if she'd done that sort of thing before.'

'Made up potions you mean?' Clement pressed gently. 'But then, she hadn't entered a beauty pageant before, had she?'

'No. No, she was all excited about that,' Vera admitted.

'And I hear she was a competitive sort of girl,' Clement chose his words carefully. He must not sound as if he was criticising her daughter in the slightest. Not only would it be cruel, it would also make her uncooperative. 'So I suppose she was determined to do well?'

'Yes, I suppose she was,' Vera admitted dully. 'She was always winning cups and prizes at school. Spelling. Running. All sorts.' She waved a hand towards the tiled mantelpiece over the open grate, where a small assortment of brightly polished cups and awards sparkled in the autumn sunlight.

'And I imagine that she would have done anything it took to actually win the crown for herself?' Clement mused, adding quickly, 'She was certainly lovely enough to win it.'

'Yes, she was, wasn't she?' Vera said, but there was more defeat than pride in her voice. Once again, Clement wondered what pills she was taking.

'Did she ever say anything to you about somebody wanting to hurt her?' Clement asked, wondering if the harshness of the question would be enough to penetrate the dull haze that the woman clearly inhabited nowadays.

'No.' Vera sounded only vaguely puzzled. 'Who would want to hurt our Abby? Oh, she was a bit of a handful at school, I suppose, but those silly complaints about her turned out to be nothing. Jealousy, that's all that was.'

'Complaints?' Clement asked delicately.

Vera Trent sighed heavily. 'It was just because she didn't fit in, at first. Coming here...' She paused to wave a hand vaguely at the fine view outside the window. 'Coming here to Parklands, was a bit of... what do they call it? Something to do with culture...'

'Culture shock?' Clement hazarded.

'That's it! Yes. We came from a big council estate in Cowley, see? So Abby grew up with kiddies just like her. Dads who worked at the car plant, mums who worked at the corner shop or did some "home help". Then we moved here, and although there's still some like us in the Crescent, the area's much finer than we were used to. Solicitors and doctors and even some old landed gentry still live around here, you know. And Abby was clever and did well in her eleven-plus and got into the local grammar school.'

103

'Oh, I see. She was bullied, was she?' Clement asked.

For a moment, Vera Trent looked disconcerted, then she shrugged and lapsed back into apathy. 'She gave back as good as she got,' she muttered. 'She had to stick up for herself, didn't she?'

Seeing that he was losing her, Clement nodded. 'So tell me about the beauty contest. What made her join in?'

Vera again shrugged. 'I don't really know. I think she wanted the prize money so she could go somewhere nice on holiday. You know, abroad somewhere? Nowadays, people can go abroad, can't they? On aeroplanes and such.'

Clement nodded. 'She was the adventurous sort, was she?'

'Oh yes. Full of ideas, and plans for the future,' Vera said. 'She always said to me, "Mum, I'm going to go places and make something of myself. You just wait and see." But now...' She shrugged helplessly.

'Do you know who she was close to, in the days before she died, Mrs Trent?' Clement asked carefully. 'Was she taking advice from anyone on beauty tips, for instance?'

'Oh, maybe, from her friends. She and Vicky, Vicky Munnings, have always been as thick as thieves. Ever since Abby met her at school here.'

'Oh. So Vicky's local to here too, is she?'

'Yes. An only child – her mother's a widow. One of those whose husbands left them a pension and a good life insurance policy. She gardens,' Vera added, as if this explained everything.

'So Abby found one friend around here then?'

'What? Oh yes – she brought Vicky home after her first day at school. She trailed in after our Abby, looking like a lost puppy. I think she was a lonely kid. She certainly perked up a bit once Abby took her in hand. They did everything together then. Ten years old, and up to all sorts of mischief between them, no doubt. They've been joined at the hip ever since. Whatever our Abby wanted, or did, Vicky had to do the same.'

Vera Trent tried to smile, but somehow couldn't seem to

remember how to do it. With a sigh, Clement admitted defeat and rose to his feet.

'Thank you for seeing me, Mrs Trent. And thank you for the tea.'

'Tea?' the other woman said vaguely. Then nodded. 'Oh yes. Tea.'

'I'll let myself out,' Clement said gently, and silently left.

* * *

DI Jennings read with distaste the anonymous letter that Trudy had just handed over to him. 'Looks like the sort of back-biting, hysterical nonsense that women like to spread around, to me. But I'll certainly hand this over to Sergeant O'Grady right away. As he is the *official* investigating officer of the Abigail Trent case,' he added with snide and telling emphasis. 'Whether or not he'll want to pursue it any further is up to him.'

'Yes, sir,' Trudy said smartly, all but standing to attention at his desk. But she had to hide a small smile. Reading between the lines, it was clear that her superior officer thought the Abigail Trent case was a low priority. No doubt he'd been expecting the coroner's court to bring in a case of either suicide, or death by misadventure, and resented having to keep on investigating it. So she rather doubted he'd be breathing down the Sarge's neck for results. Which, with a bit of luck, would leave the field clear for herself and Dr Ryder.

'And if he does decide to put in an appearance at the theatre, I'll be sure to tell him not to approach you,' the DI said reluctantly.

'Thank you, sir.' Trudy swallowed hard, sensing that more sarcasm was yet to come.

'No doubt it was Dr Ryder's idea to take up Mr Dunbar's hare-brained scheme that you entered the competition as a contestant?' he shot at her.

Trudy, for a half a second, wondered whether or not to take the easy way out and simply agree. Then her innate honesty got the better of her.

'Well, sir, it was more of a joint decision really. Mr Dunbar was eager to have someone looking into the pranks that were being played, and was most insistent that it should be me. And I thought that, if there *was* any connection between Abigail's unexplained death and the competition, it wouldn't hurt to put myself in an ideal position to explore the possibility. Sir.'

DI Jennings sighed heavily. 'Just don't do anything to make us the laughing stock of the police force, *probationary* WPC Loveday,' he gritted, stressing her probationary status with near relish. 'Don't forget, the Chief Constable won't take it kindly if the press get a hold of what's going on.'

Trudy gulped. 'No, sir.'

'All right. Well, carry on then.'

'Yes, sir!'

When she was gone, the Inspector leaned back in his chair and groaned. If it wasn't for the fact that Dunbar was a big donor to the Police Widows and Orphan fund…!

Perhaps this time the interfering Dr Clement Ryder would fall flat on his face for once? This so-called investigation into a dead girl who might or might not have been poisoned on purpose smelt like a no-hoper of a case to him. And if he brought down Trudy Loveday with him – well, the DI wouldn't be sorry to see her kicked off the force. She'd become one less headache for him to have to worry about.

He scowled down at the anonymous letter ferociously. Of course, it would be just his luck if it turned out that there *was* something iffy about the girl's death after all. Perhaps he'd better give some more thought over whether or not to make sure that Sergeant O'Grady took the poison pen threat seriously?

Just in case.

* * *

The picker of yew berries was once again contemplating murder. Of course, it couldn't be poison again. That was far too risky. Besides, all the little darlings of the competition were thoroughly alerted to that wheeze by now. Nobody would be likely to fall for that again.

The killer of Abigail Trent gave a wry smile. Not even pretty airheads were that dumb!

No. It would have to be a more direct method this time. Which, of course, presented another set of problems.

How did you kill someone easily, without getting caught, and without any risk to your own life and limb?

Drowning? Hardly.

A knife or cosh or blunt instrument? Too dangerous. What if the weapon was somehow wrested from you and used against you?

No.

It had to be more subtle than that. More crafty. More safe and sure.

But the picker of yew berries was clever, and confident that a way could be found. What's more, the killer could be patient. At some point, the right method would present itself...

Chapter 12

Vicky Munnings left her apartment by her usual side entrance and walked quickly to the bus stop. The ride into town was short, and she made her way quickly to the main library.

There, she handed back the books she'd taken out a while ago. If the librarian noticed that all the books were natural history books, mostly detailing the native flora of Britain, he made no sign of it. Probably, Vicky mused, he barely noticed the titles of books after so many years of handling them.

Vicky was not, by nature, much of a reader, and usually preferred female fiction, if anything. The books on native plants had been rather dry and boring. Even the bits about poison – which you'd have thought would be just a bit exciting.

But they'd told her what she wanted to know.

Abby would have suffered.

She stood at the bus stop, feeling cold and suddenly alone. For all that she was glad that Abby was gone – yes, she could openly admit that now – there were still times when she felt oddly lonely.

It was as if Abby was the only other person in the world who had truly *known* her. Had understood her. Had shared her darkest, nastiest secrets. Whilst it was a relief that she'd never have to think about such things again, it also made her feel isolated – as if she was living on an uninhabited moon, instead of a busy city.

Inwardly, she squirmed with shame as she thought of some of the things that Abby had made her do. They hadn't been nice. No, not nice at all.

Suddenly Vicky thought of the new girl, Trudy something-or-other, and what she'd said about having a friend of her own that had been no angel. Vicky gave a silent grunt of bitter amusement. Whatever the new girl's friend had been like, Vicky was sure she had been nothing compared to Abby.

If Trudy whatever-her-name-was knew all there was to know about Abby... But she was gone now, and couldn't cause anyone any more trouble.

Her bus came, and Vicky sighed and climbed wearily aboard.

* * *

Trudy tucked her hated recorder under her arm and poked her head into the kitchen. She was just in time to see her mum put some shillings into the milkman's canister (formerly used to keep tea) and realised that tomorrow, being Friday, was the day she paid him.

'I'm just off, Mum – I won't be late.'

'OK. I didn't know Grace played the recorder though.'

Trudy ducked her eyes so that she didn't have to meet her mother's gaze. To explain her sudden propensity for going out on a weeknight, she'd told her parents that she was going to Grace's house to help her practise her music.

'We all learned at school, Mum,' Trudy temporised. Which was true enough. Of course, Grace had no more kept up with the instrument than Trudy had!

'Give my love to her mother,' Barbara Loveday said.

'I will,' Trudy called back, feeling smaller and smaller by the minute, and she made her escape with some relief.

She walked quickly to the bottom of the road, where the coroner's Rover was parked and waiting for her. It was not another 'judging' night at the theatre, thank goodness, but Dr Ryder wanted to visit some of his fellow judges and had offered to save her a bus fare into town.

He was going to use the excuse of needing to ask for their advice on judging to probe them about what they knew of the girls' private lives.

'So it's the talent spot rehearsal tonight, is it?' the coroner asked spying the recorder right away.

Trudy sighed heavily. 'I'm terrible at it! I never was much good even at school. And it's taken me ages to find a "proper" piece to play. You know, by a real, classical-type composer. I don't think "London Bridge is Falling Down" will cut it somehow! I'm not even sure I'm reading the score right, since I've never been musical. It's going to be a complete disaster!'

Clement smiled. 'Never mind. Remember, it's not as if you're actually going to be in the competition when it plays out in front of the public, are you? So it doesn't really matter, does it?'

'No,' Trudy laughed. 'But I'm still going to look like a right nit-wit in front of the others, when they get to listen to me tootling away!'

Clement grinned heartlessly at the imagined scene, and blithely dropped her off at the theatre, before going on to the Eagle & Child in St Giles. It was the pub made famous by some of Oxford's more well-known authors, but it was also the chosen local, or so he'd been told, where one of his fellow judges often went for his evening pint.

Before he went in, he popped a breath mint into his mouth, and was still sucking on it as he pushed through the door and stepped over the threshold. Then he felt his foot catch on the uneven flooring and stumbled slightly, forcing him to catch hold of the edge of the door to prevent himself from pitching forward.

He glanced around nonchalantly and was relieved to see that

none of the drinkers already inside had noticed the incident. In fact, the haze of smoke from cigarettes was so thick in the rather small bar room that he doubted that anyone would have noticed if he'd come in wearing a tartan kilt and a tam-o'-shanter.

He checked his gait as he walked up to the bar and was relieved to discover that he hadn't begun shuffling his feet just yet – another symptom that would manifest itself sooner or later as his disease progressed.

He celebrated by ordering a small brandy, crunching and swallowing his breath mint as he waited. When he then took a sip of his drink, standing at the bar and glancing around, he had to hide a wince of distaste. The trouble with constantly having mints in your mouth was that it tended to overwhelm all other tastes – like those of a fine brandy!

'Is Ronald Palmer in tonight, landlord?' he asked the man behind the bar amiably.

'Yes, sir, that's him over yonder, by the window,' his host informed him with a smile. It pleased him when his customers ordered the finest – and most expensive – brandy.

'Thanks,' Clement said, taking his drink and approaching the table with the best view of St Giles beyond.

Ronald Palmer, according to the paperwork given to him by Grace Farley, was a member of one of the city's 'old money' families. Given that he'd been married four times, and to progressively younger brides, it was considered that he might have considerable experience of judging youthful beauty. That, at least, was how Dennis Quayle-Jones had put it to him, but no doubt, when being asked if he'd like to sit on the judging panel, the Dunbars had been rather more flattering.

That his family's most recent fortune had been built on hosiery – and thus his company could provide one of the prizes in the form of a selection of silk stockings and suchlike to the winner of the talent contest stage – had probably been an added bonus.

He was a man in his early fifties, doing his best to look as if he was in his early thirties. His hair was dyed a rather suspiciously uniform dark-brown, and he sported a tan – which he'd probably picked up in the summer months on the French Riviera somewhere. He had the beginnings of a stomach paunch, which excellent tailoring was so far managing to hide.

It looked as if he'd been steadily drinking for some time, even though the hour was early, for when Clement introduced himself, he was most effusive in his welcome.

'Well, well, so you've been forced to join our merry band of judges, have you?' he asked, with a knowing smile. 'I dare say they had to twist your arm, yes, like me?' He eyed the coroner's bulbous brandy glass enviously, and Clement, raising it so that the bartender could see, tapped it, then indicated his drinking companion.

Ronald Palmer beamed as one of the young girls serving behind the bar hastened to bring his glass over.

'Decent of you, cheers,' he said, as Clement handed over half a crown to the barmaid and told her to keep the change.

'I was hoping you could give me some pointers,' Clement said. 'I have to say, I never thought I'd find myself in the position of being a judge on a beauty pageant. It's not something I'd normally agree to, you understand,' he said, somewhat wryly. He had to wonder what some of his friends would make of it once it became more widely known! 'But the Dunbars talked me into it.'

'Oh, they would,' Ronald agreed, his dark-brown eyes closing in bliss for a moment as he savoured the brandy. 'Bit of an odd couple, of course. She has all the money – and he has all the brains and drive.'

'Yes, I gathered as much,' Clement agreed, happy to encourage the man to gossip. 'But he didn't strike me as the downtrodden sort, mind you.'

'Oh no. Not our Robert,' Ronald agreed, nodding solemnly. 'Between you and me, he's a bit of a lad. Not that he isn't discreet, mind. He lets Christine have her head most of the time without complaining, but he doesn't let that spoil his fun.'

'Ah,' Clement said. So the man kept a mistress somewhere. It didn't altogether surprise him. 'Mind you, from what I saw of her, his wife didn't strike me as the kind who'd put up with that sort of thing.' He thought of the big-boned woman with the tightly corseted figure and bright brassy hair and remembered most of all her set, tight, and rather unhappy face. 'She looked like the kind of woman who might become rather hysterical about that sort of thing.'

'Oh, probably, probably,' Ronald agreed vaguely. 'She certainly keeps a close eye on him, I know that.' He grinned. 'It's rather amusing, really, seeing her watching all those pretty young things, and watching her husband watching them!'

'Yes. It can't be easy for her,' the coroner agreed. 'I'm surprised this beauty pageant was allowed to take place at all.'

'Ah, but that's business, old man,' Ronald said easily, and with all the casualness of a man who had managers to run all his own concerns. 'Robert likes to make money, and he's determined to put his wretched honey on the map. Ever tasted the beastly stuff?'

'I'm more of a marmalade man,' Clement agreed.

'Me too. Still, mustn't grumble. It gives me the chance to go the Old Swan now and then and look at pretty girls. I remember that place when it used to put on musical variety shows.'

'Talking of pretty girls,' Clement put in smoothly, 'I had the misfortune of residing over the inquest of one of them who ended up dead recently. Abigail Trent?'

'Oh yes, dear Abby. A pretty girl, and one of the hot favourites. Such a damned shame. What a damned foolish thing to go and do – make up some dodgy potion out of berries and whatnot! Still, you can't tell 'em. The young nowadays, they think they know it all.'

'You ever see her taking herbal stuff at the theatre?'

'Good grief, no. I just sit out front and watch them parade

113

past, bless 'em. Of course, I dare say our Christine didn't shed too many tears to see her go,' he added morosely finishing his glass and then staring at it gloomily.

'Why would Christine Dunbar be glad to see one of the contestants go?' Clement asked sharply. 'Surely, anything that reflects badly on the contest, and as such, Dunbar Honey, must be a bad thing for her?'

'Hmm? Oh, yes, yes, I don't suppose it pleased them, what they wrote in the daily rags at the time. But, between you and me, there's been a rumour going around that Robert Dunbar was, er... taking a sip of honey where he shouldn't be!' He laughed happily at his own supposed wit, then slumped back in his chair. 'Of course, all the girls come on to us judges at some point or other.' He contemplated this state of affairs happily. 'Can't blame 'em, really, can you? They all want to win the prizes, and all of them want the top money prize. Well, that and a shot at becoming Miss Oxford.'

'You think the girls are willing to bribe us to vote for them?' Clement asked, not sure whether he found the prospect of being propositioned by a determined young lady amusing or horrifying.

'Oh, not all. Some of them are just good sorts. Mind you, I could tell you some dark things about one or two of them,' he muttered darkly.

Clement, aware that his witness would soon become too drunk to be reliable, asked quickly, 'And was Abigail Trent one of them?'

'Hmm? Oh, pretty Abby. Well, yes, I suppose so. To some extent, that is. But she wasn't the real dark horse. If you ask me...'

But before Clement could ask him anything, Ronald Palmer went neatly and unobtrusively to sleep.

Instantly one of the barmaids came over and turned off the lamp nearest to him – a big, pink-fringed affair – which left her inebriated customer slumped and snoring slightly in semi-gloom. 'Don't you worry, sir, we're used to Mr Palmer's little ways around here. We'll wake him up and send him home come closing time,' she assured Clement.

* * *

Trudy was in no hurry to publicly practise her recorder, and kept handing over her time slot to one of the other contestants.

Candace Usherwood did her comedy skit, and really was as funny as Betty Darville had said. Everyone had stopped to watch as Caroline, in a lovely pale rose-pink tutu, danced a piece from Swan Lake.

'Do you think she once danced professionally?' Trudy whispered to Grace, who had left her typewriter for the moment to come and watch the rehearsals.

'Maybe – but never as a principal dancer, I'd say. She'd still be doing it, if she'd been good enough to make it *that* far. Miss Tomworthy is the sort who likes to be a big fish in a small pond.'

Trudy glanced at her friend thoughtfully. 'You don't like her.'

'Nobody does.'

'Did Abby?'

'Good grief, no,' Grace said shortly. She felt tired and irritable, and not in the best of moods. It was as if being Christine Dunbar's cat's-paw was eroding everything good in herself. How long, she wondered in despair, before she began to actually hate herself? But what was the use? She had no choice. 'I need to get those invoices sorted out for Mrs Dunbar before she leaves,' she muttered helplessly, and slipped back behind the curtains and disappeared.

Trudy watched her go and felt sad. Poor Grace – she looked as if she had the weight of the world on her shoulders. She only hoped her mother hadn't taken a turn for the worse. Earlier on, Grace had told her that her mother was taking some new exper-imental drug or other. But she had sounded so depressed and resigned – as if her mother was dead already.

Trudy could only hope that the new drugs worked some sort of a miracle.

Luckily the time slots ran out before she could do her 'recorder rendition' and she was so relieved at this, that she was slipping on her coat to leave before she remembered that she still needed to chat to Vicky Munnings.

She hung about around the cloakroom where everybody left their coats and hats, waiting stoically as all the other girls began to leave their dressing rooms.

Betty Darville was first out, and donned a pretty, lightweight, pale-grey top-coat that looked rather expensive. Trudy was still admiring it when Vicky and Candace came out together. Behind them, Sylvia Blane reached for her coat and slipped it on, but before Trudy could manoeuvre herself to stand beside Vicky and think up some opening gambit, Sylvia gave a sudden, surprised exclamation.

'What on *earth*...?'

She withdrew her hand from her coat pocket and stared down at the small brown object she had scooped out, which was now sitting in the palm of her hand. 'Ugh! How could this have got into my pocket?' she demanded, glancing around her with sudden sharp suspicion.

As everyone crowded around to look, Trudy tried to get a good view, but whatever it was, it wasn't a big object, and it was hard to see in any detail.

'What is it?' It was Candace who asked the question, her big eyes opening as wide as saucers.

'It's a dead moth,' Betty Darville said blankly. 'It must have flown into your coat and just died.'

'Oh no! It hasn't eaten any of the material has it?' Candace wailed. 'I hate it when moths get into your best clothes.'

'Don't be silly,' Betty said with a grin. 'It's not *that* kind of moth! They're rather small and nondescript. This is bigger. I can't remember seeing one quite like it before.'

'Here, I'll have it,' Trudy offered eagerly and at once. 'I have a little brother who collects stuff like that,' she temporised quickly, as Betty Darville shot her a quick, quizzical look. 'Dead beetles, animal bones, you name it. Mind you, Mum wouldn't let him keep a dead grass snake that he found.'

'Ugh, little brothers are the limit,' Candace agreed. 'Well, I'm off. Night night, everyone.'

Trudy moved forward and held out her hand, and with a brief frown, Sylvia shrugged and tipped her hand, letting the desiccated little corpse fall into Trudy's open palm.

As casually as she could, she wrapped it loosely in her handkerchief and let it rest on top of the stuff in her handbag so that it wouldn't get squashed.

When she looked up, she was vexed to see that Vicky Munnings had managed to slip away. Again!

But Trudy wasn't that put out. She knew she would corner Abby's so-called best friend sooner or later.

Right now, she was far more interested in her latest piece of 'evidence'.

For her eagle eye had spotted something strange about the dead moth that she hoped that none of the others had noticed.

Namely, it's unusual markings. Markings that, to her eye at any rate, resembled the rather macabre and sinister shape of a human skull.

Chapter 13

'It's called a Death's Head Hawkmoth!' Clement said the next day.

They were sitting in his office, and he was leaning forward on his chair, staring intently at the pathetic offering that Trudy had just placed before him. 'I haven't seen one of these in years! Where did you find it?'

'One of the girls found it in her coat pocket when we were leaving the theatre after rehearsals last night. I think most of the others presumed that it had just flown or crawled in there and died. But I don't think that's very likely.'

'It's possible, I suppose,' Clement said cautiously. 'But I think, like you, it would be a remarkable coincidence if it had. Far more likely someone had put it there on purpose. Especially this particular species.'

Trudy eyed the little corpse thoughtfully. 'It's certainly got a gruesome name. I take it that it earned it because of the skull-like markings on it?'

'Yes,' Clement said. 'There was quite a bit of folklore and superstition surrounding it back in olden times. Its melancholy shriek when disturbed made it the stuff of legend – when folks were more inclined to believe in all sorts of dark and dreadful things.'

'It shrieks?' Trudy said, her jaw dropping. 'A *moth*?'

Clement's lips twitched. 'I don't suppose it's very loud – like the call of a shriek-owl or anything. But loud enough to be heard, certainly. For centuries, it was regarded as being a bringer of doom, and was always an omen of death.'

Trudy gulped. 'So this is another death threat then?' she asked uncertainly.

'It certainly could be,' Clement mused. 'Some say its appearance in King George III's bedchamber pushed him into madness.'

'Well, that's just wonderful,' Trudy huffed. 'Anything else that can be laid at its door while we're at it?' she asked, intending it to be a rhetorical question. She was appalled to hear that the coroner hadn't finished yet.

'Oh, plenty!' Clement swept on enthusiastically. 'For instance, others believed that should its wings extinguish a candle by night, those nearby will be cursed with blindness.'

'Oh,' Trudy said, beginning to feel rather chilled. At first, when Sylvia had found the moth and Trudy had noticed the skull markings, she'd been a little concerned. Now that all this stuff was coming out, she was beginning to feel as if something dark and evil might really be stalking the Old Swan Theatre. What kind of person would put something like this in someone's pocket?

'It's very name – *Acherontia Atropos* – derives from Greek mythology.' Clement carried on the lecture with remorseless relish, eyeing the moth with some fascination. 'Acheron – the river of pain, and Atropos, the Fate that severs the thread of life.'

'Please stop now,' Trudy begged. *River of pain?* She was beginning to feel slightly ill! 'Who'd have thought so much hate and bile could be represented by one little brown insect?'

Clement sighed and leaned back. As a threat, this latest offering certainly punched well above its weight. But it also revealed quite a bit about the person behind the 'pranks'.

He frowned, not liking where his thoughts were going. More

and more it seemed to him that the likelihood that Abigail Trent's death had been accidental was receding.

So if she *had* been murdered, the chances were fairly high that the joker at the theatre and her murderer were one and the same. Was it time to demand that Trudy resign from the contest?

'Well, luckily, I don't think that any of the girls really took much notice of it, thank goodness,' Trudy said, unaware of her friend's growing concern for her safety. 'If they'd known all that stuff that you just told me, they'd have been climbing the walls!'

'Yes, so I would imagine,' Clement agreed dryly.

'Do you think all this could be aimed at the Dunbars?' Trudy asked curiously. 'Because it seems to me that everyone at the theatre has a lot to lose if the contest fails. Even the theatre will be out of pocket. So it could, conceivably, be someone with a grudge against anyone involved. Maybe it's not just the girls themselves who are the target?'

'You're right, but we don't have enough information yet to say,' Clement said.

'No, I suppose not. But this all feels so… personal, doesn't it?' Trudy said, deciding then and there that she was going to leave the dead moth where it was – on the coroner's desk. She didn't want to ever touch it – or see it – again. If it needed to be logged into evidence at some point in the future, she was sure Dr Ryder wouldn't mind handing it over to the Sergeant. 'I'm beginning to get a feel for our prankster now, and I can't help but think that there's something really dark and deep behind it all. I don't know… that there's something sort of insane about him or her.' She gave a little shudder, making the older man look at her severely.

Clement sighed. 'You mustn't let your imagination run away with you,' he warned her. 'This' – he nodded at the dead moth – 'was meant to make all the contestants feel repulsed and alarmed. Whoever it is who's doing this, wants to instil fear, panic and suspicion in the theatre. Don't let them succeed.'

'No, you're right,' she agreed, stiffening her backbone and thrusting out her chin a little. 'I won't mention any of the stuff you told me about our dead friend here,' Trudy promised. 'With a bit of luck, everyone will forget it ever existed.'

Clement nodded. 'Until the next time something happens,' he added darkly.

Chapter 14

Rupert Cowper usually went home at lunchtime, leaving his flower shop in the capable hands of his assistant. His housekeeper, used to his ways, often left him a cold collation, and he was just cutting some bread when he heard his doorbell ring.

He wondered who could be calling at that hour, and when he opened the door to find a tall, grey-haired man – who looked only vaguely familiar – on his doorstep, he wondered uneasily if he'd made an appointment and had then forgotten about it.

'Hello?'

'Hello, Mr Cowper, isn't it? Sorry to bother you – I'm Dr Clement Ryder. One of your fellow judges on the Miss Oxford Honey panel? I believe I saw you at the rehearsals the other night?'

'Oh yes.' Rupert smiled, taking the hand the older man was holding out. 'Won't you come in?' he asked politely, but was clearly puzzled by his visitor's presence.

Quickly Clement spun his tale of needing judging advice, and within a few moments, they were sitting at the dining table, where Rupert had insisted the coroner join him to share his lunch.

'My daily woman always leaves out too much food anyway,' he insisted.

Clement accepted a slice of bread and some cold roast beef,

added a dash of horseradish sauce, and munched happily for a while. Then he sighed. 'The thing is, I've never done anything remotely like judging a beauty pageant contest before,' he began, with a wry smile. 'So I suppose I feel rather... er...'

'Embarrassed? Wrong-footed. A little silly?' Rupert offered, with an understanding smile of his own. As Clement nodded, he sighed heavily. 'Me too. I never wanted to sit on the panel either, but Robert insisted. Mind you, I think he only wanted me because he knew that I'd volunteer to provide the big standing floral displays on "show night". Six six-foot stands with cascades of roses, lilies, freesias... sorry, you don't want to know about that!' Rupert grinned, breaking off to cut himself a small wedge of mature cheddar.

'I understand that a lot of the judges are providing something – prizes and what-have-you,' Clement mused. 'Mr Dunbar certainly has a way of cutting down his costs and keeping an eye on his overheads.'

Rupert laughed. 'I'll say. What that man won't do for money... Still, I suppose it's a bit of fun.' But he sounded distinctly dubious, and Clement eyed him curiously.

'You sound as if you think it's anything but?' he said mildly.

The younger man shrugged, looking rather shame-faced. 'Oh, the amount of ribbing that I've taken about it from my friends! Well, male friends, that is. They seem to think I'm a lucky old so-and-so. I suppose I can see why they think that. Mind you, it's not as glamorous a job as you might imagine. Though on the other hand, a lot of the members of the fairer sex of my acquaintance are treating me with either cool amusement or downright finger-wagging. So, all things being equal, I wish I'd never agreed to sign up for it!'

'So how exactly are we supposed to do this judging?' Clement asked casually. 'Do we meet the girls and talk to them ourselves, or is there a more complicated and regimented points system?'

'Oh, it's nothing very scientific,' Rupert laughed. 'On show night, we'll all be given forms and have to fill in points out of ten for all the different categories like talent, and interview performance and whatnot. But also more general things like choice of costume, walk, grace, all sorts of rubbish really,' Rupert said, picking up a tomato and frowning at it. 'Then, at the end, you tally them up and come to a total figure. Whoever has the highest tally wins.'

'Doesn't sound that harrowing,' Clement agreed. 'But you're looking at that innocuous tomato as if you want to murder it.'

Rupert laughed, looking a little abashed. 'Sorry. Yes, I suppose I was really.' He sighed and lowered the fruit to his plate, then shot the older man a thoughtful look. Seeing only an older, presumably wiser and definitely benevolent face looking back at him, he leaned a little forward over the table, and said, 'Just between ourselves, Dr Ryder…'

'Oh, call me Clement, please.'

'I'm Rupert then. Between us then, Clement, I'm beginning to seriously wish that I'd followed my first instinct, which was to say "no". With hindsight, I would never have let Robert talk me into this whole fiasco.'

'Oh? Why? They all seemed like a pleasant bunch the first time I met them. The girls are certainly keen and eager to win,' Clement said mildly.

'Oh, aren't they just,' Rupert mused bitterly. 'But that's half the trouble. You wouldn't believe half the things that go on in that theatre sometimes.'

Clement carefully reached for a piece of cheese and took a casual bite. 'Sounds ominous. What do I need to look out for, exactly?'

Rupert had the grace to laugh. 'Sorry. I dare say I sound ridiculous – if not melodramatic! But what's a chap to do when pretty girls will, well, cosy up to one? I mean, how's a chap supposed to put them off and still be a gentleman about it?'

Clement bit back the desire to smile and instead forced himself to look serious. 'I take it you're not married then?'

'No, I'm a widower. My children are both in their late teens now.'

'Ah. So you're an eligible man again. What's more, you own your own business, and you're still in your prime. I suppose it's no wonder you come in for more than your fair share of interest.' Clement shrugged. 'There are worse problems to have, surely?'

Rupert again laughed, but Clement could see his heart wasn't in it. For such a good-looking man, he seemed rather unusually bashful and shy. Or was there something deeper and darker at the heart of his reluctance? It wasn't usual for a good-looking and still relatively young man to find the attentions of women – especially young and pretty women – so alarming.

'I know, I know. I sound like a bit of a prig,' Rupert confessed at once. 'But really, you know, it's no joke. Sometimes I feel like a character in one of those awful *Carry On* films they're making nowadays; but it's no laughing matter, I can tell you. First of all, there was that poor girl who died who kept trying to corner me, and now she's gone it's Syl… Well, never mind. Just take my advice, and don't give them even a spark of encouragement, that's all I'm saying, Clement. Otherwise you'll turn your head and find them clinging to your arm like a limpet! Here, have some mustard. It's French, and I go down to London especially for it.'

Clement spread a bit on his second, open-topped beef sandwich and looked at the florist thoughtfully.

'You know, it's odd you mentioning Abigail Trent. I presided at her inquest. Such a sad case. What do you think happened to her?'

Rupert shrugged. 'Oh, I have no doubt she made the concoction herself, thinking it would help her complexion or make her eyes shine or who knows what nonsense. Either that or someone else made it for her, promising the same thing. I tell you, these girls will do anything to win. They're all desperate to get their picture in the papers. Which seems to be the greatest thing on earth, if you ever stop and listen to their endless chatter!'

Clement nodded. 'So I take it Abigail was one of those who tried to suborn your vote?'

'Yes. But at least she was subtle about it and didn't make a pest of herself. Unlike... well, never mind. Just watch out, that's all I'm saying. Unless, of course, you're quite happy to have some female company...?' He looked at Clement with a raised eyebrow.

'Good grief, no!' Clement said, genuinely appalled. 'I'm old enough to be their grandfather!'

'Oh, that won't stop them,' Rupert glowered darkly.

'You make it sound like they're all positive man-eaters!' Clement said with a smile.

Again, the florist sighed heavily. 'Perhaps they are,' he said a shade darkly. Then, catching the older man's stare, forced another laugh. 'Sorry, don't listen to me. I'm just an old grump sometimes. Or perhaps I'm just old-fashioned. But I like women to be... well... a little more reticent. Oh, never mind. A pickled onion?'

He offered the jar of onions, and began to talk about the merits of carnations over roses.

* * *

Clement parked his car in the cobbled yard of Floyd's Row and sat for a moment, thinking hard.

His interview with the florist had left him feeling distinctly uneasy. On the face of it, Rupert Cowper was a good-looking, affluent businessman, with two grown children and not a care in the world. By his own admission, he'd been given a task to do that made his male friends envious.

And yet he seemed to be afraid of women.

One thing was for certain – Clement would be willing to bet that the good-looking florist's relationships with women were tricky, uncertain things at the best of times.

Or was he just seeing problems where none existed? Had the prankster/probable murderer got him seeing suspicious and odd behaviour where none really existed? Perhaps Rupert Cowper was nothing more than a shy, handsome widower who had never learned how to cope with women?

Angry with himself for prevaricating, he again contemplated whether or not Trudy should remain undercover at the theatre. He knew that she would be very angry with him if he pulled her out now. But if it turned out that there really was something dark and mad at work there, he wouldn't be able to live with himself if Trudy Loveday were to be its next victim.

* * *

But at that same moment in time, Clement Ryder was not the only one who was thinking long and hard about murder and madness.

The picker of yew berries was also thinking very hard indeed.

Mostly about domestic heaters and how obliging carbon monoxide could be. As a gas and a poison it really was a gem! You couldn't smell it or taste it to any great degree. And it robbed your body of oxygen so very competently, sending you into a peaceful – and permanent sleep – with the greatest of ease and the minimum of fuss and attention.

Again, a trawl of the libraries had provided such a plethora of useful information.

For instance, victims who had breathed in too much of it were left with cherry-red faces.

Now just how delicious was that?

All that pale and delicate beauty rendered an unbecoming red? It was almost poetic.

* * *

Throughout the city, many people were thinking many things.

Candace Usherwood, for instance, was sitting in front of her dressing-table mirror and thinking about eyebrows.

Ever since Betty had got that note about Abigail Trent's 'flawed' beauty, Candace had been living in a state of near panic. Because of the tiny, white, almost invisible scar on her left eyebrow, the result of a minor childhood accident... which was definitely a flaw, wasn't it?

Of course, only someone who was standing really close to her would ever know it was there.

It was not at all like Abigail's beauty mark, which had been much more obvious and visible.

Still.

Perhaps she should pull out of the competition? Winning a competition wasn't worth... well, putting your life in danger, was it?

Ever since that horrible letter had come to light, Candace had tried so hard to pooh-pooh it. After all, everyone knew that the kind of people who wrote poison pen letters weren't really dangerous, were they?

But what if that wasn't the case this time? What if, whoever wrote that note really *had* had something to do with Abby's death?

Helplessly, she vacillated.

The trouble was, she so loved being a part of the beauty pageant that she didn't want to leave it. She'd never done anything so daring before, even though for all her life she'd felt the urge to be a bit of a showman. Oh, she wasn't vain enough to think she could win the actual title. But she did so love doing the 'talent' spot and had high hopes of winning the prize for that particular category.

For her, it was the lure of performing in public at the theatre on show night that was the real, glittering prize.

And the thought of giving it up made her want to cry.

All the boys she knew were well impressed when they heard she was a potential beauty queen! For the first time in her life, the contest made her feel like someone special.

And she'd made some good friends too. Oh, not Caroline Tomworthy, but the rest were good pals. Sylvia and Betty and...

But what if Abby hadn't died because of a sad, silly accident? What if someone really was out to teach 'flawed' beauty queens a lesson?

Candace's eyes shot to her eyebrow again. Could she be next?

And so the see-saw of indecision swept over her again.

* * *

Sylvia Blane was also thinking hard – about a certain handsome florist. And she was frowning. She'd have thought she'd have got much further in her pursuit of Rupert by now, but he was proving a much harder proposition than she'd first thought.

But she wasn't sure where the problem lay, exactly. She knew she was pretty enough to attract him, and was young enough to appeal to his vanity, without being *too* young and making him feel ridiculous. Mind you, only a few of the girls in the competition were really young – since you had to be 18 or over to qualify.

He was definitely interested – she could tell that from the way he reacted when she kissed him. He wriggled like a little worm sometimes, she thought with a giggle, so that she couldn't feel how aroused he was.

But for all his fascination with her, she couldn't get him to agree to a proper date and to begin a real courtship. With any other man, she would simply suspect that he was only out to get one thing – and that putting a ring on a respectable girl's finger didn't come as part of the bargain.

But with Rupert it was almost as if she had the opposite problem. He wouldn't make any overtures to her at all. Even with her gentle encouragement. She had to do all the running, and all the kissing. And he... well, wiggled about and looked uncomfortable. Even when there was no chance that somebody might interrupt them.

It was almost as if, Sylvia thought with a puzzled frown, he didn't like her. No, not that exactly. More like... he was afraid of her.

Which was just plain silly.

* * *

Grace Farley had raced home in her lunch hour, as she did every day, and was now sitting by her mother's bedside, helping her to eat some broth – but every day she seemed to be getting only thinner and thinner, her face ever more haggard and pale and cadaverous.

In spite of the new medication she had sacrificed so much to get a hold of.

'You're doing well, Mum,' Grace forced herself to say encouragingly.

'It tastes wonderful, Gracie,' Frances said, her voice as light and ephemeral as the sunshine coming in through the window. 'You're such a good girl.'

She smiled tremulously.

Frances Cunningham had never been a pretty girl. In fact, it was generally agreed, even by those who loved her the most that she was rather a plain little thing. But that hadn't stopped Bill Farley from loving her.

Grace, as ever, had to hold back the hot, bitter tears whenever she contemplated how unfair life could be. Tonight, at the theatre, they'd all troop in again, full of youth and healthy vigour, with not a care in the world...

'How about some music, Mum?' Grace whispered gently. 'Some of those new Doris Day records I got you for your birthday?'

As she played the music for her mother, Grace walked to the window and stared out sightlessly over the city.

It was just not fair...

130

Caroline Tomworthy also had a fine view of the city from her office window, but at that moment she wasn't remotely interested in the view of Oxford's dreaming spires.

She worked as the personal assistant (she never let anyone call her a secretary) for Mr Thomas Osborne, a coal merchant on a grand scale. He paid her well, not daring to do anything else, and she ran his admin with a cold, hard and competent ease. She knew she was not liked by the other office staff, and didn't care a hoot. But now it was time to move onwards and upwards.

She'd never had an easy life, but she'd been clever enough at school to pass the exams that would allow her to earn some 'safety net' secretarial qualifications. Her first love had always been ballet though, and her grit and determination to succeed had seen her earn a place in the corps of a small company in Brighton.

But even that wonderful time had been blighted for her by the hardships inflicted by a constant lack of money and the jealousy of her fellow dancers, leading to her dismissal by the time she was just 22.

But nothing could keep her down for long.

She *was* going to live the life she wanted – which was the good life – no matter what it took. She craved not only money, but culture, glamour, and a life less ordinary than one her poor mother could ever have imagined.

At first, she'd thought she could earn it for herself as a ballerina, before deciding she would simply have to do what many women before her had had to do – namely, marry into it.

But she had learned her lessons in life the hard way, and had no illusions that it would be an easy task to catch the attention of a really rich man and get him to propose.

In her nicely appointed PA's office, Caroline Tomworthy gave a tight, cynical little smile.

But there were always ways and means.

Rich men the world over had always married women far beneath them socially – provided they could provide their would-be spouses something interesting, something that would make the rest of their set envious or intrigued. Which was why, even in Victorian times, lords of the realm married actresses!

She'd almost been on the verge of despair, working in the hated office and performing her mind-numbingly boring job, when she'd spotted the advert for Miss Oxford Honey – and she'd grasped the opportunity with both hands.

A beauty queen title would do nicely.

Now all she had to do was win it, and then she'd be entered for Miss Oxford. And that was a big enough stage from which to lure a big fish.

Looking out from her window over the city, Caroline Tomworthy smiled more happily. She had no serious doubts that she would win the title. Most of the other girls were silly, young, airheaded little things without a clue.

And her biggest rival – Abigail Trent – was now no threat.

Even so, she wasn't going to leave anything to chance. If you wanted to succeed you had to make *sure* you succeeded! You had to be ruthless, clear-headed and let nothing stand in your way.

Which is why she had made sure that she had an ace in the hole.

Already she'd been dropping certain hints in the right ear. And although that ear wasn't proving to be very responsive just yet, that would soon change.

Chapter 15

Vicky Munnings got home from work at her usual time and went straight to her 'apartment'. She liked to call it that, since it made her feel marginally better. Although most of her friends lived at home with their parents until they got married, it had always been Abigail's dream in particular to 'get a place of her own'.

In spite of how Abby had always called her a chicken, Vicky had secretly seen herself as being braver, more modern and independent than anyone else too.

Both of them had loved going to the cinema to watch the films where Doris Day was living the good life in her own fancy New York apartment and having a grand time with the likes of the dishy Rock Hudson. But it was not so easy to be a society girl in Oxford when your wages hardly stretched to new nylons every week!

But she had sort of managed it.

In truth, her 'apartment' consisted of the small annexe that had been added to the back of her parents' home when Grandma Carruthers had come to live with them. After Gran had died, the family had quickly reclaimed the two rooms – a large bed-sitting room with an adjoining bathroom – as their own, with her father (before his death three years ago) using the one room as a study, and everyone using the other whenever the family bathroom was unavailable.

It had taken her some time, and much persuading, to allow her mother to let her claim the space for her own once she'd reached the age of 18. But she had eventually relented, mostly Vicky knew, because she'd been scared that her daughter might leave home if she hadn't.

She had promptly redecorated it to her taste and had spent most of her money on refurbishing it with the latest 'in' things. Much to Abigail's tight-lipped envy! Even now, Vicky hugged that almost unprecedented feeling of superiority to herself. It hadn't been often that she'd been able to make Abigail jealous.

True, the apartment could still be accessed through the main house, with a door leading off the utility room. But it also had its own private entrance via a pair of French doors. A short, rather overgrown garden path led from this door to the rear garden, which was screened by mature shrubbery, and therefore ideal for Vicky's purposes. It meant that she could come and go unseen, at all hours, without disturbing the family or setting the gossipy neighbours' tongues wagging.

But when she came home from work that day, she entered the house normally, called out a vague greeting for her mother who could usually be found in the sitting room, and went straight through to her place.

She'd glanced at the large wooden 'sunburst' clock that hung in pride of place, then went over to the large, modern Bakelite wireless that she had to play much less loudly than she'd like. She found a station playing a rock 'n' roll tune from America and slipped off her shoes.

Her double bed took up most of the room, but she'd still managed to squeeze in a sitting area, and was saving up to buy a television set of her own. An unimaginable luxury! She could watch the programmes she preferred on her own, without her parent's supervision or censorship.

With a sigh, she draped her coat across the back of the room's single armchair, turned the heater full on to take the chill off the room and then went through to the bathroom. A shower had been installed, because Gran couldn't climb into or out of a bath. It was annoying, since Vicky rather liked lazing in a bath, but she supposed you couldn't have everything.

After showering, she emerged in a long silk dressing grown, a gift to herself after Abby had died. She'd needed cheering up and had always wanted to buy something extravagant for herself. Something that would have made her dead friend envious all over again...

She had an hour before she had to get to the theatre. Tonight, they were doing a full dress rehearsal of the ball gown section of the show, and she was looking forward to wearing her choice of dress.

It made her angry that it belonged to the theatre's wardrobe selection, as she'd have loved to be able to own it herself. But only the likes of that snooty Caroline Tomworthy, who had a really well-paid job, could afford to buy and wear their own dresses. Unless Caroline had a secret sugar daddy who bought her clothes for her? Which might well be the case. There was always something sly and knowing about Caroline.

With a sigh about the injustices of life (and rather wishing she had the nerve to find a sugar daddy for herself) Vicky sat down at her tiny vanity table, squished to one side of the French windows, and began to brush her long blonde hair.

It was the one thing that she'd always had over Abby – her naturally blonde, long, silk-straight and thick hair. She was also slightly slimmer than Abby had been – which she'd always secretly been happy about, for all Abby had maintained that men preferred curves.

Of course, now that Abby was gone, Vicky was well aware that she had to be one of the favourites to win the competition. Her and Caroline – and maybe two of the others.

She bit her lip as she contemplated the stiffness of her competition, then caught herself doing so, and quickly stopped. It wouldn't do to have chapped lips tonight – being a full dress rehearsal was bound to bring some of the judges to the theatre.

Not all the judges attended the rehearsals, of course, but most of them did. Dirty old men, Abby had called them with her usual contemptuous grin. But that hadn't stopped her flirting with them, had it?

Vicky continued to brush her hair thoughtfully and think of her dead friend. Her thoughts made her squirm.

It wasn't until Abby died that Vicky had really begun to see how much she had dominated her life. Ever since they'd met, it had always been Vicky who had done the following – Vicky the acolyte; Vicky the sidekick; Vicky the henchman.

It made her wince, now, to think how easily she'd been led, how mindlessly she'd always fallen in with Abby's schemes. At school, if anyone had ever slighted her, Abby had made sure Vicky helped her 'get their own back'. If Abby hated a teacher, Vicky must hate her too. If Abby wore her hair a certain way, Vicky must copy her – whether the style suited her or not.

Of course, that sort of thing might be tolerable when you were 10 or 11. Or even 14. But even after they'd left school and found jobs, Vicky, somehow, had remained locked in her orbit.

Take the beauty contest for instance. Vicky would never have dreamed of entering it. But Abby wanted to, and as usual, she wanted her henchman by her side to bolster her ego and keep her company.

Absently, Vicky stopped brushing her lovely hair and slowly began to smile. Well, that at least, hadn't worked out quite how Abby had wanted it, had it?

At first, after her friend had died, she'd gone around in a daze, not sure what to do. Her life seemed oddly lop-sided and ungainly. A big chunk seemed to be missing. She wasn't sure what she should be doing, or how to fill her time. But in a shockingly short time, Vicky had begun to feel better – she was free.

For the first time in her life, she felt as if her life belonged to her – and not to Abigail Trent. And it was wonderful.

And yet… Vicky felt afraid.

Feeling angry with herself, she got up and began to dress hurriedly.

Chapter 16

Christine Dunbar listened to the excited chatter coming from the dressing rooms and tut-tutted angrily. Anyone would think these girls had never worn dresses before!

Everything about them irritated her – their self-absorption, the way they took their youth for granted and most of all, their slim, unthinking beauty. She herself had never been exactly slim, for she'd always been too large and too fleshy. But she'd had a naturally curvy, hour-glass figure once – many years ago now. When she'd been in her early twenties. But middle age tended to make one spread so.

She caught herself looking at her reflection in a mirror through an open dressing-room door and was reassured that the corset she was wearing still gave her the illusion of that figure. At least her head of fine blonde hair still looked good! She patted the brassy curls (touched up just that morning by her regular hair-dresser) with satisfaction and moved on.

She had lost sight of Robert, and she didn't like that.

* * *

From a seat in front of the stage, Patricia Merriweather watched Robert Dunbar chatting to one of the girls, who had yet to change into her costume. It was that nice girl, Betty Darville, one of the old lady's favourites. But even as she watched, Christine Dunbar strode across the stage, her eye firmly fixed on her spouse.

Patricia found herself smiling wryly, and then looked to her immediate left as someone took a seat next to her – or rather, the next seat but one. British social etiquette demanded that you never be so forward as to actually come too close.

She discovered, with some surprise and intrigued delight, that a decidedly handsome older man not quite of 'her' generation was seated there. Moreover, one who had the gumption to nod across and smile at her.

'Dr Ryder,' he introduced himself smoothly. 'Are you a fellow judge?'

'For my sins,' Patricia agreed, taking up the opening gambit. 'I got roped in by way of being a "Friend of the Old Swan Theatre".' She deliberately sounded the capital letters with mock-importance. 'But how the devil did the evil fate befall you?'

Clement grinned, rather liking the twinkling mischief apparent in the old girl's eyes, and decided to step up to the challenge.

'By dint of not being quick-witted enough to dodge Robert Dunbar.'

'Ah,' Patricia nodded wisely. 'It happens to us all at some point.'

'I rather gathered that.'

'Patricia Merriweather.' She thrust out a slightly gnarled hand. 'Widow, tireless donator to charity, owner of a tediously respectable and tiresomely 'old' family name and champion of the city's rather more risqué architecture,' the old lady introduced herself.

'Pleased to meet you,' Clement said, and meant it. He was beginning to think he was the oldest person there! 'Clement Ryder. City coroner and all-round curmudgeon.'

Over by the stage curtain, Trudy had just arrived and was yet to change. She saw Dr Ryder at once, chatting and laughing in the front seats with the old lady who was something to do with preserving the theatre.

She noticed Betty, looking rather peeved, just walking away from the Dunbars, who were having a rather heated discussion about something, and saw the other girl's face clear and then smile when she spotted her.

'Hello,' Trudy said with a grin. 'I'm rather looking forward to tonight. Miss Farley hasn't said what dress I'm going to be wearing, but I'm hoping it's something swanky,' Trudy confessed. She found it very odd to have to refer to her friend Grace as 'Miss Farley'. 'She says it's really nice.'

'I'm sure it will be,' Betty said encouragingly. And then, following Trudy's glance towards the front seats, nodded. 'Looks like the judges will be out in force tonight. I wonder who the old girl is flirting with now.'

Trudy blinked in astonishment. True, she'd already seen for herself how relaxed Clement was, even laughing now and then and leaning closer to listen to what his companion was saying, but it had never occurred to her that he was being 'flirted with'! And by a woman so much older than he was!

'Really?' she asked, astonished. 'Mrs Merriweather didn't strike me that way. Didn't I hear someone say that she was from one of the city's old families?' Trudy heard herself stutter.

Betty laughed. 'Oh yes. One of the oldest and most respectable. Old money too, and the Merriweathers have managed to keep it too, despite the two world wars. A lot of the old guard went into serious decline, but not them. Mind you, it hasn't been all roses for them.'

'Oh?'

'Family troubles,' Betty said darkly. 'The Merriweathers have always had the reputation of being unlucky. My mum said a lot of them died in that bad flu epidemic after the First World War, and losing so many of their children sent some of the older generation a bit dotty.'

'I imagine it must have sent a lot of people dotty,' Trudy said sadly.

'Yeah. But the old girl's all right,' Betty said breezily. 'Besides, she married into the family. No tainted blood in her and all that. Mind you, her son, Christopher, went a bit queer in the last war, so they say. Shell shock I suppose. Or he might have been a prisoner of war.'

Trudy shivered. She had no real memories of the war, of course, having been too young to remember how bad it must have been. Her main memories concerned food rationing and the dearth of proper sweets that came afterwards! But she'd grown up listening to her parents talking about the friends and family they had lost, and those they knew who had suffered both mentally as well as physically.

'I hope he's all right now? Mrs Merriweather's son?'

Betty shrugged, quickly losing interest. 'I don't know. He must be, I suppose, because I know he got married and had a kid of his own – a girl, I think, because the old woman often talks about her granddaughter Millie. Dotes on her, like all grannies do. I think he travels a lot, and left his good old mother to raise the kiddie. Stopped her being so lonely, I expect.'

'Oh, that's good,' Trudy said. She liked a story with a happy ending. 'I've only met Mrs Merriweather the once, I think, but I liked her.'

'Yes, she's a grand old dame,' Betty agreed with a smile. 'Bit of a raver in her time, though, or so I hear. Did the Charleston with the rest of the bright young things and drank champagne out of a slipper. That sort of thing! Mind you, she's been a widow for some time now. So I don't know if that fella she's with is all that safe!'

Trudy had to hide a grin. She was pretty confident that 'the old fella' could take care of himself!

'Who's not safe?' Sylvia Blane asked, making Betty jump and Trudy spin around fast. She hadn't heard her come up behind them.

'Don't sneak up on us like that!' Betty said, betraying how tight her nerves were. Clearly the person behind the threats was having an effect on everyone's morale, and it made Trudy angry. What right did he or she have to make everyone's life so miserable?

Sylvia mumbled an apology. 'Sorry. But when you said someone wasn't safe... I sort of got spooked. Nothing' – her voice lowered a couple of decibels – 'bad has happened again, has it?' she whispered.

Betty laughed in relief. 'No! I was just telling the newcomer here about our Pat! How she was a grand old girl in her time, and how she's probably getting her claws into the new judge over there.'

'Oh, is that all!' Sylvia wilted in relief. Then she smiled. 'You've got to hand it to her. She's a game old girl. I think I like her the best out of all the judges. At least you know she'll be fair.'

'I know what you mean,' Betty said darkly.

At this, Trudy's mental antenna pinged suddenly. 'What? What do you mean? Aren't the rest of the judges fair?' she asked, hoping she sounded suitably innocent and naive.

The other two girls exchanged glances. Then Betty grinned widely. 'Well, let's just say some of us are trying to sneak an advantage. Right, Sylv?'

Sylvia opened her eyes wide. 'I don't know what you mean.'

'Right. Like you've not been vamping the lovely Rupert!' Betty teased.

'Oh well. Judges expect to be buttered up,' the other girl muttered with a sly grin.

Trudy sighed. This was getting her nowhere. 'What about Vicky?' she asked casually. 'Does she butter up the judges too?'

'Not that I noticed,' Betty said, clearly determined to be fair.

'I dare say losing her best friend left her feeling down,' Trudy fished gently.

'Yes. I suppose,' Sylvia put in. 'But if you ask me, she's got over it pretty quickly.'

But before Trudy could follow up on this interesting line, she was thwarted.

'Oh hello – the judges are heading our way.' Betty hissed the sudden warning, and Trudy turned slightly to see Clement and Patricia heading across the stage towards them.

'Hello, girls. Going to treat us to a fashion parade tonight then?' Patricia said with a smile. 'Have you met your newest judge, Dr Ryder?'

Clement politely shook hands with all three of them, Trudy not quite knowing where to look when her friend reached out and shook her own hand.

'I think I've seen all of you before, the last time I was here,' Clement said smoothly. 'But it's nice to meet you officially.'

Trudy, worried that she might give herself away somehow if she indulged in too much small talk with her friend, muttered an excuse about needing to find her gown, and beat a strategic retreat.

Grace was waiting for her in her dressing room with a gown that made Trudy's eyes pop.

It was a deep ruby-red genuine silk dress with an empire waistline and intricately beaded shoulder straps that seemed to glow like the gemstone. Sleeveless, it would leave her shoulders bare, no doubt lending her skin a pale-as-cream contrast that would hopefully catch the judges' eyes.

Then she brought herself up short. What did it matter if she caught the judges' eyes or not? She was not really in the competition!

'I thought this would suit you,' Grace said casually as she handed it over. 'It's from a play they put on last year – one of those murder-mystery things. You know, set in the drawing room of a country mansion sort of thing. I think this belonged to the actress who turned out to be the killer,' Grace added with a wry twist of her lips.

Trudy, a little taken aback by the coldness of the silk, stared down at the lustrously glowing folds speechlessly. It looked so sumptuous and glamorous that she was worried that just touching it might soil it.

'Well, go ahead and put it on,' Grace said, a shade sharply. 'The girl who does hair will be along soon. She's nearly finished with Connie Beardsley, and you'll want to get yours done before that Judith Calver gets hold of her. She takes ages, and demands that all sorts of twiddly bits and who-knows-what gets done to her precious locks.'

'Oh right,' Trudy said, shaking a leg and going behind a screen to start peeling off her clothes. She felt absurdly shy doing so, and wondered nervously if she'd be able to do the lovely dress justice. The closest she'd ever come to owning a 'gown' was when a neighbour had knocked up a white frothy dress for her when she'd been voted May Queen of her primary school when she was 10!

Grace carefully shut the door of the dressing room and then approached the screen. 'Have you learned anything yet?' she asked quietly, aiming her voice over the top of it.

'Not really,' Trudy was forced to admit. 'But there are some interesting bits and pieces we've picked up on,' she said, but didn't go into the details about the dead moth, or any of the gossip that was doing the rounds. 'I've just been chatting to the girls about Patricia Merriweather. Is it true there's madness in her family?' she asked.

For if the prankster at the theatre really *was* Abby's killer, then surely she should be looking at someone who might be insane? There was, after all, a sort of leering, nasty glee about the troubles that had beset the theatre and the pageant that smacked of someone with a sick mind.

Although the old woman seemed perfectly normal on the surface, you never could tell. Trudy had already made a mental note to tell the coroner about it the moment she had the opportunity. Since he was so clearly getting on with her, he'd be in the ideal position to get to know her better, and as a medical man he might notice any tell-tale signs if there was anything wrong with her.

'What? Mrs Merriweather?' Grace said, startled. 'No, don't be silly,' she added somewhat impatiently. Then, realising that she mustn't sound too sure about things in case Trudy started to wonder why, she quickly temporised. 'Well, I know her grand-daughter's been ill recently and is under the care of doctors,' she added casually. 'So she's probably not feeling her best. We sort of got talking about it, when she learned about Mum being so ill. She was really helpful and kind and understanding about that. Reading between the lines, I got the feeling the doctors aren't hopeful about her granddaughter's recovery. Poor thing! Mind you, the old lady isn't the sort who takes things lying down, and she has the doctors hopping to it and doing all they can.'

Behind the screen, Trudy couldn't help but smile. 'I'll bet she has,' she said.

'No, you're barking up the wrong tree there, Trudy. Besides, she wouldn't do anything that would hurt the theatre or its reputation. She's determined to stop it being knocked down to make way for a car park or whatever might happen to it, if they can't keep it going.'

Trudy emerged from behind the screen and walked tentatively towards the mirror. The dress fell in lush, gleaming folds to the tops of her feet and made a gloriously 'swishing' sound as she moved. It had a modest set of underskirts that gave it a slightly bell-shaped and very pretty line, and she hardly dared look in the mirror. But when she did, her big dark eyes rounded. 'Oh, Grace, it's fabulous!'

The beading on the shoulder straps and on the high waistline sparkled in the artificial light, and the deep ruby-red colour accentuated and made the most of her dark curls and dark eyes. When she'd got her hair done up properly – perhaps in some loose, wavy-type chignon – and had had time to get her make-up on properly, she...

Again she had to stop herself from getting excited. She was here to do a job – not get distracted by playing 'dress-up'.

Grace, who'd probably seen more than her fair share of sumptuous gowns since being roped in to oversee the beauty pageant, barely gave it a glance. 'Yes, you look lovely,' she agreed absently. Then she got back to what was really important. 'So you really have no idea who's behind all this awful business?' she persisted, unaware that there was something in her voice beside impatience, something darker and far more menacing. Or that Trudy had picked up on it.

In the mirror, Trudy looked at her friend's reflection with troubled eyes. Grace was standing just behind her and her face looked small, pale and tense in the windowless room.

Trudy was sure that she'd detected pure desperation in her friend's voice.

'Grace, nothing's been sent to you, has it?' she asked abruptly, turning around, and catching her friend unawares. 'Nobody's been making trouble for *you*, have they? Because if they have, you must tell me – you mustn't be brave and keep it to yourself.'

But the only look on Grace's face was one of genuine surprise. 'What? Me? Oh no. You mean have I had a nasty letter or something?'

Trudy nodded.

But Grace shook her head firmly. 'No. Nothing like that. Besides, I'm only the general dogsbody who does a bit of minor admin for the pageant. I'm not a competitor or anything important like that.'

Trudy wondered why Grace was so sure that only those who were in the competition were at risk. If Abigail *was* murdered (and she had to remember that, so far not even *that* had been established) then perhaps her killer had a grudge against the beauty pageant as a whole. In which case, surely, any one of them involved with it might be at risk? The judges, Dennis Quayle-Jones, the Dunbars – anyone.

146

Slowly, Trudy became aware of a slightly sick feeling in the pit of her stomach and regarded her friend uncertainly. 'Grace... do you know something about all this that you're not telling me?' she asked quietly.

She was dismayed to see a look of guilt quickly flit across her friend's face.

Inside, Grace felt a small leap of triumph that she was careful not to let show. Finally the opening she was looking for!

'What?' She forced her eyes wide in what she hoped was an unconvincing show of innocence. 'No, of course not. If I had any *proof* of somebody doing something wrong, I'd have told you right away! You know I would!' Grace avowed, hoping that her friend had picked up on the slight emphasis she'd given the word 'proof'. Because if not, this was going to be harder going than she'd hoped.

Trudy smiled with sudden relief. 'Oh I get it. You suspect someone, but because you don't know anything for sure, you don't feel right in talking about it?'

Grace looked away quickly, as if hiding non-existent guilt.

Trudy smiled. Good old Gracie! It was just like her to be so fair-minded. Gently, she reached out and touched her friend on the arm.

'It's all right, Grace. You can tell me. I won't go mentioning it to anybody but Dr Ryder and he'll be discreet. But you have to tell me who you suspect and why.'

Grace sighed gently. At last! But now, she would have to be careful. She couldn't over-do it, but she needed to get her friend well and truly hooked.

'But, Trudy, I *don't* have any real proof. Nothing I can point to and say, "look, see, so-and-so did this". It's just... I just feel... I can *sense* that this person is... *wrong*. That there's something... skewed, something... dark about them... Oh, it's no good. I can't really put the feeling into words. Trudy, it's been really awful,' she said. And meant it.

Her life, just recently, had been made pure hell.

'You just have an instinct about them?' Trudy suggested gently. 'Well, there's nothing wrong with that. In fact, in training, my tutors told me that most officers develop a sort of "copper's instinct" about things. They just can tell when something's wrong.'

Grace smiled wryly. 'Most people just laugh at "women's intuition" though, you know.'

'Well. *I* won't,' Trudy promised, reaching out to put a hand on her friend's shoulder. 'So come on, tell me. Who is it that worries you so?'

Grace glanced around uneasily, but the dressing-room door was still firmly shut. She didn't really have to feign fear, for she knew that if a certain person ever got wind of what she was doing… She shuddered.

Beneath her hand, Trudy felt the movement, and felt a tremor of fear herself.

'Gracie! What is it?' Trudy asked, feeling more and more unnerved. She knew, from her training, that panic and fear could be as contagious as the common cold, and forced herself to brace up. 'You must tell me! I won't let anybody know what you say to me. I promise. I won't even put it down in writing on my official police report.'

Even with this encouragement, Grace visibly hesitated, and Trudy, who was beginning to feel like screaming with impatience, was just about to ask her again what she thought, when her friend finally spoke.

'All right. It's… it's Mrs Dunbar! I think she might be the one doing all this. I think she killed Abby deliberately. I know she…'

148

Chapter 17

'Hello – does someone in here want their hair done up?' The voice, shocking in its mundane breeziness made both women jump guiltily apart.

The opening door revealed a plump, middle-aged woman toting a large bag overflowing with curlers, heating tongs, various hairbrushes and combs, and canisters of hairspray.

'Yes, this is Trudy. I think her hair would look nice done up, don't you, with maybe some curling tendrils either side?' Grace gabbled hastily, shooting her friend a slightly panicked look. 'I'd best go and let you get on with it.'

Trudy, feeling immensely frustrated at being interrupted at such a crucial moment, watched her friend shoot out the door. Clearly she was terrified that the hairdresser might have overheard what she'd been saying.

Was she really so frightened of Christine Dunbar?

If only she'd had time to finish what she'd been about to say! Grace, having worked for the Dunbars for some time, was in the best position to have picked up on anything that might be wrong about the situation at the theatre if her employers were somehow involved.

But what might it be?

149

Trudy had noticed for herself that Mrs Dunbar seemed rather jealous of the other girls and possessive about her husband. In fact, it was a bit of a standing joke between them that she kept such an eagle eye on her spouse.

But, now she came to think about it, was that really so funny? Or was it just sound common sense on the part of Mrs Dunbar? For Trudy had picked up several pieces of gossip and innuendo about how some of the contestants flirted with the judges in order to boost their chances of winning. Who was to say that someone – Abigail, maybe – hadn't done the same, and had chosen to flirt with Robert Dunbar?

But even if she had, would that really lead to *murder*? Well, not if Mrs Dunbar was normal, no, surely not. But was she? Wasn't that what Grace had been trying to tell her – that the woman was somehow insane?

With a sigh (and realising that she could drive *herself* insane speculating wildly without any facts), Trudy gave herself over to the ministrations of the hairdresser. Who did indeed follow Grace's advice, and commenced to sweep up her hair in a high chignon, but allowed two artfully twisted tendrils to frame either side of her face.

Such artistry, however, was lost on Trudy, who was busy making mental notes. First, she had to coral Grace after the show so that she could say exactly why she suspected Mrs Dunbar.

Secondly, she still had to talk to the rather elusive Vicky Munnings! Was it sheer bad luck that she kept missing her, or was the dead girl's friend actually avoiding her? But if that was so, did it mean that she'd guessed that Trudy wasn't all she appeared to be?

Then, thirdly, she had to…

'There you go, dear, all done,' the hairdresser said cheerfully, and so distracted was she, that Trudy barely had a chance to thank her before she disappeared out the door to help sort out her next client.

150

Absently Trudy reached for her make-up bag. The dress rehearsal started in twenty minutes, and she needed to be on time. Now what else did she need to do...? Oh yes, find out if any of the girls had been trying to vamp Robert Dunbar, and if so, had Abigail been chief among them?

* * *

The killer was also anticipating the start of the dress show rehearsal – or at least the little after-party event that would follow. It was going to be interesting to see what the pretty little darlings made of the 'gift' that had been sent to them.

But it was rather annoying that news of the biggest surprise of all had yet to be sprung upon them, and the picker of yew berries was feeling rather disgruntled that it wasn't already the talk of the evening.

Something, clearly, had prevented the news from circulating. And it was a little nerve-wracking not knowing what that something was.

But perhaps the unexpected delay was all for the best, the killer mused.

Shock following on from shock might have a better impact than all the bad news being delivered at once.

The killer began to smile. Patience...

Chapter 18

Clement Ryder took his place at the judging table, which turned out to be a set of small, wooden foldaway tables that had been placed in a straight line along the front of the stage and covered with a long white cloth. He only hoped that the foldaway chairs that accompanied them weren't the flimsy kind that always made him wince with anticipation of whether or not they'd take his weight when sitting down on them. Luckily they weren't, and although his creaked slightly when taking his seat, at least it didn't collapse and dump him unceremoniously onto his behind.

Beside him on his right-hand side, Rupert Cowper nodded with a smile of greeting as he took his seat, and he was especially pleased when Patricia Merriweather joined him on his left. If anyone could lead him through the ropes of this ridiculous judging process it would be she.

The Dunbars, he noted, sat down, not together, but one at each end of the long line of tables – like slightly disapproving bookends.

In between them, he vaguely recognised several of his fellow judges from before – the owners of various shops and local businesses. He was amused to note that Patricia Merriweather and Christine Dunbar were the only female judges on the panel.

Then Dennis Quayle-Jones stepped out from behind the curtain, hands outstretched in greeting, obviously enjoying his role as the compere.

'Hello, one and all, and welcome to the first Miss Oxford Honey beauty pageant.' He paused, then looked behind him, and said as a clear aside, 'On the night, the curtains will have swooped open to reveal a no-doubt ravishingly decorated set.'

Everyone smiled, although by now, this had all become rather humdrum. The glamour had been quick to wear off, and most of his fellow judges, he noted, looked merely resigned and patient.

However, as the manager-actor set a gramophone recording going (a gently sweeping tune of big-band music) and the first contestant swept out onto an imaginary red-carpet runway, both Clement, and his fellow judges, perked up.

Candace Usherwood was first out, wearing a coffee-coloured gown that complemented her brown curly hair and did the most to accentuate her curvaceous figure.

She walked graciously towards the table, turned, walked past them in a queenly, elegant silence and then turned, revealing that a small diamond-shaped pane was cut out of the back of her gown, revealing a pale patch of delicate skin. A little too short and plump to be truly elegant, she nevertheless glided away impressively.

Clement, seeing that a small pad and pen had been provided, and that his judges were busily scribbling away, reached for it, and, after a moment's thought, simply wrote – 'Pretty girl, a little too plump, but nice smile.' Then wondered, was he supposed to give her a mark? And if so, was it out of 10 or 100?

Then he had to quash the sudden desire to laugh. This was so absurd! That he of all people should be doing something so outlandish. He'd far rather be sitting at home with a good book.

Then his right hand began to tremble violently and he froze.

Slowly, he withdrew his hand and dropped it into his lap.

He looked out of the corner of his eye to the right, but Rupert Cowper was busy looking at the next contestant – a rather tall and skinny redhead, with a patrician nose and an air of unexpected sex appeal.

Then he looked to his left – and felt an unpleasant jolt shoot through him as he met Patricia Merriweather's concerned glance. Instantly, she looked away. Obviously, women of good breeding pretended never to notice anything that might be described as the least bit socially awkward.

But Clement felt a bead of sweat form just under his hairline, and fought the surge of panic that threatened to swamp him.

She'd seen it. He was sure she'd noticed the tremors.

Instantly, he told himself he was over-reacting. So she'd seen it. So what? She'd assume either that he'd been drinking, or maybe had a spasm of cramp. There was no reason to assume she'd understand the importance of what she'd seen. She was no medical doctor, after all.

He pretended to watch the skinny redhead as she swayed along the stage, dressed in a mint-green, crushed-velvet gown that did wonders for her pale skin and bright colouring. But he didn't reach for his pen to write anything in the notebook.

Instead he surreptitiously flexed and re-flexed his hand and fingers in his lap for a few moments, and then rested them against the top of his thigh.

To his relief, they were still and compliant.

* * *

Trudy took a deep breath and walked out from behind the curtain. She was confident that she looked good. After being so distracted by Grace's revelations, she'd slowly begun to notice what an excellent job the hairdresser had done on her long dark hair, which had in turn inspired her to be even bolder with her make-up choices than before. Consequently, she'd painted her lips with a dark-red lipstick to match her dress, and had added a sort of reddish-brown, golden eyeshadow to her lids.

Her shoes (borrowed from the wardrobe department) had only a modest heel (since she still wasn't sure she could wear the stiletto high heels that the likes of Betty and Sylvia confidently paraded in) but since they weren't visible under the long length of silk, she wasn't that worried. She was also fairly tall anyway, so it hardly mattered, she told herself firmly.

As she walked out, the sea of empty seats beyond the judging table reassured her somewhat. At least she wouldn't be doing this in front of the general public in less than two weeks' time, which was probably a good thing, she thought wryly, as she attempted her version of the catwalk 'sashay' across the stage.

Had she but known it, the fact that she didn't exaggerate her walk so much made her actually stand out from the girls who'd gone before her, and gave her a more appealing girl-next-door quality that a lot of the judges liked.

Clement, seeing Trudy appear on the stage, felt a moment of disorientating unreality. He'd never seen his protégé in such a way before. Not only was the gown eye-catching, but with her hair up like that, and wearing sophisticated make-up, she was so different from her usual self that he almost didn't recognise her. Gone was the unflattering uniform and the needful repression of anything feminine or individual, and instead, a lovely young woman swept past him.

He noticed, with a wry smile, that she very carefully didn't meet his eye and realised that, if he felt unnerved, she must be feeling positively surreal, walking past him with that over-large band around her wrist, with the number '18' visible.

Beside him, Clement heard Rupert Cowper murmur something appreciative, and curiosity aroused, glanced at his fellow judge's paper, and realised he'd given Trudy 95 out of 100.

Praise indeed. Trudy would be flattered!

Again, Clement had to resist the urge to laugh out loud.

Eventually the fashion show came to an end, Dennis Quayle-

Jones did a dry bit of speechmaking and then the backstage staff started setting up the buffet.

It was Caroline Tomworthy who noticed the lavish box of chocolates first. She was still dressed in her sleek turquoise and silver gown that had vague hints of a Japanese kimono about it, and unlike most of the others, who'd opted to have their hair intricately dressed, her long straight black hair hung down nearly to her waist.

She noticed the chocolates first because they were so different from the usual bland fare of crustless cucumber sandwiches and the little fancy cakes that the Dunbars preferred. And also because they bore the name of a very famous brand of Swiss chocolates that could only be bought in the most exclusive of shops in London's West End.

Knowing the price of such things, she found the large and heavy box (clearly containing a double-layer) intriguing. They must have cost a small fortune! The box itself was made of stiff gold card, which gleamed dully but enticingly under the stage lighting, and had been wrapped around with an extravagantly large silver and gold ribbon.

She knew that one of the judges had agreed to supply the winner of the 'interview' part of the show with a year's supply of confectionery. But she had often walked past that judge's shop, and knew for a fact that this brand of chocolate wasn't available there. And why should it be? It would have to have been ordered from London, and she doubted that many people in Oxford would buy such a high-end luxury item on a mere whim.

So who had bought it and left on the buffet table?

She was still staring at it thoughtfully, when Sylvia Blane sidled up beside her. 'Oh, they look fabulous,' the other girl said, but with a marked lack of enthusiasm in her voice.

'They are,' Caroline said shortly. 'And far too expensive for this little production.'

Sylvia, who might have said something catty (since Caroline

156

liked to give the impression that she herself was also far above 'this little show'), found any such remarks dying in her throat. Instead, she regarded the gleaming, enticing box of delicacies with growing unease.

Soon a few of the other contestants, perhaps sensing something 'off' had also gathered around, forming a tight little group at the far end of the table. Something about their tense silence alerted Trudy, who also wandered over, wondering for a moment what they were all staring at.

When she saw the box of chocolates, she too went a little cold.

'So, who's going to be the first to take one?' It was, predictably, Caroline who spoke, her words cool and amused and sharp.

'Not me,' Betty Darville said instantly, with a bit of a shudder. 'I can't see the stingy old Dunbars having forked out for those.' Unspoken, the question of just who else might have left them hung menacingly in the air.

'It might be an admirer, I suppose,' Candace offered nervously.

There was a general silence between the girls as they contemplated this, until eventually Betty Darville plucked up the courage to say what they were all no doubt thinking.

'Yes, and perhaps our "admirer" put some yew berry juice in the liquid centres too.'

Clement, who'd been standing to one side of the buffet table at the far end from the group, took a sip from an indifferent glass of Liebfraumilch and chatted desultorily with Rupert Cowper. Then he noticed Trudy turn and look around, clearly seeking something or someone out. When her gaze finally caught his and she jerked her head in a tiny movement, he excused himself and wandered over.

'Hello,' he said vaguely, and the girls, as they all did in the presence of a judge, made room for him and began to smile.

'Hello, Dr Ryder,' Trudy said, before any of the others could start anything embarrassing – like flirting with the old vulture!

'We were wondering if you knew who sent these wonderful chocolates? It wasn't one of the judges by any chance?'

Clement, taking only a bare second to catch on, looked at the sumptuous box, with its intricate ribbon and expensive contents, and felt a cool shiver run down his spine.

'I'm not sure,' he said. 'Do you want me to find out?' It was, of course a rhetorical question, and he was already turning away. It didn't take him long to find out that neither the organisers, nor the judge with the confectionery shop had had any hand in it.

His next stop was with the old man who guarded the door, but he assured him that no 'official deliveries' had been made that day.

Next, he asked around the stagehands and those responsible for setting up the table. But nobody admitted to setting out the chocolates.

Whilst he was away, Grace had joined the small group of girls, and when the coroner returned with his mostly negative news, he added that she herself, who was in charge of ordering and overseeing the catering, had definitely not splurged her tight budget on such an outstandingly lavish object.

The chocolates, it seemed, had just appeared on the buffet table at some point in the evening, as if by magic.

They had yet to be opened, but nobody offered to do the job. Eventually, not really wanting to make herself conspicuous by taking charge, but feeling prodded by her conscience into doing something, Trudy cleared her throat.

'Dr Ryder. You're a medical man, aren't you?' she asked tentatively.

The other girls looked at him almost as one person, and Clement, again fighting back the urge to smile, nodded solemnly.

'Yes, you could say that,' he admitted.

'Would you mind... I mean...' Trudy looked around at the others, and then glanced over Clement's shoulder at the rest of the assembly – most of whom seemed unaware of their dilemma.

'Could you do us an enormous favour and take these chocolates away with you and get a lab to test them for us?'

There was a slight and general restive movement among the contestants as she said this. Although all of them, Trudy was sure, approved of her request, actually hearing it made out loud seemed to bring home to them how serious things had become.

For now, they were being forced to face up to the stark but unmistakable possibility that someone might actually have tried to poison them.

Clement hesitated. He knew that if he was to 'stay in character' he should now be heartily demanding to know why on earth he should do such a thing. And if they confessed their fears, perhaps make a show of pooh-poohing it all as being ridiculous.

But he had the feeling that things had already gone too far for him to be worried about maintaining his 'cover'.

'Of course I will,' he said simply instead. If any of the girls later started to wonder just why he had been so conciliatory and helpful so quickly, they'd just have to deal with it then.

'I'll take them when I leave and ask a colleague to test them for me straightaway. Would you like me to let you and the others know, Miss... er...' He looked at Trudy with a raised eyebrow, and she quickly took her cue.

'Trudy. Yes, if you can let me know straightaway, I'll tell the others,' she promised.

Clement nodded, then strolled casually away. Mentally he made a note to keep an eye on the table, and if any of his fellow judges or stage staff showed an interest in the box, then he'd have to intercept them. But it looked as if most of the others were more interested in the free drinks than in indulging in chocolates.

But in that – at least in one instance – he was wrong.

For one person in the theatre that night had noticed the silent congregation of contestants, and had noted, with absolute glee, their consternation over the 'gift' of chocolates.

Of course, the picker of yew berries had never been hopeful that anyone would actually open and eat the chocolates. Not even such dim-witted beauties, by now, would be so silly.

No.

The killer had expected the ruse to be instantly spotted. Would any of them actually have the foresight to get the boxes' contents analysed though? The killer really hoped so. For then it would be found that none of the lovely chocolates were, in fact, deadly.

Oh, they might be found to have contained a strong laxative! Which would have proved embarrassing and inconvenient for anyone who'd eaten them.

Even so, the news that something unpleasant and undignified had been sitting on the table waiting for them – and all wrapped up in such pretty camouflage too, just like themselves – would be bound to terrify and demoralise them all even further.

Oh, to be able to see the looks on their faces…

But this had only ever been designed to be just a little diversion, a little foretaste of much worse things to come.

For the killer had already done far, far worse. And soon they would know that another member had been removed from among their ranks. And then the terror would begin in earnest…

Chapter 19

Sylvia forced herself to forget all about the chocolates, and set about steering Rupert to a quiet dark corner of the stage where she could begin to weave her magic on the handsome widower. As usual, he reacted to her overtures like a nervous horse, but, again as usual, allowed himself, eventually, to be corralled.

Sylvia, dressed in deep burnt-orange taffeta that left her shoulders completely bare, dazzled him easily enough. Although she quite liked the idea of being a beauty queen, she liked the idea of becoming the second Mrs Cowper even more.

And earning a life of ease, comfort and luxury for herself with the added bonus of acquiring a good-looking and slightly older husband into the bargain, was worth fighting tooth and nail for.

* * *

Caroline Tomworthy, holding a glass of wine that she hadn't taken so much as a sip from, was also contemplating her glorious future. And to further this aim, she watched Dennis Quayle-Jones from dark, thoughtful eyes.

Was it time to make her move?

She didn't think so. Not quite yet – these things had to be judged just right, and the timing would be key.

It hadn't taken her long to find something that she could use against the man. His lifestyle, like those of most of his kind, was necessarily a risky one anyway. And she'd hired the best, to get the best photographs.

Which meant her initial goal – that of winning this rinky-dink little contest – was all but secured. Unlike Sylvia, who was happy to settle for netting herself a wealthy local merchant, Caroline fully intended to win the competition, and find a much richer and far more cosmopolitan mate for herself.

Dennis Quayle-Jones, whether he liked it or not, was going to ensure that she was crowned Miss Oxford Honey. She'd already made it clear to him just what she expected, but so far, he'd only reacted with mild amusement – and just a little alarm.

Soon though, he'd realise how deadly earnest she was!

* * *

Grace Farley watched the little party from a gap in the curtains. She was sure Trudy would seek her out later and demand to know more about what she 'knew'.

Grace would be ready for her. Before long, Mrs Dunbar would find herself under intense scrutiny from the police. And that would give the employer's wife far more to think about than she had right now, Grace hoped.

She forced herself to breathe deeply. There was now hope of light at the end of the tunnel. Even so, she felt slightly sick. If anything should go wrong…

* * *

It wasn't until the end-of-rehearsal get-together began to wind down that Trudy finally realised something. Something she

162

should have noticed much earlier, but which had escaped her attention during the chaotic glittering whirl of the evening's action-packed entertainment.

Namely that Vicky Munnings hadn't shown up at the theatre that night.

Chapter 20

Rosemary Munnings awoke that morning, as she always did, just before the alarm clock had had a chance to go off, and slipped out of bed. Silencing the clock by turning the chrome-plated key set on top of it, she yawned briefly, rose, had a quick wash, brushed her teeth and then got dressed.

She was a small, rounded woman, who mostly managed to enjoy her life. A widow for three years now, her husband, Douglas, had had the foresight to leave his wife and only child fairly well provided for, and she was happy with her home and her adopted city. She'd been born in Leicester, but much preferred the élan that an Oxford address gave her.

She padded down into the kitchen in her favourite fluffy slippers, and contemplated her day. She'd spend some time in her precious garden, of course, but after that, a trip to the library to change her books was always a pleasure. She was addicted to romance novels, where she could travel the world and meet all sorts of exciting men! She also often met up with friends there, and would probably have lunch in a café somewhere with one or two of them to help pass the time.

She had the church flowers to see to that afternoon, and only hoped that old Mrs Crowther wouldn't insist on incorporating asters from her garden again. They were usually rife with earwigs, and sometimes rather tatty-looking, but the vicar seemed loath to put his foot down. He was a kind-hearted soul, but really, his parishioners could walk all over him.

She sighed as she waited for the kettle to boil for morning tea, keeping one eye on the clock.

Where on earth had her daughter got to?

Usually Vicky would be up and about by now, bustling into the kitchen to give her mother a quick kiss before giving her a hand to help make the breakfast. She started work at nine on the dot, and if she didn't put in an appearance soon, she might miss her bus.

Yesterday had been her day off, and Rosemary hadn't seen hide nor hair of her all day. Not that that was surprising, since nowadays her daughter seemed to have less and less time for her poor old mother. She sometimes wished her only child hadn't insisted on having the annexe to herself, since Rosemary could feel rather lonely at times. But she understood that young girls nowadays valued their independence.

She went to the kitchen door that led off into the annexe and stood there, hovering uncertainly.

It was a household rule that she never go into what Vicky called her apartment without being asked. Not even to clean. But another quick glance back at the kitchen clock assured her that Vicky really would be late if she didn't come and have her breakfast now.

Even so, she didn't want to actually open the door, so instead, Rosemary tapped sharply on it. 'Vicky love – do you know what time it is?' she called out loudly.

She listened intently, but there was no response.

Perhaps she'd risen early and had already gone out? Rosemary dithered at the door, frowning uncertainly. Surely Vicky would have found time to mention if anything at work meant that she'd needed to make an extra early start today? As a rule, Vicky liked to sleep late, and would have moaned about having to leave her bed before the usual time.

'Vicky, if you want to eat, you'd better get a move on, darling,' Rosemary called again.

This time, she actually put her ear to the door, but again she could hear no movement.

With a sigh – and fully expecting to be told off by her temperamental offspring for stepping inside – Rosemary opened the door and peeped in.

The first thing she noticed was that the bed/sitting room was in semi-darkness, which meant that the curtains were still drawn. And since Vicky was in the habit of opening them first thing, it meant that she was still in bed.

The second thing she noticed was a very faint but odd mustiness to the room that she couldn't quite place.

With a sigh, Rosemary passed through the open door and made her way to the curtains, aware of a sense of mild relief. It was all right – her daughter had simply over-slept. So she'd have no reason to blame her mother for coming into the apartment uninvited and rousting her out.

She pulled the curtains – which were pale cream with large pink roses on them – noisily apart and called briskly, 'Come on, our Vicky, you're going to be late.'

As she spoke, however, something seemed to catch at the back of her throat, and she found herself coughing for a few moments. As she did so, she became aware of vague, slightly metallic taste in the back of her mouth.

It wasn't until she turned and glanced at the bed that she realised her daughter hadn't stirred.

Which was rather odd. Vicky had never been a light sleeper – even as a child, she'd been restive and fidgety.

'Vicky?'

Rosemary Munnings started to approach the bed and her daughter's sleeping form. As she did so, she became aware of

166

feeling just a touch light-headed. She hoped she wasn't coming down with something. It was surely a little early to be getting a winter cold, wasn't it?

'Vicky, come on, sweetheart, wake up,' she admonished, a shade impatiently.

Her daughter was lying on her side, her back towards the room, her face to the wall against which the bed had been placed.

Rosemary reached out and shook her daughter's shoulder. As she did so, Rosemary noticed two things at once. Firstly, the movement of her shaking made her daughter turn slightly in the bed, turning her more onto her back – but that she was making no other movement. And secondly, that her face was looking very flushed – in fact, quite rosy.

'Vicky, love, have you got a fever?' For a second, the girl's mother wondered if her daughter, not feeling well and coming down with something, had spent all of yesterday not out and about and enjoying herself as she'd previously thought, but in bed.

'If you've been coming down with something you should have told me, you silly girl,' Rosemary said, more sharply than was her wont. Because she was beginning to feel afraid. Very afraid indeed. Why wasn't she waking up? Why wasn't she demanding to know what was going on?

Why was her daughter so still? It almost looked as if she wasn't even breathing…

And then Rosemary realised that she was having a little trouble breathing herself. Suddenly, the awful truth hit her and she began to scream. Then the frantic screams turned to a fit of violent coughing, and she sank down onto her knees, retching helplessly.

Chapter 21

Grace Farley awoke well on time that morning, and was up and about to get her father's breakfast, as usual. He was always the first to leave for work, and for years he'd left the house with a smile on his face and with a cheerful whistle as he went down the garden path. Nowadays, of course, he was silent and pale.

Grace, dressed in a smart skirt and jumper, ready to take her place in the offices at Dunbar's, took up her mother's morning tray. As usual, her mother was awake and smiled up at her from the bed.

Her father had obviously seen to her having a bath, since her hair was still slightly damp at the ends, and she had a soft flush on her usually pale cheeks.

'Here we go, Mum,' Grace said, placing the tray on the bedside table, before helping her to sit up. 'I've made the porridge with lots of milk and a bit of cream, and some brown sugar, just the way you like it.'

She handed her a spoon and watched hopefully as her mother began to eat. Usually, she had more strength first thing in the morning, but after only a couple of spoonfuls, she saw her mother's arms were starting to fail.

Forcing a cheerful smile onto her face, she sat beside her on

168

the bed and took over. 'And now for the magic pills!' she said brightly, as, little more than half the porridge eaten, her mother indicated that she was full.

Grace reached towards the table beside the bed, which had a long, thin, narrow drawer incorporated underneath it, and extracted from it a bottle of tablets. She spilled two out, her face never by a flicker indicating just how much trouble she'd had to go to in order to obtain them.

Her parents both thought they had been prescribed for her, free of charge, by the NHS, because that's what Grace had told them.

In fact, they weren't available in the country on the NHS, and she'd bought them privately, from an expensive clinic in High Wycombe. The drugs were strictly experimental, and could only be obtained from shipping them in from the United States. Over there, although it was still early days, they had gained the reputation of being helpful to people with her mother's rather rare condition.

Mrs Merriweather had found out about them for her after Grace had confided in her about her mother's devastating illness.

Of course, the likes of Patricia Merriweather and her ilk would have thought nothing about paying the bill for the pills – it probably amounted to petty cash to them. However, to Grace, the exorbitant cost of the medication had been crippling – and still was.

But she didn't resent the burden they placed on her. In her heart of hearts, she knew that her mother was only still alive because of these wonderful pills. And she'd do anything – pay any price – to make sure that she could carry on providing them for her, for however long her mother had left. They not only helped ease her pain, but gave her what little energy she still maintained.

She filled a glass with the barley water and watched her mother take them, her heart filled with love and despair in equal measure.

With one final plump of the pillows to make sure she was comfortable, she turned and fled.

She knew that Mrs Crawfield next door would pop in every hour or so, just to check on her. The Crawfields and the Farleys had been friends and neighbours ever since Grace could remember.

As she left, running a little down the pavement to make sure that she caught her bus, she tried not to feel overwhelmed by everything.

But it wasn't easy.

In order to pay for her mother's pills, she'd had to do something that she never thought she'd do. Something her family would be ashamed of, if they ever found out – something that would break her mother's heart for sure.

Well, she was paying the price for it now, wasn't she? Grace thought defiantly. She was in a real mess, and wasn't sure she'd be able to get out of it, even now. Things might or might not work out as she hoped on the Trudy Loveday front, but at least there was some hope now.

Last night, as she'd known she would, her friend had sought her out and demanded she tell her more about her suspicions. Grace had been careful to tell her exactly what she needed to hear – and no more.

How Abigail had flirted openly with Robert Dunbar, and was clearly and openly disdainful of his wife. How she'd watched Christine Dunbar's jealousy and hatred for the girl grow and boil. And how she, Grace, had come to believe, on hearing that Abigail had died from yew berry poison, that Christine had been the one responsible. How she'd even seen Mrs Dunbar smile with satisfaction on hearing the news of the girl's death.

Trudy had been fascinated, as Grace had known she would be.

But would that be enough?

She knew Trudy was only a lowly WPC, and didn't have the

power, really, to arrest anyone. But surely her friend would report back to her superiors? And then they must act!

As she caught the bus and rode towards the office – a place that was now almost unbearable to her – Grace wondered what she would do if Christine Dunbar wasn't arrested soon. If she was allowed to carry on her campaign…

But the consequences of that were almost unthinkable, and instead Grace forced her mind to think of other, nicer things.

She'd buy some nice red onions to go with the soup she was going to make to tempt her mother's non-existent appetite. Maybe she could find some nice fresh herbs too…

Chapter 22

Trudy was out on patrol most of the morning, for there'd been reports of a spate of shoplifting in the covered market. So it was nearly lunchtime by the time she got back to the station. She'd barely had time to sit down at her desk and start typing up her reports before the door to DI Jennings' office opened and she was summoned peremptorily inside.

'Sit down, Constable,' the Inspector said briskly.

Trudy obeyed, taking off her policewoman's cap and setting it neatly on her lap, as she'd been trained to do. But her eyes immediately darted to those of Sergeant Mike O'Grady, who was already sitting beside her in front of the DI's desk.

At 41 years of age, he was a slightly chubby man, with a quiff of sandy-coloured hair and pale-blue eyes.

'Sergeant,' Trudy said respectfully.

The Sergeant smiled and nodded back at her. Unlike the DI, he didn't actively resent her presence, but he too felt that women in the police force were only good for certain things – such as searching female suspects and acting as family liaison.

Now he watched her with curiosity. Clearly, the Inspector had been telling him all about her latest 'case' with the old vulture, and she doubted that the Sarge would have approved.

But she had to break off her gloomy thoughts as Harry Jennings began to speak.

'All right, Constable,' the DI began flatly. 'I understand you were at the theatre last night, with all this beauty pageant business?'

'Yes, sir,' Trudy said, wondering what this was all about. Usually the DI was happy to wait until the end of the day for her reports, and she had no idea why the Sergeant was present.

'I want you to tell me anything of interest that happened there,' her superior officer demanded abruptly.

Trudy blinked, wondering what was up. For something definitely was. Up until now, the Inspector had showed no real interest in what she had to say about the Abigail Trent case, only wanting to be reassured that Dr Ryder wasn't making any trouble that might rebound on him.

'Well, sir – there was the incident about the chocolates,' she conceded. Concisely, but leaving nothing out, she told him about the discovery of the expensive 'gift' that had appeared on the buffet table, and how she and the coroner had been unable to ascertain how they had come to be there.

'But, sir, it had to be someone at the theatre. No stranger could just have wandered in and left it without attracting attention,' she concluded. She wouldn't have been human if she hadn't wanted to make sure that her DI knew her undercover work at the theatre was proving to be fully justified, and was now paying dividends.

'I hope you kept this box as evidence?' DI Jennings snapped, when she'd finished.

'Yes, sir,' Trudy said smartly. Then, before he could demand that she produce them, added smartly, 'Dr Ryder took them with him, sir. As a medical man' – she rushed on, seeing that the DI had already opened his mouth to blast her, and not wanting to give him the chance – 'he was in the ideal position to take them to a laboratory and get them tested. As you know, sir, sometimes, our own police lab reports can be... well, a bit slow with their results. Whereas Dr Ryder promised he'd light a fire under someone's er... posterior... and would have preliminary results today. He said he knew someone who owed him a favour. Sir.'

Beside her, she was aware that Sergeant O'Grady was a hiding a grin behind his hand.

Jennings, perhaps seeing the sense in what she said, subsided somewhat. Although he was fuming, he did have to admit that it made a nice change for the old vulture to be giving someone else a headache and making their life miserable, instead of his own. To be fair, the coroner probably was the chap you wanted on your side when you wanted to get things done.

'All right,' he agreed gruffly. 'It'll be interesting to see if there was anything actually wrong with 'em, though,' he growled.

'Oh, sir?' Trudy asked. 'Do you have reason to suspect that there might be?' she felt bold enough to ask. 'Only before, you seemed to think that the possibility that there might be anything really dangerous going on at the beauty pageant was rather remote.'

Jennings scowled fiercely, sensing criticism lurking somewhere underneath her mild and inoffensive tone, and he shifted uncomfortably on her seat. 'That was before another contestant turned up dead,' he had to admit flatly.

For a second, Trudy felt her heart contract and she went cold. Her thoughts flashed to her recent, newly-made friends. Who was it? Candace, who had been so pleased with her comic turn in the talent contest? Betty Darville, everyone's big sister? Or the fiery and full of life Sylvia Blane?

'Who...' Trudy found her voice came out rather strangled, cleared her throat and tried again. 'Who has died sir? And may I ask, how?'

'Vicky Munnings was found dead this morning by her mother,' Jennings said flatly. 'The preliminary findings by our medico and forensic chaps say that she'd been dead since some time the night before. Apparently, yesterday was her day off work and her mother didn't see her. She has some rooms of her own within the house, or some such nonsense. Until the post-mortem has been done the doctors can't be sure, but they think she died of carbon monoxide poisoning. There was a heater in her room, one of those that uses a big cylinder of gas. They think it had a faulty valve or something.'

Trudy leaned forward, her lips unknowingly parting as she looked intensely at the Inspector. The Sergeant, watching her, had to admit that the girl didn't lack either intelligence, diligence or commitment. She was concentrating intensely.

'They believe,' Harry Jennings swept on, 'that she probably died the night before last, in her sleep. So at least that's something. The poor girl didn't know anything about it and didn't suffer. The canister of gas was empty when the technicians tested it, so they think it was probably only half-full or so when it developed the fault. The gas continued to leak all during the night and the next day, when the girl's mother assumed she was out and about and enjoying her day off. Luckily, most of it had had time to dissipate somewhat during the next twenty-four hours, so that by the time the mother went into the room, only some remaining traces were left.'

Jennings sighed heavily. 'As it is, she inhaled some of it when she went in the next morning and found her daughter dead in her bed. But not enough to cause her any harm. She had a bit of a coughing fit, but she was able to stagger out and raise help from her neighbour. Her doctor has attended her, and she's currently staying with the neighbour whilst we're investigating at the house.'

'Oh, that poor woman,' Trudy said. 'So that was why Vicky wasn't at the dress rehearsal then? She was already dead!'

'Yes. Naturally, this second death casts a different light on things,' the DI continued briskly. 'Mind you, there's nothing to say that this isn't still an accident.'

175

'But sir, the coincidence of th—'

'People *do* die as a result of faulty gas heaters, Constable,' he reminded her sternly. 'And there's nothing to say that this isn't still the case here. However' – he held a hand up in a "shushing" gesture – 'in light of the fact that another girl from the same beauty contest has also died in… well, ambiguous circumstances… I've come around to yours and Dr Ryder's way of thinking, and am inclined to think this business needs further action. Certainly a more rigorous – and *routine* – proper police investigation.'

Trudy blinked, not sure whether to feel relieved or disappointed by this announcement. At least the DI was taking the whole case more seriously now. But it was beginning to sound as if her days undercover were going to come to an end. Worse still, she suspected that she might be about to be reassigned. When it came to 'proper' investigation, she was sure the DI didn't have one probationary WPC in mind.

The sheer frustration of it all made her want to scream, but of course, she did no such thing. Instead, she set her mind to thinking of how she could stay involved in the subsequent investigation.

'To this end, I've asked the Sergeant to take over the running of the case,' the DI said flatly.

'Yes, sir,' Trudy said smartly. 'Sir, I'd like your permission to carry on playing my role at the theatre. As a "contestant" the girls are more likely to talk to me and tell me things. Things they might not tell the Sergeant here, or someone in uniform.'

Jennings sighed heavily and glanced at O'Grady. 'Well, Sergeant – do you have any objections?'

To Trudy's immense relief, the older man was already shaking his head. 'No, sir. I think WPC Loveday is right. As you know yourself, witnesses very often get scared when they see a police uniform. Confidences are seldom given when every word they say is being written down in a notebook. If something sinister is going on with this beauty contest… well, it's happening to a bunch of young women. So it makes sense for the constable here to stay undercover. She's far more likely to find out stuff than we are.'

Trudy could have kissed him. (But again, she did no such thing!)

'But if there is a killer lurking about, or even just a nasty prankster, I think we need to take steps to make sure nothing happens to our officer,' Sergeant O'Grady added, which tempered Trudy's relief and joy somewhat.

She regarded him uncertainly. Why did she have the sudden feeling that she wasn't going to like where this was leading?

Jennings nodded. He could just imagine the bad press – not to mention the ire of his superiors – should something fatal happen to a young woman police constable.

'But, sir, I can look after myself,' Trudy began, only to realise, furiously, that neither man was taking the least bit of notice of her.

'Yes, yes,' Jennings said to O'Grady. 'What did you have in mind?'

'Well, sir, I think we need to keep an official presence at the theatre as well, whenever this pageant is holding its rehearsals. Someone fit and strong and in uniform – someone that WPC Truelove can rely on and call on for help, if she finds herself in any difficulties.'

At these words, Trudy felt her heart plummet. For she could already guess what was coming next.

'Yes. PC Broadstairs should fit the bill,' O'Grady said complacently.

Trudy bit back a groan.

Rodney Broadstairs was the station's blue-eyed boy. A bigheaded, bone-headed, good-looking buffoon who thought he was every girl's dream. He'd be like a kid in a sweet shop, surrounded by women in bathing costumes! And the thought that he would get to watch *her* in *her* bathing costume didn't bear thinking about!

She'd never live it down.

Trudy could have wept.

'Of course, there will have to be another inquest on this Munnings girl,' the DI ruminated, then looked at Trudy severely. 'And this time I think we'll have to make sure it's another coroner that hears the case.'

Instantly Trudy opened her mouth to object, knowing how irate Clement would be when he learned that he was going to be deliberately kept out of things, but again, her superior officer swept aside any of her entreaties before she could make them.

'After all, it was Dr Ryder who insisted on initiating his own investigation into this matter, so he can hardly be called objective now. No, he's bound to have some preconceived ideas about this latest death, and we simply can't have a coroner's court presided over by someone who is biased. I'm sure everyone will agree on that,' he added tellingly.

Trudy flushed but remained silent. She could, reluctantly, see that he had a point, and that the powers-that-be would agree with him.

But she had no doubt that Dr Clement Ryder would have something to say about it when he was told that he couldn't oversee the inquest into Vicky Munnings death. And she only wished she could be a fly on the wall when he did it!

Chapter 23

The theatre that night, unsurprisingly, was buzzing with the news of Vicky's demise.

When Trudy arrived, most of the girls, both of the Dunbars and Dennis Quayle-Jones were clustered together in the middle of the stage, arguing about something, and she didn't have to listen long to find out what it was all about.

Should they call the beauty pageant off, or not?

The leading proponent for cancelling the show, funnily enough, was the theatre owner, which Trudy found a little odd. Wouldn't that mean he would lose a considerable amount in revenue if the show didn't go on? 'I'm just not sure if it's in good taste to continue any further,' the actor-manager said clearly, his trained voice easily rising above the babble of the others. 'After all, that's two of our young ladies *hors de combat* as it were. Don't you think it's just a teeny bit insensitive to carry on?'

This comment caused a slight pause in the hubbub. Nobody wanted to be considered lacking in sympathy for Vicky and her family, and a certain sense of uneasiness and embarrassment snaked through assembly.

Robert Dunbar sighed heavily. 'Well, naturally, I don't want our customers to think we're being hard-hearted,' he began uncertainly, and it took Trudy a confused moment to realise that he was thinking and talking about the people who bought his line of honey and jams.

'I agree,' Christine said quickly – very quickly. 'The whole point of this contest is to bring our products to the notice of a wider buying public. But that's no good if they associate our honey with something... well... tragic. I think we should just forget about the whole thing.'

At this, some of the girls looked at one another sceptically. Apparently, they all thought that her reasons for wanting to cancel the show had nothing to do with public opinion, and far more to do with finally having an excuse to keep her husband away from pretty young girls.

Trudy wondered if Grace was right to be so sure that Christine Dunbar was the prankster.

She'd discussed Grace's fears, among other things, with Clement Ryder that afternoon. She'd also spent her lunch hour in the coroner's office warning him that moves were afoot to keep him from presiding over the Vicky Munnings case, and bringing him up to date on everything else that she'd learned that morning.

As expected, Clement had been furious to think of the Munnings case going to one of his colleagues, but once he'd made some phone calls – and for once, been unable to get his own way – he'd calmed down in a surprisingly short time.

He'd then told her that fighting a losing battle was pointless, and it was far better to keep your powder dry for the battles you could win. And, as Trudy had pointed out in consolation, it wasn't as if they didn't have enough things to keep them busy.

Surprisingly, he hadn't seemed to give Grace's revelations that much credence, pointing out that she hadn't actually offered them any sort of *proof* of Christine Dunbar's involvement. Now she looked around to see if Clement was at the theatre, but couldn't see him. Perhaps none of the judges had been called in for that night?

'Well, I for one, think that we definitely *should* carry on with the contest,' Caroline Tomworthy's clear voice rang out, and she was quickly backed up by most of her fellow contestants.

'So do I!' Sylvia Blane said. 'I want my shot at that Miss Oxford title. And I don't think Abby or Vicky would mind! They'd want us to carry on.'

Trudy wasn't quite sure how true that might be, and Sylvia was probably being less than candid with her assessment of her fellow competitors' largesse. Or was she just getting cynical? Perhaps the two dead girls really wouldn't have begrudged the rest of the girls their shot at 'fame' and a modest fortune.

But the other girls fastened on eagerly enough to this somewhat questionable premise.

'Yes, it seems a shame to stop now,' Betty Darville said, a little less certainly. And Trudy noticed that Candace and one or two others, made no comment at all. Perhaps they were actually considering pulling out of the competition? Clearly, some of the girls were more scared than the others, and for a while the debate continued.

Suddenly Trudy was distracted by the sight of Rodney Broadstairs swaggering down the centre aisle of the seating and coming to a stop in front of the stage. Not quite six feet tall, he removed his helmet, showing off a head of full blond hair, and grinned up at her.

Square-jawed and classically good-looking, with big blue eyes, it didn't take long for the other girls to notice him.

When they did, the conversation faltered.

'Hello there, ladies,' Rodney called up. 'I'm PC Broadstairs. I've been assigned to keep you all company for the duration,' he declared confidently, his eyes moving from one pretty face to another.

Trudy gave a mental groan, and bit back the urge to kick his shins. No doubt he was wondering which lucky lady he would try and woo first. She only hoped that all of them had more sense than to fall for his obvious charms. He was known at the station for being a bit of a love-'em-and-leave-'em type.

'See, we now have a police presence.' It was, not surprisingly, Caroline who again picked up the baton and ran with it. 'Nothing can go wrong now. Whoever's been playing these silly pranks will have no choice but to stop it or risk getting caught.'

There was a vague murmur of happy agreement that helped to swell Rodney's head even more, for he again grinned as dozens of thankful female eyes turned his way. He gave a brief bow.

Trudy felt vaguely nauseous.

Then she wondered. Why was Caroline Tomworthy, of all of them, so determined to carry on? More than all the others, she seemed hell-bent on making sure the show continued. Was she so confident that the pranks that had been played at the theatre were totally unrelated to the death of the two girls? In which case, what did she know that nobody else did? Or did she simply not care if they were? And if that was the case, why was she being so brave? Did she think she was immune from being a third victim?

'Perhaps we all need to calm down and think things through.' Robert Dunbar tried to take back control, but nobody now seemed willing to listen.

In truth, he wasn't sure if stopping the contest was the best thing to do. Surely doing so would only bring *more* unwanted attention to the beauty pageant? If they pulled out now, would it send the message to the press that he *did* think the deaths of the two girls were down, in some way, to the Miss Oxford Honey contest?

After all, the death of this girl Vicky Munnings sounded like a very sad, but simple, accident – and one that happened often enough. You could open a newspaper any day and once or twice a year read about how people were found dead in their houses due to faulty gas heating. Nobody suspected foul play then, did they?

And at Abigail Trent's inquest, no real connection was made to the beauty contest either. Oh, some newspaper articles had been a bit snide, saying that if she hadn't been entered, she wouldn't have been looking for herbal remedies to give her an edge over her competition. But he'd been sure that most right-minded people wouldn't blame them for that!

But the publicity might turn bad with this second death. The press could be so silly sometimes, inventing stuff to sell papers. Look at all that 'curse of the pharaoh' stuff they came up with back when Howard Carter found Tutankhamun's mummy!

The last thing he needed was for Dunbar Honey to be associated with a curse in the minds of the public.

On the other hand... handled right, could this turn into a goldmine for him? If only...

Trudy noticed that most of the judges had now arrived – including Clement. She backed away as the debate continued to roar around her, and went to meet him.

'I see things are heating up,' Clement said wryly.

'I know. I'm worried they might call the whole thing off. And then we might never get to the bottom of things,' Trudy said worriedly.

'Never mind. Perhaps my news might help calm the nerves,' Clement said, somewhat mysteriously, and walked onto the stage.

'Ladies and gentlemen, please, your attention,' he said, not particularly loudly, but such was his strong personality that everyone fell obediently silent.

'As you know, I was asked to have the contents of a box of chocolates, sent to this theatre last night, analysed.'

The Dunbars, who hadn't been informed of either the mysterious box of chocolates, or the request for the coroner to get its contents checked, looked at one another in surprise, as did several of the judges, who also knew nothing about it.

But the majority of the contestants suddenly perked up, and listened intently – as did Trudy, who was feeling a little miffed that the coroner hadn't told her first!

'I can tell you now that nothing deadly was found in any of the chocolates,' Clement said, and Trudy, along with everyone else, felt her shoulders suddenly loosen. Until then, she hadn't realised just how tense she'd felt.

There was a general susurration of relief that swept across the stage, and several of the girls began to smile and even laugh.

'However,' Clement swept on, and again the stage became deadly quiet. 'We did find traces of a laxative in all of them. So clearly, someone was playing a trick on you.'

In the silence, it was yet again Caroline Tomworthy's voice that spoke up. 'But only a trick! A silly little trick. I for one won't let someone with a warped, schoolboyish sense of humour spoil the contest for us. Why should they? Right, girls? We want to carry on, don't we?'

Trudy wasn't surprised when all of them – albeit some with less enthusiasm than others – agreed with her.

It was as if learning that the chocolates contained only laxative and not deadly yew berry toxin, gave them some sort of permission to carry on. She was no psychologist, and so didn't really understand the forces that were at play now, but even she too felt reluctant to let some unknown malignant stranger dictate what she could or couldn't do.

Whatever the phenomenon was, it affected Robert Dunbar too, for after being badgered by the girls for a few minutes not to pull the contest, he finally agreed that the Miss Oxford Honey beauty pageant should, indeed, go ahead.

'It's only a week next Saturday before it's put on anyway,' he concluded. 'And with the police here to see that nothing else happens, I think we should go ahead.'

Dennis Quayle-Jones shrugged, and turned away, metaphorically but clearly washing his hands of the whole affair.

And watching and listening to it all, a killer smiled cynically.

Oh yes. The show would go on all right.

Chapter 24

Clement, not unnaturally, became the centre of attention for some time after his unexpected and dramatic announcement, as the rest of his fellow judges and some of the theatre staff gravitated around him to try and find out what was going on.

Clearly not everyone had been aware that the Miss Oxford Honey contest had been running into difficulties, and Clement found it interesting to see how most of them reacted to news of the prankster's efforts to upset the show.

One judge decided then and there to withdraw from the panel, but Robert Dunbar was all charm and understanding, and promised that there were no hard feelings, and that he was sure that he could find someone else to replace him at short notice.

Most of the theatre staff looked uneasy, as if worried that someone would try to pin the saboteur's tricks on them, and generally the atmosphere became rather morose.

It had been a long day, and Clement was frankly thankful when Robert finally clapped his hands together and brought the meeting under control.

'All right, everyone,' he said with forced cheerfulness. 'Since we're going to carry on – and the show does its public performance next Saturday...' There was a general rumpus as everyone was forced to consider, nervously, how close the final performance was becoming. '... I suggest we crack on with rehearsals. Tonight it's a dress rehearsal for the swimwear section. So off you go ladies and change into your costumes. Judges, if you'd care to make your way to the panel. Grace... Where's Grace...? Oh, there you are. Grace, if you could find us some suitable music for the record player... thank you. All right then...'

Trudy barely listened to the rest of his pep talk, for suddenly the full calamity of her situation hit her. She was going to have to parade about in her swimming costume and high-heeled shoes right now and in front of Rodney Broadstairs of all people!

Her heart sank. As if it wasn't hard enough getting her colleagues to see her as a police officer on an equal footing with everyone else at the best of times. But dressed for a day on the beach, parading around with that humiliating number strapped to her wrist...

Trudy could have screamed. Or wept. Or both!

* * *

Clement made his way to the table in order to have another word with Rupert Cowper. He wanted to know if any other of the contestants besides Sylvia had been making a serious play for him. And if they had, had Abigail and Vicky been in their number, and had they made him feel hunted and uncomfortable?

But as he approached the end of the line of trestle tables, he felt his left foot barely move from the ground, but simply shuffle along the wooden flooring of the stage, causing him to stumble slightly and pitch forward.

As he did so, he reached out and forward, automatically putting a hand out to the table to save himself. Luckily, flimsy though it was, it was enough to save him from an embarrassing fall, and as he looked quickly along the line of tables, where most of his

187

fellow judges were already sitting, only one person seemed to have noticed his stumble.

Gently, Patricia Merriweather smiled over at him.

'Dr Ryder, it seems you've been very busy,' she mused, in a clear and evident attempt to put him at his ease. 'I had no idea about this prankster that we seem to have acquired! Putting laxatives into chocolates indeed!'

Clement carefully sank down into a chair, but his heart was thumping uncomfortably in his chest. This was twice Patricia had noticed him in difficulties. She was nobody's fool, but a woman who was more than capable of putting two and two together and coming up with the right answer.

He'd been hearing from fellow medical men over club lunches and spells on the golf course, that due to an illness in the family, Patricia Merriweather had made it her business to learn a fair bit about medical matters. She was a shrewd and vastly experienced woman in the ways of the world. So what were the chances that she'd known someone else with Parkinson's and had recognised his early symptoms?

Forcing himself not to panic – after all, even if she *did* suspect something, he would have bet his last guinea that she wasn't the sort to go blurting other peoples' woes about willy-nilly – he smiled back across at her.

'I know – someone has a deplorable sense of humour!' he agreed.

The old lady gave him a shrew look. 'They certainly have,' she agreed blandly. 'And how lucky we were to have you on hand – such an experienced man – to deal with it,' she added archly.

Clement grinned at her. 'Oh, I like to be useful,' he agreed, equally blandly.

Giving him a bright and knowing smile, she turned to look at the stage as the first of the girls made her appearance.

* * *

Trudy knew her face must be flaming with embarrassment as she stepped out onto the stage, careful to follow the chalk lines that had been put down, depicting where the red carpet would be on the night.

She was glad she had to concentrate on walking properly in her high heels, as it took her mind off the fact that she was wearing a one-piece costume that clung to every part of her.

She resolutely refused to look to the front row, where she knew PC Rodney Broadstairs would be watching and no doubt grinning up at her like the village idiot.

Somehow she got through it, and was heartily relieved to finish her stint and walk back behind the curtain and out of sight. Then she went straight to her dressing room and put on a long white robe and tied the belt at her waist with a tight, vicious movement. Forcing herself to concentrate on the task at hand, she tried to forget her own predicament and decide what her next move should be.

Naturally, she was as relieved as everyone else to hear that the chocolates hadn't contained anything deadly. But it did raise the obvious question – *were* the prankster and the killer the same person? For Trudy could no longer believe they were dealing with two fatal and tragic accidents.

Or could they be dealing with two separate people – someone who had a grudge against the two girls and had killed them for whatever reason, and didn't even know, or care, about the beauty competition. And another individual who liked tormenting the beauty contestants, and had latched on to the two deaths as yet another way to make life miserable for the Miss Oxford Honey people?

Or was it possible that the killer of the two girls was simply using the beauty pageant as some sort of cover or smokescreen? Could the deaths of Abigail and Vicky have nothing to do with the fact that they were in the competition at all? After all, Trudy reasoned with growing excitement, if you wanted someone dead, you presumably had to have a motive for wanting those people dead. And if the police found that motive, your goose was well and truly cooked. But if you could set them off after a false hare, you would be sitting pretty. Whilst everyone was searching for someone with a crazy fixation about the beauty contest, the real reason behind the murders would never be suspected or sought out.

Trudy felt a growing buzz of excitement lance through her. Was she really onto something at last? She couldn't wait to discuss this theory with Clement, but even as she thought about it, she felt her confidence begin to waver. She knew from past experience that the coroner – quite rightly – tended to try and rein her in whenever she produced theories without any corroborative evidence.

So she needed to start testing her hypothesis.

For a start, she could talk to Grace again, to see if she knew anything more about Mrs Dunbar's movements on the day and night when Vicky Munnings must have succumbed to the gas from her faulty heater. If she could begin to rule out people who were connected with Miss Oxford Honey, she would be closer to proving her new theory. Of course, even if she was right, the killer of the two girls must have *some* connection with the pageant, in order to take advantage of it as a cover for their murderous activities. But if she could begin to eliminate those without a real motive, she might start getting somewhere.

She now knew, thanks to Sergeant O'Grady keeping her in the loop, that the rubber tubing that had carried the gas from the canister to the valve in Vicky's bedroom heater had developed a rupture, thus allowing the gas to escape directly in the room uncontrolled, filling it with carbon monoxide and various other chemicals.

Although there was no evidence of a clean 'cut' in the tubing – which would at least be unambiguous – it was still undergoing tests to see if the 'rubbing' that had thinned and then split the tubing, could have been caused deliberately. On the face of it, it seemed unlikely that the general wear and tear incurred by the changing of the cylinders could alone have been enough to cause such damage. But then mice had been known to nibble things, and the tubing might have become brittle over time and degraded. It could be argued either way – and the Sergeant was not happy with the 'boffins' who couldn't seem to pronounce definitely one way or another.

Clearly the killer was being very careful and clever about their methods, and not to leave a scrap of forensic evidence behind. In fact, so far they had not a scrap of proof that either girl had actually *been* murdered.

Only Grace seemed to be sure that it was murder, and that Mrs Christine Dunbar was the killer, and Trudy could only hope that her friend had been trying to keep a record of her movements as much as possible.

Although she would be careful not to tell Grace that she was hoping to find proof that Mrs Dunbar *wasn't* the culprit after all!

So Trudy made her way to one of the small back offices, where she knew Grace kept on top of the admin and took charge of the Dunbars' paperwork. As she approached the closed door, she was suddenly very aware of how quiet and claustrophobic it was back here. The bright lights and gaiety of the stage might be a hundred miles away. Dim lightbulbs barely helped illuminate the windowless corridors and once or twice, Trudy could feel the hairs on the back of her neck rise, as if someone was creeping up behind her.

But both times, when she quickly turned her head to see, nobody was there. Perhaps she just felt extra vulnerable because she was wearing so little! Even her feet were bare, as she'd kicked off her shoes with relief the moment she'd gone into her dressing room. Although she'd been practising walking in them for nearly a week, she still hated them. They were like devices of torture, pinching her toes and forcing her weight forward in a weird and unnatural way.

Give her a pair of her good, sturdy, flat, black constable's shoes any day!

As she approached the office door, she noticed that it was very slightly ajar. Good. It meant Grace was there.

Not realising just how quiet she'd been in her bare feet, she pushed open the door and looked inside.

Chapter 25

The picker of yew berries was having an enjoyable time. The hysterical debate about whether or not to continue the show had been very amusing, and they had not been at all surprised by what the consensus had been.

Whenever greed and the opportunity to make money were concerned, finer feelings or sentiments would never win out. Ally that with the vanity of a young girl's desire to be admired, and 'doing the decent thing' would never stand a chance.

The killer, gathered around the buffet table for the usual after-show nibbles, hooked a glass of indifferent white wine, and contemplated the complication that was Dr Clement Ryder.

Of course, his appointment as a judge had always been suspect, and now he'd shown his colours so clearly, it might be a good time to act a good deal more circumspectly. The man had the eyes of an eagle, and missed nothing. It would not do at all to underestimate so clever and competent an adversary.

The killer sipped the wine and contemplated a stuffed tomato thoughtfully.

* * *

Caroline Tomworthy had changed out of her gold and black bikini into a gold and black sarong that had a long slit at the side, allowing flashes of her elegant left leg to show whenever she walked.

Unlike Trudy, she hadn't removed her extremely high stiletto heels, enjoying the added height they gave her. A matching, roomy black-leather shoulder bag hung from one arm as, slim and elegant as a reed, she watched and waited for her opportunity to act, which wasn't that long in coming.

The first Dennis Quayle-Jones knew of her proximity was the subtle wave of jasmine that reached his nose. Turning, he eyed the raven-haired beauty beside him with the detached eye of a connoisseur, and the unmistakable lack of sexual interest of a man whose interests lay elsewhere.

Naturally, Caroline had guessed his leanings the moment she'd met the man. It had hardly required any great leap of intuition on her part. In these men, there existed an amiable tolerance and a determinedly-turned 'blind eye' that wasn't to be found anywhere else in society.

All of which had offered up certain opportunities for her that she'd been quick to understand and turn to her advantage.

Now she approached him and wasted barely a flash of a smile on him. 'Dennis,' she purred quietly. 'Just the man I wanted to see.'

'Oh? Not here to try and twist my arm yet again, are we?' the actor-cum-theatre manager drawled with an insincere smile of his own. 'Now why do I suspect you've hardly been champing at the bit to keep me company because you appreciate my charms, Caroline dear?'

'Now, now, don't be so catty,' Caroline said with a small laugh.

'Sorry, sweetheart – I was forgetting, that was *your* prerogative. You do know that most of your fellow competitors have given you a rather feline nickname, don't you?' He couldn't resist putting in a little dig. The truth was, overly confident and beautiful women had always annoyed him.

'I dare say they have,' Caroline said, with genuine indifference. 'It hardly matters. And please, don't call them my competition. As if any of them are actually that!' This time, her smile was one of near-genuine amusement.

'Oh, I don't know, dearie,' Dennis shot back. 'One or two of them are nipping at your heels, according to my fellow judges.'

Caroline's eyes flashed suddenly. 'Ah yes – how clever of you to mention that, Dennis. As it happens, that's exactly what I wanted to talk to you about.'

'Oh?' Of course, this little minx had been pressing him to try and swing the competition in her favour for some time. He'd pretended to be shocked, and had played it with a light hand, but now he rather suspected that the determined little madam was about to up her campaign.

'As the owner and manager of this quaint little theatre, you have the most influence over what goes on, Dennis. I do hope you've been giving my request some serious thought?'

She watched, amused, as the other man began to lose his smug, affected air.

'Not sure I know what you're getting at, dearie,' Dennis prevaricated.

'Oh, don't be so modest! I'm sure you're always very quick on the uptake! Now I happen to know for a fact that you gave old man Dunbar a very good deal on the rental of the theatre for his one-night show. So he must be feeling very grateful towards you, yes?'

Dennis shrugged his best Noel Coward shrug, and drawled, 'My darling girl, I doubt that man knows the meaning of the word. As long as he gets to sell pots and pots of his awful honey, he couldn't care less!'

'Ah, but you could make him care, Dennis darling, couldn't you? Very easily in fact,' Caroline mused.

They were standing close together on the far side of the stage, watching the 'gannets' (as Dennis always thought of them) gathered around the buffet table. For himself, the food was so bland and atrocious that he wouldn't be caught dead eating so much as a cheese straw.

Now he began to wish that they weren't quite so out-of-the-way and secluded. He had a feeling that this rapacious woman was up to same major mischief, and instinct told him that he wasn't going to like it. Surreptitiously, he tried to manoeuvre them away from the back and edge out towards the lights and the crowd.

'Now why on earth would I want to do that? Believe me, I might have to sell my theatre's soul to mammon sometimes in order to keep the doors open, but that doesn't mean that I have any influence over the likes of Roger Dunbar and his tawdry little pageant,' he wheedled.

'Come on, Dennis, being modest doesn't suit you,' Caroline said sharply. 'And stop shuffling away – I'll only have to raise my voice, and you won't like it if others have to hear what I'm going to say. That's better.' She smiled, as her quarry suddenly froze.

'Now, if you were, say, to withdraw the use of your theatre for next Saturday night, I think our Roger would be very upset indeed. And very inclined to do whatever you say in order to ensure that you change your mind and the show goes on!'

Dennis gaped at her, genuinely appalled.

'I can hardly do that, dearie. The man does have a contract, you know,' he said briskly. 'Now, if you...' He tried to extract himself again, but he didn't get to take a single step away before her long, elegantly slim-fingered hand reached out and grabbed his forearm.

'Oh, but I'm sure that can be circumvented,' she purred. 'These things always can be, can't they? If, say, you noticed a fire regulation not being met – or a problem in the wiring that would need to be fixed before a performance could go on. You must know ways and means of wangling out of a contract when it suits you, Dennis,' she purred.

Her companion, halted mid-flight, shifted uneasily on his feet, and regarded her doubtfully. What on earth was the awful woman getting at? 'And why would I want to do that? Even if such a thing were possible,' he added hastily, 'it would be professional suicide. After all, once a theatre gets a reputation for not honouring its commitments, it's just asking for trouble.'

Caroline smiled grimly. 'Oh, I'm not suggesting that you *would* do it, Dennis,' she said with a wide smile that was so full of malice it almost made him wince. 'Only that you *could*. And that Robert should be made aware of that fact.'

Dennis took a long, slow breath. Playing at being catty with the likes of a fellow cat was one thing. But as he was becoming alarmingly aware, Caroline Tomworthy was a different species altogether – far more cobra than cat, in fact. Getting a dose of her toxin was not something that was high on his agenda.

'And why would I want to get Robert over a barrel exactly?' he asked, affecting amusement, but feeling only very real trepidation.

'Oh, relax, Dennis! It's nothing major.' Caroline sensed his growing panic, and reeled him in carefully. Now that she had him thoroughly rattled, it was just the right psychological moment to offer him hope. 'It's just so that he would then have to do you a little favour in return, that's all. A bit of *quid pro quo*, and all that.'

'Oh? And just what favour would I want him to do me?' Dennis asked archly.

Caroline smiled gently. 'What do you think, dearie?' she mocked him gently. 'I want him to have a word with all his fellow judges and make sure that it's understood that they can vote for their favourites once or twice – just so long as it's understood that, overall, I'm to be the winner. Of course.'

Dennis began to laugh. 'Oh, of course.'

Caroline let him laugh for a few moments, and then reached into her shoulder bag and withdrew a large, buff-coloured envelope.

'And what makes you think exactly that Robert Dunbar could influence his fellow judges in that way?' Dennis demanded.

'Oh grow up, Dennis,' Caroline snapped, all sense of playfulness leeched from her voice now. 'They're all men of the world. They know Dunbar has done them a huge favour letting them in on his little PR scheme, and they'll probably be expecting to have to ante up somehow. Everyone knows these things are all a fix anyway.'

'Are they?' Dennis asked, genuinely curious.

Caroline shot him a simmering glance. 'Of course they are. And in this particular instance,' she said, opening the envelope carefully, 'it's going to be fixed in my favour.'

'Oh, is it?' Dennis said, beginning to feel riled by her attitude. 'What makes you so sure? And just why the hell do you think I'm going to do *you* any favours?'

'Because of these, Dennis, dearie,' Caroline said, pulling out a sheaf of photographs and handing them over with a theatrical flair that, in other circumstances, the other man might have appreciated. 'After all, what you get up to with your... friends... is very illegal, dearie. Isn't it? I can't think prison garb would suit you, Dennis.'

* * *

Candace was worried about her tummy. Did it look too obvious in her swimsuit? It wasn't much of a bump, but her tummy definitely wasn't as flat as Caroline's was.

Was that another 'flaw'? Did that mean that whoever it was that was being so mean, would target her next?

And had Vicky's death really been an accident as everyone was saying?

198

Rodney Broadstairs was having a whale of a time chatting to pretty girls in swimming costumes. So much of a good time, in fact, that he'd totally forgotten that he was supposed to be watching out for Trudy Loveday. Who had now been missing from the stage for some considerable time.

Trudy, in fact, was staring at her friend Grace, open-mouthed and in a state of shock.

When she'd pushed open the door to the office, the first thing she'd seen was Grace rooting through a large black-leather handbag – a handbag that Trudy recognised instantly as belonging to Mrs Christine Dunbar.

'Grace!' she breathed.

Her friend gave a little shriek, her hand going up to her heart, and spun around. Seeing only her friend standing in the doorway, she slumped back against the desk.

'Oh, Trudy! You gave me such a scare. I thought you might be...' Her voice trailed away guiltily.

'Your employer's wife?' Trudy asked sharply, coming in and shutting the door firmly behind her. 'What are you doing searching through her things?' she demanded.

Grace paled. 'She's just nipped into the ladies' loo.'

'I don't care where she *is*,' Trudy hissed. 'What are you doing going through her stuff? And don't lie to me,' she almost shouted. She was beginning to feel hurt and betrayed, as the sudden realisation hit her that her friend had been playing her for a fool. For although part of her wanted to believe that her friend was just so convinced that Christine Dunbar was dangerous that she'd stooped to searching her handbag for evidence, common sense and instinct told her that something else was going on here.

Grace, seeing her friend's open suspicion, suddenly caved in. Months of sleeplessness and stress overtook her in a mighty wave, and she felt all her strength go. She slumped back against the desk, like a puppet with its strings suddenly cut, and began to cry. Not only a few pretty tears either, but gut-wrenching, ugly, hopeless sobs that seemed to come from the pit of her stomach and carry on and on.

Trudy was beside her in a flash. Aware that Mrs Dunbar could return for her violated handbag at any moment, she quickly steered her distraught friend out into the deserted corridor and into what seemed to be a rumble room, where scenery and cast-off props from previous shows were stored. She gently steered Grace to a loveseat that had probably last been used in an old restoration romance and sat her down, rooting about in her robe pocket for some tissues, and luckily finding them.

Eventually Grace, looking exhausted and beaten, stopped crying. She was pale, her nose and eyes red from tears, and looked curiously blank-faced, as if incapable of forming a single thought. Trudy was no psychiatrist, but she could easily guess that her friend had been bottling things up inside her for far too long, and now it had all come gushing out, leaving her feeling empty and blank.

When Trudy thought that her friend might finally be able to speak, she knelt down in front of her, and took Grace's cold limp hands in her own, and said, 'What's going on, Gracie? What's the real story behind you and Mrs Dunbar? Do you *really* think she killed Abigail and Vicky?'

Listlessly, her friend shook her head. Then she shrugged and nodded, but finally admitted dully, 'I just don't know. She might have. But probably not.'

'So why did you tell me you thought she did?' Trudy asked gently. 'Why did you come to me in the first place? What did you expect to achieve by bringing me into all this?'

Grace sighed heavily. 'I was hoping you could get something on her. Or just frighten her. Give *her* something to worry about, for a change.'

Trudy frowned. 'Grace, that doesn't make sense. Why would you want any of that?'

'To get her off my back,' Grace said, too spent to sound even resentful or afraid, let alone angry.

Trudy shook her head. 'I still don't understand, Gracie,' she said gently. 'Just tell me what it's all about, from the beginning. It'll be easier once you've got it all off your chest, I promise. Whatever it is, I'll do my best to help you. You've done something wrong, haven't you?' she proffered tentatively.

Wordlessly, Grace nodded.

'And Mrs Dunbar knows about it?'

Again, Grace nodded.

'All right. What was it? What did you do wrong?'

'I've b-b-borrowed money from the petty cash,' Grace said, beginning to sob again. 'Oh, Trudy, don't look at me like that. I had to! For Mum! I'm not a thief. I intended to pay it all back. Really I did.'

'All right. All right, Gracie,' Trudy tried to soothe her. 'But why did you need the money so badly?'

'It was for Mum's new medicine. Everyone thinks the pills came from the NHS doctors, but they didn't. I had to pay for them privately, and I just couldn't afford them on my wages. I intended to pay the money back later, after Mum... When I could save more money from my wages again... But Mrs Dunbar got suspicious and audited the petty cash.'

'Oh, Gracie,' Trudy said helplessly. But she could hardly blame her friend for being tempted. Wouldn't she have done the same if her own mother had been so ill?

'Why didn't she report you to the police?' Trudy asked, puzzled.

'Oh, she probably would have done,' Grace said dully. 'But then she got a better idea.'

'What idea?' Trudy said, but she thought she already knew the answer to that.

'She wanted me to spy on her husband,' Grace confirmed.

'And *was* Mr Dunbar having an affair with any of the girls in

201

the competition? With Abigail or Vicky?' she asked quickly.

But Grace was already shaking her head. 'No, I don't think so. He's a bit of a flirt, but I think he's too clever to do anything so obvious.'

Trudy nodded.

'I thought, once she was convinced that her husband wasn't straying, she'd have no further use for me, and would go to the police about my... borrowing the money from the petty cash.' Grace gulped. 'Then, when Abby died, and odd things began to happen at the theatre, I saw a possible way out of things. I thought that if I could get the police to suspect her of crimes of her own, it might make her think twice about everything.'

Trudy smiled wryly. 'In other words, that she might have too much to worry about to bother with you?'

'Exactly. After all, if you know you might be a suspect in a murder case, you wouldn't want to draw any attention to yourself in any way, would you? Not even by accusing someone else of something.'

'Plus, admit the fact that you've been a blackmailer,' Trudy said cynically.

At this, Grace brightened a bit. 'Yes, she is, isn't she? And blackmail's a crime, isn't it?' she asked wonderingly.

'It certainly is,' Trudy said, getting to her feet. 'If I were you, Grace, I'd point that out clearly to Mrs Dunbar and come to some sort of arrangement. Tell her if she doesn't get off your back, you'll accuse her of blackmail. She might guess you're bluffing, but she'll have as much to lose as you do. People of her class, in my experience, will do anything to avoid a social scandal, as well as prison! If both of you can keep your... arrangements from the attention of the police, the better it will be for both of you.'

Even as Trudy spoke, she could imagine DI Jennings' face if he could hear her now. She was supposed to arrest petty thieves and bring in blackmailers – not advise them to sort themselves out!

But there was no way she could arrest Grace for doing what she had had to do in order to try and prolong her mother's life. She might be an officer of the law. But surely she had to be a human being first? Or was she just trying to justify herself?

Suddenly Trudy felt on very uneven ground indeed.

But what else could she do?

Chapter 26

Trudy wasn't that surprised, on walking out of the side door and emerging through the small alley onto Walton Street, to see the coroner's 'Aunty' Rover car parked at the kerb and waiting for her.

Taking a quick look around to check that nobody she knew was watching, she quickly slid into the passenger seat. Smoothly, Clement slipped the car into gear and pulled away.

'Boy, have I got a lot to tell you,' Trudy said excitedly, and commenced to tell him everything – from Grace's circumstances to her own theories. By the time she was finished, they were just pulling into her street, so the coroner parked by her front gate and turned off the ignition.

'You know, I'm beginning to think I hate beauty contests,' Trudy said with a tired sigh.

'Oh? Why?' Clement asked curiously.

Trudy, reluctant to admit to her feelings of humiliation at having to parade in her swimming costume in front of Rodney, simply shrugged. 'It just seems so silly. I mean, how would you men feel if we women asked you to parade up and down in your shorts, so that we could judge how handsome you were?' she demanded.

Clement Ryder gave a great bark of laughter. 'If I paraded

about in my shorts, I'd be had up for public indecency. Nobody would want to look at my knobbly knees!'

Trudy had to giggle. 'That's not the point!' But by now she was too busy laughing to hold on to her angst. Eventually the mirth subsided, leaving her feeling just a little flat.

'So,' Clement said, shifting slightly in his seat to a more comfortable position, 'what have we learned? Grace has been pilfering, Mrs Dunbar has been blackmailing, Mr Dunbar is probably innocent of being involved with either of our two dead girls, and the prankster didn't intend to kill anyone with the chocolates. What does it all add up to?'

Trudy sighed. 'You haven't said anything about my idea that the killer might just be using the beauty pageant as a means of sending us on a wild goose chase,' she pointed out, feeling just a little miffed.

'Oh, no doubt it's a good thought – and one I've had too,' he admitted, perking her up instantly. 'The trouble with this case has always been the uncertainties. Did Abigail accidentally poison herself – or was it murder? Was Vicky's death a tragic accident and a large coincidence – or again, was it murder? If we are dealing with murder, is the prankster at the theatre the same person, or are the two things unconnected? I think it's high time we started making some firm decisions about these things, based on what we've learned, common sense and instinct.'

'All right,' Trudy said eagerly, always glad to take action. 'First, I'm sure we're dealing with murder – in both cases.'

'Agreed.'

'Secondly, I think the prankster and the killer are one and the same.'

'I do too.'

'Third – I still think that we haven't even begun to discover the real motive behind this case. Taking it as read that the prankster is the killer, why do you suppose he or she started up with the pranks in the first place?' Trudy asked.

Clement gazed out at the dark street ahead of him, eyes narrowed in thought. 'Well, on the face of it, either the killer has a twisted mentality and enjoys tormenting people, in which case, we're dealing with a case of madness, or the killer is targeting the contest, as you suggest, as a means of obscuring their true – and totally sane – motive.'

'Which do you think it is?'

Clement smiled somewhat ruefully. 'I'm not exactly a mental health expert, Trudy,' he pointed out genially. 'I was a surgeon – I dealt with blood and bone. Diseases of the mind, I've always left to my colleagues in the psychiatry department.'

'But you must have seen a lot of things since you became a coroner,' Trudy insisted stubbornly. 'Besides, you're a man of the world, and you've dealt with people all your life. Now that you've got to *know* the people at the theatre, what does your instinct say?'

Again, Clement smiled ruefully. 'You're asking for my best guess?'

'I suppose I am,' Trudy admitted meekly. 'Oh, I know you're a man who prefers science and facts and all that. But this case isn't going to be solved by that, is it? We have no hard, forensic evidence at all! So we need to think like the killer, don't we, if we're to get anywhere?' Trudy pressed.

Clement sighed. 'All right – let's drop down the rabbit hole and theorise a bit. I don't *think* that anyone I've met in this case is truly insane.'

'So the killer's just playing the part of being unhinged? The threatening letters, the dead moth, the doctored chocolates… that's all so much window dressing to make us think we're dealing with a certain type? And that all this is not the result of a diseased mind at all? Oh, I know anyone who can commit murder is sort of mad in a way, but… Oh, you know what I mean!' Trudy enthused. 'Basically, they're just bad people, and as sane as you or I. Yes, I think that's what we're dealing with too. So, if we rule out some madman or woman with a grudge against beautiful girls, what are we left with?'

'A plain and simple killer,' Clement obliged her.

'Right. And why do people kill people?'

'The usual suspects are love, money, revenge and self-defence,' he obliged.

'All right. Well, we can surely rule out self-defence, can't we? And none of the girls were from what you'd call really well-off families. Oh, they lived in a nice area, and all that. But… I don't see how money or gain can come into all this. So that leaves us with love and revenge.'

'With love being the most obvious?' Clement mused. 'After all, we are talking about beautiful young women. And I know from experience and memories of my own turbulent youth just how much havoc they can cause! What's more, we know that a lot of the girls have been flirting with the judges. Somewhere in that mix could lie a few broken hearts or feelings of betrayal. Especially since, from what I can tell, one or two of them are determined to find themselves a rich husband.'

Trudy grinned. 'Like Rupert Cowper you mean? Yes, I know Sylvia is very keen on him. He *is* rather good-looking.'

'And unwilling,' Clement said thoughtfully. He gave Trudy a brief summary of his talks with the other man, and when he'd finished, Trudy was silent for a moment.

'So… what? You think he's afraid of women?' she asked cautiously.

'I wouldn't go that far,' Clement said judiciously. 'But I definitely sense that he's ambivalent. I think he's the kind of man who shouldn't have been born so attractive to the opposite sex. Who knows, perhaps he was raised by a mother who had issues of her own, and that affected him. Apart from that, I'm not willing to venture,' Clement said soberly.

'So could he have some sort of complex then? You know – could he have snapped, and killed Abby and Vicky because they were coming on to him?' Trudy demanded impatiently. Sometimes the older man's cautious and considered approach irritated her considerably.

'Were they?' Clement asked sharply.

Trudy thought about it, then sighed and shook her head. 'No, I don't think so. I've heard they could be a little daring, but I think Sylvia was the main one chasing him,' she was forced to admit. 'She's certainly possessive of him and may have warned them off him though.'

'And she'll probably catch him, and make him very happy in spite of himself,' Clement said dryly. 'Besides, I thought we'd decided to take the line – for the moment – that this *isn't* the work of someone with a mental quirk? Which rules out Cowper.'

Trudy sighed. 'You're right. I think it all has to come down to motive. And really, when you take into account all that we've learned, who really has a *proper* motive for wanting the girls dead?' she asked, her voice as frustrated as she felt.

'How about Grace's favourite – Mrs Dunbar? A jealous wife, desperate to keep her husband, she might resort to killing off her younger, lovelier rivals. It's been done before.'

Trudy sighed. 'But she's had Grace reluctantly spying on him all this time, and Grace admitted to me that she's had to report back that Mr Dunbar *wasn't* straying. At least, not with the girls in the competition. Besides, I get the feeling that Mrs Dunbar is the type to put up with a straying husband, rather than risk scandal and social humiliation. Would she take the risk of actually resorting to murder?'

'All right – let's, for the moment, scratch the Dunbars from the list,' Clement agreed. 'Who else can we cross off?'

'I can't see that Mr Quayle-Jones has a motive,' Trudy said after a moment's thought. 'If things blow up at the Miss Oxford Honey contest, his beloved theatre gets dragged through the mud, simply by association.'

'All right. We'll shelve the theatre manager. What about Rupert? Have we definitely finished with him?' Clement asked.

'If he's not insane and has a mad grudge against women, he doesn't have a motive either,' Trudy pointed out.

'We're rapidly running out of suspects,' Clement said wryly. 'I take it you don't include Grace on your list?'

Trudy shot him an appalled look. 'What possible motive could she have for wanting them dead?' she asked defensively. She rather suspected that the coroner hadn't been quite as taken in by Grace as she had, and she still felt a little raw about her naivety on that score. She certainly didn't want him finding out about the unorthodox advice she'd just given her friend. She'd never live it down – the old vulture would tease her mercilessly. 'How about the old lady – Patricia Merriweather?' she asked quickly.

Clement shrugged. 'What about her? She's a rich old woman from a prominent local family, who's on the board to keep the theatre open. I can't see what she has to gain. Unless you think that she might resent girls for being young and pretty, when she's old and not? In which case, we're back to her having some sort of mental condition.'

Trudy sighed heavily. 'We're not getting anywhere, are we?'

Clement shrugged. Unlike his young companion, he'd learned the importance of patience. 'We're agreed our killer is very sane and very clever, yes? So far he or she has managed to murder two girls, leaving us unsure even if it's murder or not. And so far, I take it, no traces of a killer or any evidence at all has been found at the so-called crime scenes?'

'No,' Trudy sighed, giving him a quick run-down on what Sergeant O'Grady had told her about the verdict on the heater in Vicky's room. 'There were no fingerprints found at either of the crime scenes that couldn't be accounted for and no sign of a break-in, or of anything out of the ordinary. But then, it's believed the French doors leading to Vicky's room were probably unlocked.' Trudy shrugged helplessly. 'After all, who locks their doors?'

Clement nodded. Maybe he was a cynic, but he could foresee a time coming when everybody would do so. But not, he hoped, in his lifetime.

'You know, we really do need to go and talk to Vicky's mother, now that she's had some time to get over the worst of the shock,' Trudy continued. 'And see the room where it happened, since the lab people have finished going over it. I can go in uniform – make it official.'

'I think that's a great idea,' Clement said. 'Because as things stand at the moment, we don't seem to be getting anywhere.'

Trudy glumly agreed, bid him goodnight, and climbed from the car.

Chapter 27

The next morning dawned bright and clear – one of those crisp lovely autumnal days, when the sky seemed as blue as possible, and the sunlight had a mellow yellow tinge that made everything look as though it was bathed in a spotlight.

Trudy, after reporting to DI Jennings, had pedalled her bicycle to Floyd's Row, and after waiting half an hour for the coroner to finish up some paperwork, had climbed back into his car for the trip to Parklands.

It wasn't until they were turning down the long, leaf-strewn road, that Clement, silent until now, suddenly perked up. 'You know, this really is a nice area of town. I thought of buying here when I first moved back to the city, before deciding I wanted to be nearer the centre of things.'

'Summertown was too far out for you?' Trudy teased. But looking around the avenue, with its ranks of lime trees now shedding their leaves, she could see what he meant. A spacious 'village' green swept away to the right, whilst a mix of Georgian, Victorian and Edwardian buildings lined up in genteel elegance to the left. Large, well-maintained front gardens led to mainly Cotswold-stone buildings, with large sash windows and an air of respectable, but not showy, affluence.

A man nodded at them as he passed the car on his way to the green, the little Yorkie he was walking pausing to bark at them with the ferocity of its kind.

'So this is where Vicky lived,' Trudy mused, checking from her notebook to make sure that they had the right address. The house was one of the younger ones, set a little apart from its neighbours and surrounded by a garden predominantly given over to shrubs. 'Abigail didn't live too far away either,' she noted. 'Just go further down the road, then turn right and then left. Of course, they must have lived near each other in order to have attended the same school. St Bart's, I think it was.'

'And that, if I'm not mistaken, is the old Merriweather place,' Clement said, nodding across the green to a large, square, uncompromisingly Georgian edifice, gleaming like old gold in the autumnal sun. 'I dare say, in times gone by, the family owned the land and houses for miles around.'

Trudy nodded thoughtfully. 'In the real old days, I suppose they were proper lords of the manor with a minor title or something.'

Clement sighed. 'Well, Mrs Munnings is expecting us. I called ahead to make sure she'd be in.'

With a small sigh, Trudy nodded and got out of the car. It was always one of the worst parts of her job – dealing with the bereaved.

* * *

Rosemary Munnings looked pale but composed as she served them tea in the front room, which overlooked the small front garden and the green beyond. She had accepted Trudy and Clement on face value when they'd presented themselves at her door, seeming not to notice Dr Ryder's rather unclear role in the proceedings.

'Everyone's been so kind,' the woman said now, somewhat

helplessly, as she left her own cup of tea steaming gently and untouched on the tray. 'My next-door neighbour has been an angel and Dr Ranking has been round every day.'

Something about her rather dreamy look and apathetic voice made Clement wonder what kind of pills she had taken, and he felt a distressing sense of déjà vu. Abigail Trent's mother had just this same air about her. Just what right did anybody think they might have, to cause such pain and misery?

Angrily, he let his eyes wander around the room as Trudy began to question her gently.

'I knew Vicky slightly,' Trudy began, making the other woman instantly smile.

'Oh, did you? My Vicky had a lot of friends,' she said proudly. 'She was always so popular at school.'

'I'm sure she was. Abigail Trent was her closest friend, wasn't she?' Trudy asked, surprised to see something unhappy and uncertain flicker across the other woman's face.

She realised the coroner had seen it too, for Dr Ryder's gaze suddenly halted its appraisal of the room and sharpened instead on the older woman.

'Didn't you like Abigail?' Trudy asked in her best casual voice.

Rosemary Munnings sighed. 'I'd rather Victoria had chosen not to become so close to her,' she admitted, sounding tired. 'As you know, her family moved here from… Cowley, I think it was. Oh, I'm not being snobbish! I just never really thought that the Trents fit in here, and that can cause such problems, can't it? I know Abigail especially felt it somewhat keenly. Well, children do, don't they?'

'Oh? Was she ostracised then?' Trudy asked. 'Children can be so cruel sometimes, can't they?'

To her surprise, the other woman suddenly flushed angrily. 'What do you mean? Who have you been talking to?' she demanded. Her eyes seemed to move to the window, and her look became definitely pensive.

213

'I just meant that, starting another school as a new girl can sometimes be daunting, Mrs Munnings, that's all,' Trudy said, a shade confused. She had obviously touched a raw nerve, but wasn't quite sure what it was or how she'd done it. 'It sounds as if your daughter was being quite kind – you know, going out of her way to make friends with the odd one out and helping her fit in and everything.'

'Oh. Oh yes, that's right.' Mrs Munnings' shoulders relaxed slightly. 'That's exactly what Vicky was. A very kind girl at heart – and don't let anyone tell you anything different,' she demanded fiercely. But it was as if any strong emotion quickly drained her, for again her shoulders slumped and she looked ineffably weary. 'Of course, Abigail was so grateful to her for that. I suppose that's why they became such firm friends. I just wish… Oh well, they're both gone now so what does it all matter?' She shrugged hopelessly.

Trudy nodded but glanced quickly across at Clement. From all that they'd learned about the girls, it seemed clear that it was Abigail who'd been the driving force in their friendship, and Vicky very much the follower. Did her mother really not know this?

'I got the impression that Vicky only entered the beauty contest because Abby asked her to,' she began cautiously, and again seemed to have said the wrong thing.

'Oh, that ridiculous competition!' Rosemary said fretfully. 'I begged Vicky not to enter it. So cheap and low-class! It was typical of Abigail to want to get involved. And as ever, she had to drag Victoria into it. But then, she was always getting Vicky into some scrape or other—' She broke off abruptly, and again her eyes seemed to gravitate towards the window.

Clement, curious as to what kept snatching her attention, got up and went to the window, ostensibly to admire a large African Violet plant that was growing on the windowsill there. In truth, he looked outside to see what Mrs Munnings found so fascinating, but could only see the green, where the man who'd passed them was now walking his Yorkie. And beyond that, the old Merriweather place.

Thoughtfully, he returned to his seat.

Trudy kept her thoughts focused on Vicky's mother. 'Well, children will be children, Mrs Munnings,' she said with a smile. 'I expect when I was in school I got dragged into the odd scrape or two myself.'

With an effort, Rosemary forced herself to smile. 'I find that hard to believe, my dear. It's so unusual for a young girl to join the police force. Your parents must be very proud of you,' she said. But she didn't sound particularly sure. Trudy could well understand how this woman would have reacted if her own daughter had told her that she wanted to make a career in the police service!

'I understand Vicky had her own apartment here?' Trudy changed the subject slightly. 'Do you mind if we see it?'

'Oh of course not, I'll show it to you.' She got up and led them through the kitchen, where a utility room had an internal door set in one wall. There she paused. 'If you don't mind, I won't go in.'

Trudy nodded hastily. 'No, that's quite all right, Mrs Munnings.'

She pushed open the door and she and Clement stepped through into Vicky's much-admired 'apartment'.

It was, in reality, a large bed-sitting room with a small bathroom off to one side. It overlooked the side garden, and large shrubs crowded close to the French doors and large single window, cutting out a lot of natural light and making it all rather gloomy.

Still, it was her own private space, and Trudy could well understand why she had cherished it. The fatal heater had, of course, been taken away for examination, and fingerprint powder covered everything in a fine dust. Clearly, the girl's mother hadn't been able to bring herself to clean the room yet. A bottle of perfume, half-full, stood on the small dresser, and a pair of stockings had been draped, causally, across the back of a chair, as if its occupant would return any moment to don them.

Trudy felt tears start to come to her eyes, and quickly blinked them away. 'She had no idea, did she, when she went to bed that night, that she'd never wake up in the morning,' she said sadly.

Clement said nothing. He went instead to the French doors, opened them up and stepped outside to look around. As he'd thought – anyone could have crept through this garden unseen – especially at night, when it was dark by seven o'clock.

'I don't think we're going to get anything useful here,' he said quietly.

Outside, Mrs Munnings waited for them with listless patience in the kitchen. When they reappeared, she looked at them without curiosity, and led them back to the front room and their cooling cups of tea.

Once they were settled, it was Clement who had things to ask her.

'I understand you've lived here for some time, Mrs Munnings,' he began pleasantly.

'Yes. My husband was an Oxford man, born and bred.'

'Ah. He'd have known the Merriweathers then. Across the green.' He nodded to the window.

Rosemary's shoulders visibly became tense again, and her washed-out expression showed signs of a frown. 'Oh yes,' she said, her voice still light and polite, but somehow strained. 'They're a marvellous old family.'

'But they've had their difficulties, I hear,' Clement said. 'Didn't someone tell me one of them – a granddaughter of the old lady – was rather ill?'

Trudy nodded, remembering that Grace had mentioned that too.

'Oh yes. Millie. Her son Christopher's child,' Rosemary said. And for the first time, she sounded a little frightened.

Trudy shot the coroner a quick, surprised look.

'It's always frightening when a child falls ill,' Clement said carefully. 'How old is the little girl?'

'Oh, she's not a little girl, exactly. She's Vicky's age.'

'Oh. So she would have gone to school with your daughter and Abigail? Or didn't she live around here?' Clement asked, taking a sip of his cold tea.

'Oh yes, she did. She lived with her grandmother – well, all the Merriweathers shared the old house. It's so big, and...' As if running out of breath, Rosemary simply trailed off.

'Her poor grandmother must be worried about her,' Clement mused. 'Is she very ill?'

'She's under the care of doctors, I believe,' Rosemary said vaguely. 'In a clinic somewhere in... I can't quite remember where now. All this... with Vicky... My mind doesn't seem to... I'm sorry.'

'No, we're the ones who are sorry,' Clement apologised smoothly. 'And we mustn't take up any more of your time,' he added, getting to his feet. 'Thank you so much for agreeing to speak to us.'

Trudy, a little disconcerted at having the interview cut off so abruptly, nevertheless got to her feet and allowed herself to be ushered out.

Outside on the pavement, she followed the coroner to his car, but instead of getting in behind the wheel, he stared out across the green towards the imposing old house.

'What was all that about?' Trudy asked, when she realised that he wasn't about to break his silence. 'Was it my imagination, or was she trying to hide something?'

'No, I don't think it was your imagination,' Clement said slowly. 'Come on, let's go back to my office. I have some phone calls I want to make to various colleagues.'

* * *

A half-hour later, Clement hung up the phone on the last of his contacts, and leaned back in his chair thoughtfully.

Trudy, who'd been forced to listen to his one-sided conversations, had nevertheless already discerned the way his mind had been working, and had already guessed what he was going to say.

'Millie Merriweather is in some sort of mental institution, isn't she?' Trudy asked flatly.

'Yes. A private clinic in Littlemore,' Clement agreed. 'According to my sources, she was always what you would call a "highly-strung" girl, but nothing particularly out of the ordinary. She did all right at the local primary school, although she had a bit of a reputation as a loner. Her parents put things down to her being a bit of a dreamer, and always having her head in a book. In truth, she was probably, even by the time she was 11, beginning to build a fantasy world of her own to live in.'

'Lots of children do that,' Trudy mused.

'Yes – but in her case, it seems the fantasy began to take over. Even so, for a year or so, she seemed to do all right at St Bart's – the local grammar school. But then things seemed to go downhill suddenly. She was taken out of school and given private tutors. But last year she had to be committed for her own good. There were instances of self-harm, followed by a suicide attempt.'

'Poor girl,' Trudy mused. 'Grace said that she and Mrs Merriweather became friends when the old lady learned about Grace's mother being so ill. So I thought that it was something physical with the granddaughter too. Maybe cancer, since it seemed as if it was something that nobody liked to talk about. But mental illness is also a taboo subject…' Trudy broke off and looked at the coroner thoughtfully.

'Do you suppose it's mental after all? Do you think old Mrs Merriweather…' She trailed off delicately, with one eyebrow raised.

'What? Has mental health issues too?' Clement asked dryly.

'Hardly.' But there was something in his voice that made her look at him sharply.

'What?' she demanded.

'Did you get the impression from talking to people about Abby in particular, that she was a bit of a bully at school? Because I did – especially when we talked to her young man, that one time. He almost came out and said that she could be very cruel to plain girls. I wondered at the time if you'd picked up on it.'

Trudy slowly nodded. 'Yes, I did. One or two other people also mentioned it. And Vicky was always her right-hand man, so to speak.' She slowly leaned forward on her chair. 'Are you thinking what I'm thinking? That the two of them might have bullied Millie Merriweather?'

'Well, it makes sense. Abigail, as the new girl to the school – and already suffering from the stigma of being "not quite one of them" – would have been unsure and aggressive, and would have felt the need to establish her dominance quickly. She began by recruiting a willing acolyte in the easily-led Vicky. And what better target would there be for them, than the "slightly weird" and rather plain girl at school? Especially since poor Millie came from such a prominent local family? Nothing would have set Abigail up as top dog so fast as gathering a gang about her and picking on the odd girl out.'

Trudy blinked. 'Bullying would have been bound to make Millie's already precarious mental condition worse... and if it was the final straw that broke the camel's back and led to her family having to finally commit her to a mental home...' Trudy paused, looking a shade appalled. 'Are we really saying that we think that nice old lady deliberately set out to kill the girls who helped drive her granddaughter over the edge?'

Clement rubbed a hand over his face. 'First, we have to find out whether or not any of this is true. We need to visit the school and talk to the teachers.'

'Which won't be easy,' Trudy predicted, sounding and feeling

219

a shade world-weary. 'Nobody at the school will be willing to admit to that sort of thing going on – their instinct will be to deny it and cover it up. Especially since one of the girls involved has a prominent, powerful family behind her.'

'Hmm. In which case, whilst I tackle the teachers, you need to find out the names of some of the other pupils attending the school at the same time and talk to them. They might be far more willing to give us an accurate picture of what actually went on there.'

'OK,' Trudy agreed, leaping up. This was better. They might finally be getting somewhere at last!

Chapter 28

Saturday night and showtime! After a month of rehearsals, it was finally time for the real thing. The theatre was beginning to fill with paying customers, and Dennis Quayle-Jones was very much aware of the growing excitement that a full house always generated. He was at his most affable and competent, and glowing with anticipation.

This was what he lived for – a live audience and a theatrical show, even a small-time, amateur-driven beauty pageant such as this one. At least he was confident his theatre looked its best. The stage scenery he had generously donated for the occasion had come from various past plays – a backdrop of glamorous Venice for the evening gown section, and a backdrop of a beach for the swimwear slot. The flowers had arrived and would bedeck the stage when it came time for the interview section, and a small band of musicians would provide the mood-music.

Most of the girls were now feeling horribly nervous, of course, and Dennis regarded them with somewhat impatient benevolence. They were, after all, amateurs – and not real theatre people at all.

The Dunbars, as hosts, were personally ushering in those members of the audience who were in 'their circle' and had come more or less by personal invitation, whilst the less blessed were filtering in, tickets clutched in hand, through the main entrance.

But Trudy, who was back to being dressed in uniform, wasn't interested in any of that.

Over the past week, both she and Dr Ryder had been steadily gathering evidence, and, like most things in life, once you knew where to look, had been finding it in steady dribs and drabs all over the place.

To begin with, they had gathered several written statements from former students of St Bart's school, who had all agreed that both Abigail Trent and, to a lesser extent, Vicky Munnings had indeed bullied Millie Merriweather extensively during her last two years at school. Millie, unfortunately, had been a rather plain girl, and they had made much fun of her 'ugly duckling' features, as a running theme in their torment.

They'd also confirmed from various libraries around the city, that Mrs Patricia Merriweather had withdrawn several books on native British flora that were poisonous, as well as more books from which she could have learned how to distil poisons. These library withdrawals had all been within three weeks of Abigail Trent's death from yew berry poisoning. Not only that, just a week before the death of Vicky Munnings, she had also withdrawn several technical manuals from which she could have learned how to sabotage the heater in the second victim's bedroom.

A walk-through from the Merriweather mansion to Vicky's ground-floor bedroom, confirmed that the old lady could easily have made the short journey, under cover of darkness, to the dead girl's 'apartment' without being seen.

None of which, Trudy now mused gloomily, had seemed to impress her DI to any great extent. Although Sergeant O'Grady, at least, seemed convinced that they had a valid lead and solid suspect, even he had had to point out how circumstantial it all was.

222

The motive was valid enough, but as he'd insisted, *anyone* at all could have used darkness and the cover of the shrubbery in the Munnings' garden in order to sabotage the heater inside. Just because the old lady had taken out books that showed how to create the yew berry poison that had killed Abigail, didn't *prove* that she had. All of which Trudy, although frustrated, understood all too well.

What's more, she was well aware that all the old lady had to do, if taxed with things, was to say something along the lines that she was worried about what poisonous plants might be growing in her garden, and who could call her a liar? And that she'd been thinking of purchasing a heater, and wanted to learn how to use it.

She was, after all, Mrs Patricia Merriweather – matriarch of an old and much-respected family. She had wealth and powerful friends, and social influence. And besides all that, who would ever believe such a nice and affable old lady would go about killing pretty young girls?

Even Trudy sometimes had trouble believing it.

She was standing now in one of the backstage corridors waiting for Clement to join her, and feeling highly anxious. Not only was she feeling a little sick-to-her-stomach for her friends, who would have to perform for the first time in front of a packed theatre, she was even more worried about what was to come, and the scene that would be carried out in a far more private arena.

When she had reported back to Clement that her DI was not going to even countenance bringing in Patricia Merriweather for questioning, let alone charge her with two counts of murder, he had not been at all surprised. In fact, looking back on it, Trudy was sure that he had always known what her superior's attitude would be.

And even though she could admit to herself that the Inspector had a point, she still felt frustrated in the extreme that they were so helpless. *Knowing* who had killed the girls and why, was no good if you couldn't bring the crime home to the killer.

Which was why she was hoping that Clement's scheme to confront the old lady here at the theatre might bear fruit. But she wasn't feeling particularly hopeful.

'What time does the show start?'

Trudy gave a little yelp and nearly leapt into the air. She'd been so deep in thought that she hadn't heard the coroner walking up behind her. Now she turned towards him with a brief apology, noting vaguely how handsome and distinguished he looked in his black tie.

'Sorry, I didn't realise you'd arrived.' She looked at her watch. 'It's still half an hour until the initial opening ceremony and parade – which is all in "normal" daywear. It's designed to be a general introduction of the girls to the audience, and each girl has a quick "chat" to the compere.'

'And the judges?'

'All making themselves comfortable in the "green room" so far as I know,' Trudy said, leading the way to a small backstage room where various drinks and snacks could be served, and a group of large, comfortable chairs were available for anyone who needed to relax.

'Shall I go and see if she's inside?' she whispered to Clement outside the door. 'Only I'm in uniform now,' she pointed out, 'and they might be a bit confused – especially if they recognise me as once being a contestant.'

'No, I'll go and lure her out. Is there somewhere we can talk privately?'

'Not really,' Trudy said with a sigh, looking vaguely around. 'It'll have to be out here – and before long, the girls will be coming out of the dressing rooms, so we'll have to make it quick.'

Clement nodded grimly. 'I'd prefer to have more time, but...'

'Do you really think you can make her confess?' Trudy asked nervously.

Yesterday, when they'd been discussing their options, he had come up with an idea that had sounded very tenuous indeed to her, but she'd eventually been forced to agree that it was better than doing nothing.

Now he shrugged. 'It all depends on how much the family name means to her. How deep and strong her love for her granddaughter really goes. How vain she is. What moral compass – if any – she has.' Clement shrugged. 'There are too many variables to know. We'll just have to play it by ear. She might just laugh in our face.'

'And if she does, she just gets away with it?' Trudy demanded angrily.

Clement looked at her a shade helplessly. Sometimes the young could just break your heart. 'People do get away with murder, Trudy,' he said, his voice more severe and rough than he'd meant it to be. Quickly, he carried on more mildly. 'Any serving police officer of any years' standing will tell you that. It's not like it is in the films or in penny dreadfuls, where everything gets to be tied up in a neat ribbon at the end. Life is much messier than that. No doubt, if you asked them, any of your colleagues could tell you indignant tales of people they knew to be guilty of all sorts of crimes, but they simply lacked the evidence to act. It's just one of those nasty little facts of life that you're going to have to face and come to terms with at some point or other, if you want to make a career out of police work.'

'Yes, I know,' Trudy said, but still reluctant to listen to such advice. 'But… *two murders*? Two young girls, with everything to live for…' She trailed off helplessly. It would do her no good now to start thinking of the anguish of the girls' families and what they were going through. She'd only want to start crying, and she needed to concentrate all her efforts on the task that lay ahead.

'Oh well, let's get on with it,' she muttered fatalistically.

Clement nodded, took a deep breath himself, and pushed open

225

the door. She heard a small murmur as his fellow judges greeted him, then had to wait for what seemed like an eternity, but was probably only a minute or so, before the door re-opened, and Clement, closely followed by Patricia Merriweather, emerged.

The old lady looked resplendent in a shimmering grey silk evening dress. A professional hairdresser had put up her white hair into an elegant chignon, and rather large and very sparkling diamonds glinted at her earlobes and hung around her throat. She was also wearing long white gloves that reached above her elbows, and she carried a small evening bag by Chanel.

'Trudy! My word, you're in a policewoman's uniform! I'd heard you pulled out of the competition, but I had no idea you were one of our splendid boys – or in your case, girls – in blue!'

Trudy found it hard to look the other woman in the face. On the one hand, she felt almost sure that Patricia must be mocking her; that she must have guessed long ago who Trudy really was and what she'd been doing, and was now just playing a game with her, taunting her with the mock-pretence of surprise.

Yet, perversely, she still found it almost impossible to believe that this friendly, slightly mischievous, larger-than-life old lady was a cold-blooded killer.

What if they'd got it all wrong?

'Hello, Mrs Merriweather,' Trudy forced herself to say politely. 'Would it be possible for Dr Ryder and myself to have a quick chat with you before you have to begin your judging duties?'

'Of course.' The old woman's eyes moved speculatively between the two of them before she moved a little away from the door. 'What can I do for you?'

Trudy looked helplessly at Clement. She had no idea what he intended to say, or how he'd say it, and she had the rather depressing feeling that he didn't know either. What she hadn't expected him to do, however, was just to come straight out with it.

'Did you murder Abigail Trent and Victoria Munnings?' the

coroner asked flatly. 'Because, frankly, Mrs Merriweather, we believe that you did.'

The old woman blinked and her face went completely expressionless. For a moment, Trudy felt almost dizzy, so surreal did the moment seem. Were they really standing in a gloomy corridor in the back of the Old Swan Theatre, with the loud buzz of a waiting audience permeating from somewhere behind them, whilst asking an old and respectable lady if she was a double murderess?

'I see,' Patricia finally said. She sounded almost – but not quite – amused. 'And why do you imagine I would do such a thing?'

She was looking only at the coroner, and concentrating on him so fully, that Trudy got the feeling that she'd been totally forgotten.

'Because they bullied your granddaughter Millie mercilessly at school. Tragically, at a time when she was already so mentally fragile and vulnerable, wasn't she?' he added, a note of compassion clearly creeping into his voice now. 'Which pushed her over the edge into some sort of full-blown mental breakdown.'

'My granddaughter is no concern of yours,' Patricia said stiffly. She was now standing very rigidly, all hint of amusement gone. Even Trudy, who was not the recipient of it, could feel the arctic chill of her disapproval.

'I agree,' Clement said quietly. 'But she *is* very much *your* concern, isn't she, Patricia? She's your whole life, in fact, since you practically raised her yourself after her mother walked out. You've never been particularly close to your son, but various sources have told me that Millie has always been the light of your life.'

'Have they indeed?' Patricia mused, forcing a lighter note into her voice. 'It sounds to me as if you've been poking that rather Roman nose of yours into places where it isn't wanted.'

'It must have been heartbreaking for you,' Clement carried

on, ignoring the insult completely. 'Not being able to protect her from the slings and arrows of life. You've always been so strong yourself, haven't you? A bit of a wild child in your own day, I bet. A free and independent spirit, so different – so much *stronger* – than Millie ever was. It must have hurt you intolerably to see her slip further and further away from life and reality. And those two girls making her life so miserable, just at the worst time of her life. Adolescence isn't easy to negotiate, is it, even at the best of times? But having two harpies pecking at her constantly, making her life intolerable – that must have driven you almost insane.'

Patricia Merriweather pulled in a long, audible breath. Her shoulders swept back and her chin lifted haughtily into the air. 'I didn't know about it at the time, Dr Ryder,' she said, her voice almost vibrating with anger. 'If I had, I can assure you, I would have done something about it. But Millie never spoke to me about it. Not at the time, she kept it all bottled up inside. It was only a year later… after her first attempt at suicide – that she told me what they'd done. The verbal taunts, the mental bullying, the physical punches and pinches, the tripping her over into stinging nettles…'

She was almost panting now, but suddenly she stiffened again and got herself back under control. 'But as I've remarked before, this is none of your business.'

'But the death – the unlawful killing of two girls – is very much my business, Mrs Merriweather,' Clement said remorselessly. 'I am the city coroner, remember? I resided over the inquest into the death of Abigail Trent.'

Patricia managed a bleak smile. 'So? Is that supposed to worry me? Or scare me? Why should it?' she asked flatly. 'As I recall, everybody believed the silly little chit either committed suicide, or poisoned herself by accident.'

'We know you took out library books in order to research poisons,' Clement said flatly.

But, as Trudy had always feared she would, the old lady merely gave a brief, bitter bark of laughter. 'So what? It's hardly a smoking gun, is it?'

'No.' Clement surprised her by agreeing flatly, and Trudy felt her shoulders, already stiff with tension, tighten even more as she realised that her friend was about to play their only card – their last-ditch attempt at getting some sort of justice for two dead girls.

'But we'll keep digging, Patricia,' he went on flatly.

Once again, their eyes locked in a duel, and once again, the old man met her unflinching gaze stoically. 'We've already presented our findings to Trudy's superior officer. And now we know where to look, it's only a matter of time before we find proper evidence,' he bluffed magnificently. 'Maybe somebody saw you that night, when you sneaked across the green and into the Munnings' garden, intent on turning the heater in her room into a deadly device. Can you be *sure* nobody noticed you? Or what about the day you picked the yew berries? What if you were seen and your activities noted? What about your servants – can you rely totally on their loyalty? You must have concocted the poison somewhere – probably in your own kitchen. Can you be sure none of them noticed anything?'

Again, Patricia gave an elegant, ladylike snort. 'You're wasting your time and breath. You and I both know you won't find a thing.'

'What about the tricks you played here?' Clement swept on, indicating the theatre around them. 'Trailing red herrings across our path, trying to make us think there was a prankster or poison pen lurking about. Can you be certain nobody spotted you up to your tricks? Are you confident those chocolates can't be traced back to you? Or maybe someone saw you slipping that dead moth into that girl's pocket. It might not have meant much to them at the time – but in hindsight, it would be a different thing. By the way, that was a bit of a giveaway that, don't you think? Only people of our generation would remember the old wives' tales surrounding that insect – modern day youngsters wouldn't have a clue about it.'

But again the old lady was scornful. 'Good luck going into a court of law with piffling little trifles like that!' she jeered. 'Any barrister would make mincemeat of you! Don't forget – I could afford the best defence available should you be so arrogant and pig-headed to try it. Oh, I know all about you, Dr Ryder,' Patricia mused, almost cordially. 'You've not been the only one to make discreet enquiries here and there. You're a man with a reputation for not suffering fools gladly. In fact, as odd as this may sound, in many ways, I rather admire you. So please do me the same courtesy and start treating me as someone with at least a modicum of intelligence and backbone!' she flashed.

'Oh, but I am, Mrs Merriweather. Believe me, I am,' Clement said, so mildly that both Trudy and the old lady were taken aback in equal measure. 'Because everything you say is quite right. We almost certainly *wouldn't* be able to bring home the murders of Abigail Trent and Victoria Munnings to you in a court of law with the evidence we have at the moment. But then, you and I, as people who've knocked about the world for a fair old bit, already know,' Clement carried on, still in that mild, almost friendly voice that seemed somehow far more menacing and frightening than an angry shout would have done, 'that isn't really the point. Is it?'

Again, the old woman blinked, her face going almost completely blank. But then Trudy was sure she saw a flash of fear cross Patricia's face, and she could almost hear her brain frantically working, seeking out the answer to the conundrum and trying to anticipate what was coming next.

Trudy, who knew exactly what *was* coming next, felt her head literally begin to throb with a tension headache, so intense was the pressure she felt.

Patricia took a step back, as if literally rocked on her heels.

'Isn't it?' she asked sharply, but the trace of uncertainty and indecision in her tone was clearly audible.

'No, it isn't. Not to someone like you, Mrs Merriweather,' Clement said flatly. 'How long, do you suppose, would it take for the rumours to start? With the police talking to your neighbours, interviewing your staff and questioning your friends. How long would it be before the thread was taken up by the people who use the libraries, where more questions will be asked, allowing them to put two and two together? Then would come the reporters, sniffing around with their sensitive noses on the alert for any whiff of scandal and picking up on a promising spoor. The Merriweathers – the doyens of Parklands – suspected of murder. How marvellous, how titillating would that be? Regardless of what could be proved or not, how long would it take before the whole city knew what you were suspected of?'

But the old lady, though shaken, was made of sterner stuff. 'Oh pooh! What would I care what people said or whispered behind their hands?' she asked, her chin once again rising haughtily and her spine stiffening in defiance.

'Your family might not be so cavalier,' Clement chided gently. 'After all, most of them are of the stuffed-shirt variety, aren't they? They never had your *joie de vivre*, did they? I'd be willing to bet none of them ever danced the Charleston in *their* day.'

Again, she merely shrugged magnificently. 'It hardly matters. It's not as if they can do me any harm – I hold the purse strings remember? Or enough of them at any rate not to have to worry about what they have to say.'

Clement nodded, then said, devastatingly, 'But what about Millie? At the moment, she's in the care of doctors. But if she's to have any hope of recovery, of one day leaving them and coming back to your home on the green, could she do that and be able to cope with all the rumours and innuendo? With all her neighbours and friends convinced that her grandmother is a murderess? Come to that, would your son, Christopher, even let her come

231

back to you? Because he'll move out the moment the going gets tough, won't he? Maybe even to another country on a permanent basis. He might even take steps to ensure you'd never be able to see her again. The doctors would be bound to back him up. You'd surely be regarded as a malign or harmful influence on a vulnerable young girl.'

Even watching only her profile, Trudy could see how deathly white the old lady had become. Her mouth slowly opened, but no words came out.

Suddenly, shockingly, right at this moment of high pathos, they were farcically interrupted. Three girls, two dressed in fabulous day dresses and one in a colourful combination of skirt, blouse and jacket, came around the dog-leg of the corridor, chattering brightly and nervously, and rushed past them.

As they did so, the faint call of the 'prompt' began to come down the corridor.

'Judges to the stage area, please. Judges to the stage.'

Trudy leapt back out of the way as the door to the green room opened and Rupert Cowper and his fellow judges began to file out.

Suddenly, the corridor was full of brightly chatting, nervous girls, most of them looking startled to see Trudy in her police uniform, and almost equally excited middle-aged men, and Patricia Merriweather, with a last contemptuous look at Clement, let them sweep her away with them.

* * *

Trudy, forced to stand at the back of the theatre and watch the Miss Oxford Honey beauty pageant unfold, could hardly drag her eyes away from watching the backs of the heads of the judges at the tables. Since Clement was at one end of the long table, and Patricia Merriweather the other, it was impossible for them to converse.

She was distracted from her vigil once or twice during the next few hours – once by Candace's comedy skit, which brought the house down. Unsurprisingly, it won her the first prize for that segment – a brand new record player (donated, of course, by one of the judges who owned an electrical store) plus vouchers that would allow her to purchase ten 45-records over the course of the next year. Although she was happy enough with the prize, she was clearly far more delighted by the warm and enthusiastic applause she was given.

A little while later, she found herself listening to Betty Darville, talking to the compere and being by far the most interesting and engaging girl of the entire evening. Again, she won first prize, and Trudy, along with the rest of the audience, applauded wildly.

Slowly, as the competition wound on, she began to stare less and less at the two white heads of Patricia and Clement at the table, and take more interest in what was happening on stage. When the final line-up was called, and it came time for the great moment to arrive, she was feeling almost as nervous as most of her new-found friends must have been feeling, up on the stage.

The final segment had been the beachwear competition, and now all the girls were lined up, waiting nervously in their swimming costumes and bikinis, as the compere hammed it up and made a great show of gathering the voting slips from the judges.

Christine Dunbar went up on stage, carrying an ostentatious and glittering tiara, which rested on a plump, dark purple velvet cushion, very much the cynosure of all eyes. The girls looked at the glittering crown hopefully, the audience with tense speculation.

When the name of the first runner up was called – a tall red-headed girl called Veronica Palmer – Trudy clapped with the rest of them as she accepted a huge floral bouquet from Robert Dunbar, along with a discreet envelope containing the cash prize for third place.

The second runner up was Sylvia Blane – who, it seemed,

233

couldn't quite make up her mind whether to be delighted at coming so close, or chagrined not to have actually won. She accepted the flowers and cheque graciously, of course, and gave the judges' table – and a certain handsome widowed judge in particular – a long and lingering look as she went by.

It was time for the winner to be announced, and Trudy, along with everyone else, felt herself holding her breath.

'And the winner of the first Miss Oxford Honey – who will automatically be entered for the Miss Oxford round of the Miss Great Britain competition – is… number fourteen, Miss Caroline Tomworthy!'

There was a roar of general approval from the audience, which carried on as Caroline, dressed in a deep, ruby-red costume walked forward elegantly to claim her prize. She smiled dazzlingly as the sparkling crown was placed on her ebony locks, and then sashayed gracefully and elegantly across the stage.

But by now, Trudy's gaze was once again fixed on the judging table – and the two white-haired individuals who, along with the rest of the panel, had politely risen to their feet in order to add their applause to that of the auditorium.

Trudy couldn't help but wonder. What on earth were they both thinking?

Chapter 29

The evening ended with a celebration backstage, but when Trudy made her way there, she found that Patricia Merriweather was conspicuous by her absence.

Working her way towards Clement, she handed out hearty congratulations to everyone who stopped to talk to her. By now, they all knew that she was an 'undercover' policewoman – a phrase that still sent thrills down her spine and made her feel faintly embarrassed in equal measure. They all wanted to thank her for 'looking out' for them.

The glow of a successful show – helped by a free-flowing variety of wines and spirits – gave everyone a rosy glow, and it was almost as if the prankster who had cast such a long shadow over their lives had never existed.

Trudy, with a pang, wondered what the two dead girls would have made of all this merriment and triumphant celebration. She made a mental promise to herself that – no matter what happened – she would call on the families of those dead girls and tell them what she suspected. Even if they could never have justice, they would know what had happened to their daughters.

And if that resulted in her being reprimanded by her superiors… well, she just didn't care.

'Have you seen her?' Trudy hissed as soon as she'd managed to make her way to the coroner's side.

'No,' he admitted bleakly. 'She must have left the moment the judging finished. I don't like it. We didn't get the chance to finish our conversation.'

Trudy shrugged helplessly. 'I don't know what more we could have said or done. I think she's just going to call our bluff,' she added gloomily.

It was only now that she realised how much she'd been taking for granted. Just because they'd successfully solved their first two cases, and brought the killers to justice, she'd assumed and always blithely believed that they'd do the same this time.

But now everything felt so… wrong, somehow. So unfinished. So… anti-climactic. 'I just can't believe we've come this far and now…' She gave a graphic shrug. 'Nothing. It's all over.'

Clement shook his head. 'Oh, something tells me it's not over yet,' he said bleakly. Something in his tone made her look at him nervously.

'What do you mean? You don't think she's going to kill anybody else, do you?' she whispered appalled. 'From all we've learned, it was only Abby and Vicky who did the bullying. There's no one else she can have in her sights, surely?'

'No, it's not that so much,' Clement said. 'And with the beauty pageant over, she's not even going to carry on with the pretence of being someone with a grudge against flawed beauty queens. So everyone here can breathe easy.'

Trudy slowly nodded, letting out a long-relieved breath of her own. 'You're sure then that all that prankster stuff was just a smokescreen?'

'Oh yes,' Clement said. 'None of the girls here were ever in real danger. The odd note, laxative in chocolates, a dead moth! That was nothing but so much window dressing designed to lead us up the garden path and obscure the real motive. Oh, I don't doubt she probably had no time for them all. After all, they were young, healthy and pretty girls, and her granddaughter was a plain, poor little thing. I dare say whenever she thought of them it was with a certain amount of bitterness and she probably quite enjoyed upsetting them. But she had no intention of ever harming anyone else, I think.'

Trudy nodded, abruptly aware that she was feeling exhausted. She wanted nothing more than to crawl into bed and sleep for a week.

Noticing the signs, Clement said with a smile, 'You might as well go home now, WPC Loveday. I'm sure that sergeant of yours and his boggle-eyed PC shadow will stay on and keep everyone safe until the theatre finally shuts down.'

Trudy gave a wan smile. She wouldn't have been human if she hadn't been delighted that someone else as well as herself had noticed Rodney's over-enthusiastic attitude for his latest assignment.

'All right.' She gave a huge yawn. 'I think I will. I'll call around at your office tomorrow?'

Clement nodded somewhat absently, and watched her go. His mind, however, was racing. Unlike Trudy, he was far from convinced that everything that needed to be said to Patricia Merriweather had, in fact, been said.

On the contrary, he was very much worried that it hadn't been.

For after pointing out to the old lady the dangers of having the police investigate her activities, and the consequences it could have on her family, he'd wanted to go on and tell her how much better it would be if she would just quietly confess and admit her guilt. That way, things could be handled with much more discretion.

True, the scandal would still be great – but at least it could be managed better. For a start, there wouldn't be the need for a prolonged period of investigation, and the media speculation that would generate. Nor would there have to be the spectacle of a long, drawn out public trial, which could often linger in the public mind long after the event.

Who knows, he could have pointed out to her, there might even be room for some sort of a deal to be made – a life-long commitment of herself to a secure mental home maybe? Given poor Millie Merriweather's predicament, he could well see how the old woman might find the ironies of that particular solution a source of bitter amusement.

Now he looked at his watch, and wondered. Should he call in at her house and discuss all this? Or should he leave it, and give her time to think things through –and perhaps come to some of these same conclusions for herself? As she herself had pointed out, she was intelligent enough to figure all this out without his help.

For a long while he pondered the problem.

In the end, he decided to leave it.

* * *

Patricia Merriweather had indeed left the theatre immediately after the judging. She'd secured a taxi with ease, and now she paced restlessly about her quiet, all-but-deserted home, still dressed in her finery and steadily drinking her way through a decanter of rather nice Cognac.

Her housekeeper – who slept in a converted flat over the stable block – had long since retired, and her son, as usual, was pursing his own pleasures somewhere on the Algarve. Not that he would have been of much use to her now. He had always been something of a dilettante, and happy to leave the management of his offspring, the family business interests, and all the tough decisions to his mother. Clement Ryder had done his homework into her family dynamic very thoroughly.

She marched agitatedly up the stairs, and in her bedroom, began to alternately curse the coroner, her son, Abigail Trent,

Victoria Munnings, fate, and finally herself, in about equal measure.

However, by the time the grandfather clock in the hall struck midnight, and sent its mellow chimes upwards, she was sitting in the chair beside a large sash window, looking out over the dark green, and thinking quietly and steadily.

She was not quite drunk, but neither was she quite sober.

But she was feeling tired. Dreadfully tired.

When she'd heard from the doctors three months ago that Millie had again attempted suicide, and that, in their opinion, the chances of her ever recovering enough to lead a full and happy life were all but zero, she'd felt nothing but a cold and overwhelming rage. A rage that had swept everything else out of her mind but the need for revenge.

For some time now she'd borne an immense burden of guilt whenever she thought about her granddaughter leaving this house to go to school, and stepping into a nightmare world of fear and bullying. And she, the girl's own grandmother, had never even guessed or dreamed that such a thing might be happening. That *her* granddaughter, a *Merriweather*, was being bullied by a pair of local, insignificant upstart harpies!

At first, it had been almost fun to plan the removal of the two heartless witches who had ruined Millie's life and happiness forever. At times, she'd even wondered if she herself might not have been a little insane, so intense was her glee as she'd gathered the yew berries and researched the sabotage of domestic heaters.

But now she felt only old and tired and, really, rather stupid.

She'd thought she was being so clever, but Dr Clement Ryder and that pretty little WPC sidekick of his had worked it all out, seemingly with no trouble at all. And now… now she was faced with the ultimate humiliation of a trial – either in a court of law, or, far worse in many ways – the court of public opinion.

The wily old coroner was right in what he'd said. Her neighbours would delight in seeing the Merriweather family name dragged through the mud.

No, it was intolerable.

Oh, she knew very well just what that cold-hearted and hard-headed coroner had been hinting at all along, damn him. That she should just do everyone the favour of putting an end to things once and for all – with no fuss and no mess, thus making it easy on everyone concerned. And with the unspoken but tacit understanding that, if she did, no charges would be pursued and the whole affair would be allowed to drop, with no smear on the Merriweather family name.

Right now, feeling pleasantly squiffy and too old and tired to care, she had no real objection to killing herself and fulfilling her part of that bargain. After all, she was old and would probably die soon anyway. She'd never have Millie come back to live here with her and brighten her days. What, really, was the point of carrying on?

But she'd always been a fighter and the thought of being bested by someone, anyone – even as worthy an opponent as Dr Clement Ryder – sat very uneasily on her shoulders. In fact, it made her feel downright spiteful.

In the old days, when she'd been young and determined to grab the world by the throat, the thought of just throwing in the towel would be anathema to her.

But there was, perhaps, one way she could kick over the traces still. Something she could do to make sure that Clement Ryder didn't have things all his own way, and that would leave her having the last laugh!

Yet, as she thought about how she would take her revenge, she felt a moment of near-shame sweep over her. After all, it was hardly playing the game, as her poor old, long-dead spouse, would have said. He'd been a gentleman through and through. And she'd always agreed with his philosophies – up to a point. There were certain things that went beyond the pale. Ratting out one of your peers was definitely high on that list.

But in the end, that night, the picker of yew berries was in no mood to be sporting.

And so, before gathering together a nice little collection of sleeping powders and a variety of medications that had been prescribed for her by her doctor (it was so handy to be old – you had so many pills to choose from!) Patricia Merriweather sat down at her desk and began to write two letters.

One was addressed – irony of ironies – to the coroner. She had no idea whether Dr Ryder himself, or one of his contemporaries, would get to read it, but in any case she kept it short and sweet. She merely stated that she was taking a mixture of pills and alcohol, which she fully expected to end her life, of her own free will and that no other persons were involved in this enterprise. She gave no reasons whatsoever for her decisions – because it was none of their damned business! She offered only a brief apology to her maid, who, she expected, would be the one to discover her tomorrow morning.

As she signed it, she smiled briefly and viciously.

The other letter she addressed to the police. This took her more time to compose, but, in the end, she was happy with what she wrote:

To whom it may concern

I, Mrs Patricia Merriweather, feel it my duty to inform the Oxford City Police that I have, on a number of occasions, observed Dr Clement Ryder, a coroner of the city, to show symptoms of what I firmly believe to be some kind of morbid disease.

I have noticed him to suffer from hand tremors on several occasions, and also a dragging of his feet, leading him to almost stumble.

Since a coroner is an officer of the law and holds a position of great responsibility, I feel it incumbent on me to point out that, very unfortunately, it may be possible that he is unfit to continue to serve in his present position.

I therefore advise, very strongly, that he be assessed by one of his fellow medical practitioners as soon as possible.

Faithfully – Mrs Patricia Merriweather.

She carefully dated the letter, slipped it into an envelope, and folded the flap neatly inside the back. Then she placed both letters where they would be easily seen, propped up against her dressing-table mirror, and finished her final glass of Cognac.

By now it was almost one o'clock in the morning.

She stood at the window for a while, swaying slightly and taking one last long look at a moonlit Oxford. Beautiful! Then she slipped under the covers of the bed and began to steadily swallow pills.

Chapter 30

Trudy arrived at the station well in time for her 7 a.m. shift. After getting her assignments from the officer on duty, she slipped out into a cold, still dark city, and made her way towards Parklands.

Her first official assignment could wait. She knew Clement probably wouldn't approve, but she wanted to go one more round with Mrs Merriweather.

She took the bus to Summertown, then walked the rest of the way, greeting people who were setting out for work with a reassuring nod. She knew the PC who walked this beat, and hoped she wouldn't encounter him (as she might end up with some explaining to do), but she was lucky, and made it to the Merriweather place unchallenged.

She went straight to the rear entrance and knocked at one of the back doors. She wasn't surprised to find it opened by a woman who was obviously the cook, but she was surprised to be all but dragged in and greeted so effusively. Normally, in her experience, nobody liked to see a police officer on their doorstep.

'Oh, you've got here ever so quick! I'm so glad. She's upstairs. Beatrice, Mrs Merriweather's maid, is staying with her until someone comes.'

The woman was middle-aged and comfortably plump, but her round face was rather pale and her eyes were round with suppressed panic.

Trudy allowed herself to be compelled out of the kitchen, down a long corridor and out into the hall. She managed to restrain the desire to ask what on earth was going on or what it was all about, and when they got to the foot of the steps, and her escort pointed upwards, she merely nodded and ascended the stairs. These were comfortably carpeted in a deep red and brown pile, and the dark mahogany banisters glowed with much polishing.

'Second door on the left it is,' the woman below called up helpfully and then quickly darted away.

Trudy, her heart hammering in her chest, turned the corner at the top of the stairs and saw a young woman standing just outside a door. She was dressed in a traditional black and white maid's uniform, and Trudy could tell she'd been crying recently.

'My, that was quick. I've only just t-telephoned for the p-police.' She gulped, her voice slightly raspy. She was a slender girl, with pale hair, pale eyes and a pale complexion, blotched red now from weeping. 'M-madam is inside. I didn't touch an-anything.'

'That's good,' Trudy said, her mind racing. Clearly something had happened to Patricia Merriweather, and her maid had just sent out a 999 message. Which meant her colleagues would soon be on the scene, and she would be quickly dismissed as irrelevant.

But she couldn't let herself be sidelined just yet. This whole case had been so frustrating and unsatisfying, she needed to be in at the end of it, at least.

'I'll just go inside. When my colleagues arrive, show them up,' she said, marvelling at how cool and in command she sounded. The maid nodded, and glanced away as Trudy opened the door and slipped inside.

The bedroom was still rather dark, even though the maid had drawn back the curtains. It was extremely spacious, with room

244

for a huge bed, a desk under the window, two bedside ta.
and a large wardrobe.

The bed itself was a large one – even bigger than a double
bed, but it wasn't a four-poster, in which Trudy had always fondly
believed that all landed gentry must sleep.

She approached the slight hump under the blankets slowly
and cautiously. She wasn't sure why, but she half expected the
occupant of the bed to suddenly sit up and laugh at her, making
her jump out of her skin. Just one last prank, with the joke firmly
centred on a certain WPC.

But as she got closer, she could see that the old lady was
beyond all that. Her face looked peaceful, but Trudy could see
that she had vomited some time in the night, which had discol-
oured the pretty lace-lined pillow below her head.

When she reached out and touched the old lady's hand, her
skin was clammy and cold.

Silently, Trudy looked at her. On the bedside table was a carafe
of water, and several empty pill bottles. So she had taken the easy
way out, for she had no doubts that this death was a natural one.
What had been going through her mind? How desperate must
she have been? And then, out of the blue, the thought hit her
with all the cruel force of a thunderbolt.

She and Clement had driven her to this!

Last night, all that talk of pursuing her, dragging her family
name and reputation through the mud…

Trudy staggered back with a soft cry. What on earth had they
done?

Then she remembered the coroner's troubled face last night,
when he'd told her that he'd been worried that they hadn't had
time to finish their conversation with this woman. Bitterly, and
feeling like an utter fool, she finally understood. *This* was what
Clement had been afraid of all along. That the old lady would
think they had been suggesting she take what was euphemistically
called 'the honourable way' out.

_ne put a hand up to her mouth as tears shimmered in her _yes, blurring her vision, feeling sick with guilt.

They had, albeit unintentionally, driven an old lady to suicide.

True, she was also the cold-blooded murderer of two young women.

Even so...

She continued to back away until she bumped into the desk behind her. It was only then, as she turned around, grateful to tear her eyes away from the pitiful sight on the bed, that she spotted the two white squares that stood out in the gloom of the room, propped against the back of the desk behind her.

She leaned closer and saw two white square envelopes. She picked up one, marvelling at its weight and good quality. It even bore a crest – the Merriweather family crest, she supposed, embossed in a dark-coloured ink in the lower right-hand corner.

It was addressed, simply, to 'The Coroner'.

Trudy dropped it as if it had been white-hot, as something ancient and superstitious shot through her. She quickly glanced around, as if expecting to see the old lady's ghost standing there, pointing an accusing finger at her. It was as if, with this last message, she was reaching out eerily from beyond the grave to denounce them both.

Then she took a deep breath, told herself not to be so silly, and nervously put the envelope back where it had been. Apart from anything else, Clement should be the first to read it.

Then she noticed the second envelope and supposed it must be a letter to her family. But when she peered more closely at it, she saw that it was addressed to the police.

Once more, her heart rate ratcheted up a notch. Was this a confession of her crimes? She glanced out the window anxiously, torn between the desire to do her duty, which was to safeguard the scene – _without any interference_ – until the proper officers got here, and to open it and read the contents whilst she still had the chance.

After all, it was *her* case, Trudy reasoned. She and Clem
had been investigating it long before DI Jennings even believed
there was anything to investigate. And, in a way, it *was* addressed
to her wasn't it? It could be argued that she *was* the police, in
manner of speaking, right?

Quickly, before she could change her mind, she picked it up
and saw with relief that the envelope had not been sealed down,
but that the flap had merely been tucked in at the back. She
pulled it out, knowing that she would have to admit to handling
both envelopes anyway, since her fingerprints would be on them,
and pulled out and opened the single page that had been inside,
and began to read.

But, holding it up to the window and the growing daylight
coming through it, she quickly realised that it was not the confession to murder she had been expecting and hoping for.

It was something far more startling. And vindictive.

At first, as she read the spiteful words, Trudy couldn't quite
take them in. Then, slowly, all the sense of guilt that she'd been
feeling began to finally drain away.

As her last act before dying, Patricia Merriweather hadn't been
thinking of redemption at all, or putting things right, or even in
easing her conscience. No. All she'd wanted to do was make
trouble for the man who had bested her.

She heard the sound of a car, and glancing outside, saw that
it was a police vehicle, which was pulling up by the front door.
Suddenly, the importance of the words on the page began to sink
in.

She herself had seen Dr Ryder's hand tremble. She had also
noticed him drag his feet on occasion. Until now, she'd always
suspected that he had a drinking problem. But what if her friend
really was suffering from some potentially incapacitating illness?

She shook her head, trying to clear it and think. Surely this
was just the final parting shot of a bitter, murderous old lady?

Even so, she could still imagine how DI Jennings would pounce

...s with glee. He'd never liked Dr Ryder, and would absolutely
...ow over it. What's more, he would be sure to take the opportunity to argue that it couldn't hurt for him to submit to a
medical.

And what if it *was* true? Clement might be forced to retire
before he wanted to.

She could hear men climbing the stairs now and the slight
babble of voices. Within seconds the door would open and she
would have to account for her presence here.

She had only a moment to make a decision.

One part of her mind was screaming at her that it was unthinkable for her to tamper with evidence, even as she thrust the paper
and envelope in her hand into her satchel, burying them deep
beneath her accoutrements.

Suddenly, she felt a chill creep up her spine. What if the maid
who had discovered her dead mistress had noticed that there had
been two envelopes on the desk? And said so?

If she was forced to submit to a search, and the envelope and
letter were found in her possession, she'd be instantly dismissed.
She might even be prosecuted as tampering with evidence and
impeding a police investigation.

Her parents would be mortified! She'd be publicly shamed.
She felt suddenly extremely nauseous. A moment of panic hit
her.

What on earth was she going to do?

As the door to the bedroom opened, Probationary WPC Trudy
Loveday stood stiffly at attention, her face a careful blank, and
nodded calmly as a plain clothes detective she didn't know walked
through the door.

'Sir,' she said briskly.

248

Acknowledgements

The author would like to thank all those who have been kind enough to share their memories of the 1960s (and especially of Oxford during that era) with her.

Dear Reader,

Thank you so much for taking the time to read this book – we hope you enjoyed it! If you did, we'd be so appreciative if you left a review.

Here at HQ Digital we are dedicated to publishing fiction that will keep you turning the pages into the early hours. We publish a variety of genres, from heartwarming romance, to thrilling crime and sweeping historical fiction.

To find out more about our books, enter competitions and discover exclusive content, please join our community of readers by following us at:

🐦 @HQDigitalUK

📘 facebook.com/HQDigitalUK

Are you a budding writer? We're also looking for authors to join the HQ Digital family! Please submit your manuscript to:

HQDigital@harpercollins.co.uk.

Hope to hear from you soon!

Turn the page for an extract from *A Fatal Obsession*

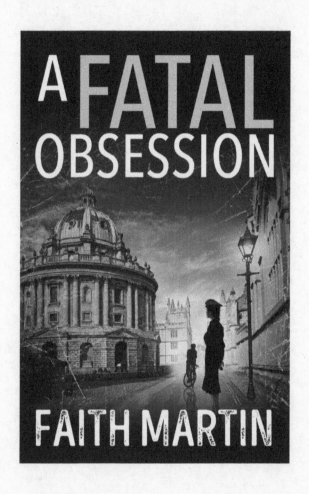

Turn the page for an extract from A Fatal Obsession.

Prologue

The body on the bed lay sedate and demurely silent as the middle-aged man looked slowly around the room. It was a lovely room – large, well proportioned and lavishly decorated in tones of blue and silver. One of two large sash windows was partly open, allowing a warm summer breeze to blow in, gently wafting the fine net curtains and bringing with it a faint scent of honeysuckle from the lush and well-tended gardens below.

The man wandered slowly around the opulent bedroom, his eyes greedily taking in everything from the quality of the silk bedsheets to the bottles of expensive perfume on an ornate antique dresser, while being careful not to touch anything. Having been born into a working-class family, he knew nothing about the pedigree of the paintings that adorned the walls. But he would have been willing to bet a week's wages that the sale of just one of them would be more than enough to set him and his family up for life.

He'd never before had cause to visit any of the mansions that proliferated in the swanky streets that stretched between the Woodstock and Banbury Roads in the north of the city, or any of the leafy avenues in the area. So now he took his time, and a considerable amount of pleasure, in looking around him, luxuriating in the deep tread of the plush blue Axminster carpet beneath his feet, which was so reminiscent of walking on mossy lawns.

His eyes turned wistfully to the jewellery box on a walnut bedside table, left carelessly open. Gold, pearls and a few sparkling gemstones winked in the summer sun, making his fingers positively itch.

'Very nice,' he muttered quietly to himself. But he knew better than to slip even a modest ring or two into his pocket. Not this time – and certainly not with *these* people. The man hadn't reached his half-century without learning there was one law for the rich, and one for everyone else.

Thoughtfully, his eyes turned once more to the body on the bed. A pretty little thing she was. Young too. Just out of her teens, perhaps?

What a damned shame, he thought vaguely.

Then the breeze caused something on the bedside table to flutter slightly, the movement instantly catching his eye. He walked closer to the bed and the dead girl, again careful where he put his feet, and saw what it was that had been disturbed. It had clearly been deliberately propped up among the pots of face cream and powder compacts, lipsticks and boxes of pills.

Bending ponderously at the waist, the man, who was definitely beginning to run to fat, squinted down at it and read some of the words written there.

And slowly, a large, beaming smile spread over his not particularly attractive face. He gave a long, slow, near-silent whistle and then looked sharply over his shoulder to make sure nobody from the house had come upstairs behind him and could see what he was about to do. Confident he remained alone and unobserved, he reached out for the item and put it safely away in his large inside jacket pocket.

Then he lovingly patted the place over his heart where it lay. For, unless he was very much mistaken, this precious little find was the best bit of luck he'd had for many a year – if not in his whole life. And it was certainly going to make his imminently approaching retirement years far more pleasant than he'd ever previously anticipated.

He walked jauntily to the door, leaving the dead girl behind him without a second thought, and stepped out confidently onto the landing.

Time, he rather thought, to tackle the man of the house.

Chapter 1

Oxford, January 1960

Probationary WPC Trudy Loveday shouted, 'Oi, you, stop right there. Police!' at the top of her lungs, and took off at a racing sprint.

Needless to say, the young lad she'd just seen snatch a woman's handbag as she was standing below the clock face on Carfax Tower did nothing of the kind. She just had time to catch a fleeting impression of a panic-stricken young face as he shot a quick look at her over his shoulder, and then took off down The High, like a whippet after a hare.

He nearly got run over by a taxi as he crossed the main road at the intersection but, luckily for Trudy, the traffic that had screeched to a halt to allow him to cross meant she could take advantage of the gap to race across herself, in rather more safety.

On her face, had she but known it, was a look of sheer joy.

Sergeant O'Grady had given her the task of trying to find the man responsible for a spate of bag-snatching in the city centre that had been going on since before the Christmas rush, but this was the first time she'd actually caught sight of her quarry in all that time. Though the thief had been active enough, and the list of outraged complaints from housewives and shoppers had grown steadily longer, neither she nor any of her fellow constables walking the beat had yet been lucky enough to be in the right spot at the right time.

Until now.

And a month of pounding the freezing pavements, taking statements from enraged or tearful women, and hiding behind shop doors on increasingly aching feet while keeping her eyes peeled for mischief, had left Trudy with a proper grudge against this particular villain.

Which meant she was in no mood to lose him now.

She was aware that many of the people in the streets were watching her race by with open mouths and round, astonished eyes. Some of the men, indeed, looked as if they were going to try and interfere, and she could only hope and pray that they wouldn't. Although they no doubt meant well, the last thing she needed was for some chivalrous, middle-aged bank manager to try and stop the fleeing thief for her, only to be roughly tossed to the floor, punched, or worse.

The paperwork involved in that was something she definitely didn't want to think about. Not to mention the look of resigned fury that would cross DI Jennings's face when he learned she'd somehow managed to muck up such a simple arrest.

Less than a minute of mad chasing had passed so far, and rather belatedly she remembered her whistle and debated whether or not she should use it.

At 19 (nearly 20), Trudy Loveday still remembered her glory days at the track and field events at her school where she'd always won cups on sports day for her racing – be it sprinting or cross-country. And she could still run like the wind, even in her neat black shoes and police uniform, with her leather satchel of accoutrements bouncing on her hip. Moreover, she could tell she was gaining ground on the little villain in front of her, who had to deal with the added obstacle of shouldering pedestrians out of his way as he ran, leaving the pavements rather less clogged for her.

Her legs and arms were pumping away in that satisfying and remembered rhythm that allowed her to eat up the yards, and she was reluctant to alter that flow, but training and good sense told her she must. So, trying not to lose momentum, she reached her hand across her chest, swung the silver whistle on its chain up to her lips, and blew hard on the outward, expelling breath.

The distinctive, loud-pitched whistle promptly resounded in the cold, frost-laden air, and would, she knew, bring any of her colleagues within hearing distance running to her aid. Which might be just as well if the bag-snatcher decided to give up his attempt at a straight flight and tried to lose himself in the city's narrow, medieval back streets, or by dodging in and out of the shops.

But so far he was intent on just running down The High, no doubt confident he could outrun a mere woman. But this hardly made him the first man to underestimate her.

With a confident grin, Trudy put on an extra burst of speed. He was so close now, she could almost feel the moment when she'd rugby-tackle him to the ground, hear him grunt with surprise and then see the look of dismay on his cocky little face as she slipped her handcuffs on him and gave him his caution.

And at that moment, just as she was reaching out and getting ready to grab him, he turned and glanced over his shoulder, saw her and swore. And immediately began to dodge to his right, between two parked cars.

Trudy cast a swift look over her shoulder, saw that the road was clear, then looked ahead as far as Magdalen Bridge, noticing the familiar outline of a red bus chugging along, coming towards her. But she had plenty of time before it reached them.

Anticipating the fleeing thief's intention of crossing the road and trying to lose her down one of the side streets opposite, Trudy gave a final blast on her whistle. This was as much to warn the gaping, watching public to keep out of the way as it was an attempt to attract further help from her colleagues.

Then she leapt sideways.

Her timing, as she'd known it would be, was near perfect, and before he could gain the middle of the road, she was on him, swinging him around and back towards the pavement. She hit him hard, putting all of her slight weight into it. Luckily, at five feet ten, she was a tall girl, and had a long reach.

The thief landed unluckily on his nose on the icy tarmac, and yelped in shock. He was a skinny, wiry specimen, all arms and legs, and already his nose was bleeding profusely. Comically, he was still clutching the lady's handbag he'd snatched back at Carfax.

Trudy felt her police cap fall off as she landed on top of him but, mercifully, her long, wavy, dark-brown hair was held up in such a tight bun by a plethora of hair pins and elastic bands that it remained contained.

Reaching behind her, with one knee firmly positioned in the middle of the thief's back, she groped for her handcuffs. She was vaguely aware of a male voice shouting something only a short distance away, and that the public, who had begun gathering in a curious little knot around her, were now moving back, when the thief beneath her suddenly bucked and twisted violently.

And before she could even open her mouth to begin to caution him, his elbow shot upwards, smacking her firmly in the eye.

'Owwww!' she yelled, one hand going up instinctively to cup her throbbing cheekbone. This provided the bag-snatcher with the opportunity he'd been waiting for, and he gave another massive heave, sending her sprawling.

Nevertheless, she had enough presence of mind to reach out and grab him by the foot as he attempted to get up. He turned, drew back his free leg and was clearly about to kick her in the face when she became aware of another figure looming over her.

'All right, matey, hold it right there! You ain't going nowhere,' a triumphant voice said. And a pair of large male hands came into her view, hauling the bag-snatcher to his feet. 'I'm arresting you for assaulting a police officer in the course of her duty. I must caution you that anything you say will be taken down and may be given in evidence.'

Trudy, her large, dark-brown eyes watering as much in frustration as in pain, watched as PC Rodney Broadstairs – the Lothario of St Aldates police station – slipped his handcuffs onto *her* suspect. Stiffly, she got to her feet. Only now that the adrenaline was wearing off was she beginning to feel the scrapes and bruises she'd sustained in the tackle. Although, fortunately, her gloves, uniform, and the heavy black serge greatcoat she wore over it had saved her from losing any actual skin.

A brief and polite smattering of applause from the public rang out as PC Broadstairs began frogmarching the thief back to the pavement. One member of the public diffidently offered Trudy her cap back, which she took with a smile and a weary word of thanks.

She also retrieved the lady's handbag for evidence.

But the admiring looks from the bystanders and the murmuring of approval for 'the plucky little thing' as she limped grimly after PC Broadstairs and the bag-snatcher did little to improve her now sour mood. Because she knew, after nearly a year's bitter experience, just how things were going to go now.

Broadstairs, having been the one to deliver the caution and put on the cuffs, would be accredited with the arrest. It would be the good-looking PC, not the humble probationary WPC, who would get the nod of approval from her superior officers.

She would no doubt be told to go home to her mum and dad and get some rest, nurse her burgeoning black eye and then type up her report first thing in the morning. Oh, and to go and get the deposition of the woman whose bag had been snatched. And all the time having to endure the whispers and snide asides about how that was all WPCs were good for.

Disconsolately, as she trooped back to St Aldates, she could only hope that DI Jennings wouldn't use her minor injuries as an excuse to put her back on desk duty again.

In front of her, PC Rodney Broadstairs looked over his shoulder at her and winked.

As WPC Trudy Loveday wrestled with the desire to swear in a most unladylike manner at her male colleague, five miles away, in the small and pretty village of Hampton Poyle, Sir Marcus Deering had stopped work for his elevenses.

Although he was still nominally in charge of the large chain of department stores that had made his fortune, at the age of 63 he now worked two days a week from the study in his large country residence in Oxfordshire. He was confident his managing directors, plus a whole board of other executives, could safely be left to do the bulk of the work without any major mishaps, and now rarely travelled to the main offices in Birmingham.

He sighed with pleasure as his secretary came into the book-lined room with a coffee tray laden with fresh-baked biscuits and that morning's post. A rather portly man, with thinning grey hair, a neatly trimmed moustache and large, hazel-green eyes, Sir Marcus liked to eat.

His appetite, however, instantly fled as he recognised the writing on one large, plain-white envelope. Addressed to him in block capital letters, it had been written in a rather bilious shade of green.

His secretary deposited the tray on his desk and, noticing the way his lips had thinned into a very displeased line, hastily beat a retreat.

Sir Marcus scowled at the pile of correspondence and took a desultory sip of his coffee, telling himself that this latest in a line of recent anonymous letters was nothing more than a nuisance. No doubt written by some crackpot with nothing better to do with his time, it was hardly worth the effort of opening and reading it. He should just consign it straight to the wastepaper basket instead.

But he knew he wouldn't do that. Human nature wouldn't let him. The cat wasn't the only creature curiosity was capable of killing, after all. And so, with a slight sneer of distaste, he snatched the offending envelope from the pile of correspondence, reached for his silver paper knife, and neatly slit it open. He then pulled out the single piece of paper within, knowing what it would say without even having to look at it. For the letters always made the same preposterous, ambiguous, infuriatingly meaningless demand.

He'd received the first one a little under a month ago. Just a few lines, the implication of a veiled threat, and unsigned, of course. Nonsense, through and through, he remembered thinking at the time. It was just one of the many things a man of his standing – a self-made, very wealthy man – had to put up with.

He'd crumpled it up and tossed it away without a second thought.

Then, only a week later, another one had come.

And, oddly enough, it hadn't been more threatening, or more explicit, or even more crudely written. The message had been exactly the same. Which was unusual in itself. Sir Marcus had always assumed that nasty anonymous letters became more and more vile and explicit as time progressed.

Whether it was this anomaly, or sheer instinct, he couldn't now say, but something about it had made him pause. And this time, instead of throwing it away, he'd kept it. Not that it really worried him, naturally.

But he'd kept the one that had come last week too, even though it had said exactly the same thing. And he'd probably slip this one, also, into the top drawer of his desk and carefully lock it. After all, he didn't want his wife finding them. The wretched things would only scare her.

With a sigh, he unfolded the piece of paper and read it.

Yes, as he'd thought – the same wording, almost exactly.

DO THE RIGHT THING. I'M WATCHING YOU. IF YOU DON'T, YOU'LL BE SORRY.

But this letter had one final sentence – something that was new.

YOU HAVE ONE LAST CHANCE.

Sir Marcus Deering felt his heart thump sickeningly in his chest. One last chance? What was that supposed to mean?

With a grunt of annoyance, he threw the paper down onto his desk and stood up, walking over to the set of French windows that gave him a view of a large, well-maintained lawn. A small brook cut across the stretch of grass marking the boundary where the formal flower garden began, and his eyes restlessly followed the skeletal forms of the weeping willows that lined it.

Beyond the house and large gardens, which were so colourful and full of scent in the summer (and the pride and joy of his wife, Martha) came yet more evidence of his wealth and prestige, in the form of the fertile acres being run by his farm manager.

Normally, the experience of looking out over his land soothed Sir Marcus, reassuring him and reminding him of just how far he'd come in life.

It was stupid to feel so bloody... well, not frightened by the letters exactly; Sir Marcus wouldn't admit to being quite *that*. But unsettled. Yes, he supposed that was fair. He definitely felt uneasy.

On the face of it, they were nothing. The threat was meaningless and tame. There wasn't even any foul language involved. As far as nasty anonymous notes went, they were rather pathetic really. And yet there was something about them...

He gave himself a little mental shake and tramped determinedly back to his desk, sitting down heavily in his chair. And with a look of distaste on his face, he swept the letter into a drawer along with all the others, and locked it firmly.

He had better things to do with his time than worry about such stupid nonsense. No doubt the mentally deficient individual who'd written them was sitting somewhere right this moment, chortling away and imagining he'd managed to put the wind up him.

But Sir Marcus Deering was made of sterner stuff than that!

Do the right thing… Surely, it couldn't be referring to the fire, could it? A spasm of anxiety shot through him. That was all so long ago, and had had nothing to do with him. He'd been young, still working in his first executive position, and had no doubt been wet behind the ears; but the fire hadn't even occurred on his watch, and certainly hadn't been his responsibility.

No. It couldn't be about that.

Defiantly, he reached for a biscuit, bit into it, opened the first of his business letters and pondered whether or not he should introduce a new line in wireless sets into his stores. The manager at the Leamington Spa emporium was all for ordering in a large batch of sets in cream Bakelite.

Sir Marcus snorted. Cream! What was wrong with Bakelite that was made to look like good solid mahogany? And what did it matter if it *was* 1960 now, and the start of a whole new exciting decade, as the manager's letter insisted? Would housewives really fork out their husband's hard-earned money on cream Bakelite?

But at the back of his mind, even as he called in his secretary and began to dictate a reprimand to his forward-thinking executive in the spa town, his mind was furiously churning.

Just what the devil did the letter mean by 'do the right thing'? What *was* the right thing? And what would happen if he, Sir Marcus, *didn't* do the right thing?

The next book from Faith Martin
is coming in 2019

**If you enjoyed *A Fatal Flaw*, then why not
try another exhilarating read from HQ Digital?**

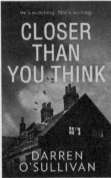

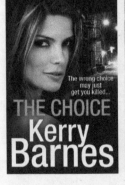

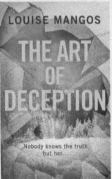